Educating Alex
by
Jacob Morrison

This book is dedicated to my wonderful husband and also to my 'top', my lovely locked attentive 'boy', my playmates and the many friends without whose support, honest feedback and encouragement it would not have been produced.

ABOUT JACOB MORRISON

Jacob Morrison has been an SM practitioner and educator for over 30 years. During that time he has enjoyed both top and bottom roles in a wide range of SM activities and set up numerous SM community web sites and organisations. He has also been involved in a number of organisations in the UK and elsewhere campaigning for the legal protection of SM activities and the rights of those who take part in them.

PREFACE

The world of sexual sadomasochism, or SM as it is usually referred to, is one little understood by those who do not take part in its sensuous delights of pain as pleasure, dominance and submission.

From the outside, SM play can appear as pure violence: one person forcing another, against their will, to endure what would otherwise be deemed torture. But SM is a game, a consensual game of erotic sensuous play, of mutually exploring the boundaries of pain and pleasure. It is a power exchange where one party willingly and eagerly relinquishes control and the other takes it in order that both can enjoy intense physical, emotional and sometimes spiritual pleasures.

What distinguishes SM sex from torture and violence is consent. To a bystander, SM activities may look identical to violence, and they may conclude that the participants are out of their minds for engaging in them. But once you appreciate the consensual, mutually pleasurable nature of what is going on and look beyond the externals – the SM paraphernalia of floggers and whips, hoods and gags, ropes and chains, the marks and the screams – you will discover tenderness, love and mutual respect, and an intimacy that can go beyond everyday sexual intercourse.

This is a story of two men, Damian and Alex.

Damian is an SM Master and Alex is his 'boy' – a term referring not to his age (he's 27) but his position as Damian's slave. It is a romantic story, which follows the growth of their deeply loving relationship, with SM sex providing the means by which Damian, in control at all times, teaches Alex how to take control of his own life and to discover his self-confidence and potential, inside and outside the SM playroom, to please others and ultimately himself.

It is an arrangement Alex consents to because before it his life was unfulfilled. Not that all submissives are feeble wastrels. Many are proud, confident and assertive, and get great satisfaction from relinquishing control to another for an hour, a day, a year or longer so their lives can be complete.

All the activities in this book are intended to be safe, sane and consensual. They are based on the author's experiences over more than thirty years as an SM player and educator. He has engaged in all the activities described in this book, either as the dominant 'top' or the submissive 'bottom' or both.

CHAPTER 1

Tap. Tap. Alex scrolls his way through the thumbnails of SM video porn on his smartphone. He's looking for something new, but he's watched all these before. This isn't surprising as he revisits these sites every ten minutes of his waking life. "Why can't these damned people add new stuff more often?" he thinks. "Don't they know I have needs as well?"

He's sitting at the kitchen table, naked but for a ragged pale blue t-shirt, covered in holes through being mangled in the local laundrette, and a once white pair of jockey shorts now distinctly grey as he can't afford to wash his whites and coloureds separately like his mother always told him.

Alex's limp dick hangs out of its front opening fearing his next assault.

Not that finding something new would help Alex much. He cums so often his prostate and balls are well drained and if he manages even a few drops from a faint echo of an orgasm it makes his day. However, that doesn't stop him attempting some level of arousal at least once each waking hour.

But what else is an unemployed, skill-less, no-hoper like Alex to do? Look for a job? He lost one job on the second day when he was found browsing porn on his phone when he should have been boosting the nation's cholesterol levels frying chicken at the local fast food outlet. He didn't do much better at the previous burger place where something similar happened. And his knee has now recovered from falling off his employer's moped delivering pizza on his most recent job when his phone pinged him to say that there was a new porn video on one of the many photo-sharing sites he subscribes to.

Any sane person would have waited until they were stationary. But this is "desperate" Alex and he tried to watch it doing 40mph in the middle of the South Circular with obvious consequences. Fortunately, it was late at night so no other vehicles were involved and he escaped with a sprained knee.

His injured knee is his excuse whenever the job centre tries to force him to apply for some work. You can't fry burgers or stack supermarket shelves sitting down he tells them, feigning a limp whenever he's called for an interview. He just hopes he can string it out a bit longer before they insist on a medical examination.

As is obvious to everyone but Alex, he is a porn addict par excellence.

For Alex, porn isn't a rehearsal or inspiration for sex. Or even a reminder. For that would require Alex to have had sex.

At the age of 27, Alex Jenkins is a total virgin. Never been kissed. Never even been naked with another person since the changing rooms at school. So for him, wanking over porn is his sex life from start to finish. It's unlikely he'd be any good in the sack anyway. He'd just lay there and expect Hollywood-style perfect sex to happen at the click of a bedside button.

Alex has always been aware of being aroused by watching muscular dominant men engaging in heavy painful sex. But a flabby, smelly, 5ft 7in wreck of a man isn't going to turn anyone else on, however much they might turn him on.

So for most hours of the day Alex can be found alone, sitting at the kitchen table or in bed, smartphone in one hand, dick in the other, and his miniature porno playmates filling the void that is his whole life, punctuated occasionally with a few seconds of arousal when he can manage it.

Just a few miles away, Damian Hall is in his office, monitoring activity on the gay SM porn web sites run by his company, DH Productions, one of the leading publishers in the field. As usual, there are thousands of visitors watching Damian's carefully choreographed video creations. The simple, sexually-charged scenes of SM activity are enacted by men recruited from the ranks of eastern European army conscripts eager to supplement their meagre state wages, and filmed in the rough-looking disused warehouses, barns and workshops that litter those countries.

But Damian is bored and feeling not just in need of some real-life sexual excitement of his own, but a bit lonely as well.

Damian enjoys the heavier side of gay sex, and his profitable business enables him to acquire the very best in SM toys and maintain a well-equipped play space in which to use them.

Over the years, he's entertained hundreds of men in his dungeon, tying them up, flogging and caning them, pumping electricity through their tender parts and generally sharing with them the perverse experience of pain as pleasure.

But he is still not satisfied. For any man that Damian will consider playing with tends to come with baggage: a job, a partner, friends and family. And Damian has a need to totally own someone else in the way that others have children or pets.

What he yearns for is a real-life slave whom he can mould and torment and, in a way most don't understand, care for and love.

Some of the DHP porno websites are interactive, enabling visitors to insert themselves into the action in a porn video; sometimes they appear as animated figures, in others they can insert their own live webcam feed into the movies.

Damian rarely monitors these interactive films as he employs plenty of people whose job it is to ensure that nothing remiss happens. But this late summer Sunday evening, idly looking through the activity logs, he notices that a particular visitor had been there 18 hours that day, jumping from one video to the next.

And a look at the history files shows that this isn't uncommon for this man.

Damian doesn't have to wait long for the log to

show that the visitor is back and into which interactive porno film he has placed himself. He turns on his supervisor view of the film and the people inserting themselves into it and decides to investigate further.

The visitor looks like the usual trolls for whom the site is their only chance of being within 1000 miles of any intimate human contact. But this one looks different. Despite his grubby appearance, there is something about his eyes, which suggests potential – a puppy-dog like glint piercing the sad unshaven face.

With his usual evil imagination, Damian has an idea which might alleviate his boredom and provide some amusement. He sends the visitor a private message, a facility occasionally used to warn people off misbehaving.

The text appears in big letters on Alex's screen, obscuring the action.

"Hey boy, what are you looking for?"

Damian's use of the word 'boy' is deliberate. If the visitor were into any sort of role-play, he would know what was expected.

At his kitchen table a few miles away, Alex jumps back. Nothing like this has ever happened before – he assumed he was anonymous. So maybe this is a new feature in the porno system. He ignores it and switches to another film.

A second message appears: "I asked what you were looking for, boy".

Alex now wonders if this is part of some online game he's being invited to join and so types back: "I don't know, Sir". He'd heard actors in SM porno films respond this way and being so immersed in them the word 'Sir' sort of got added instinctively.

Damian bashes out a few commands on his keyboard and suddenly Alex finds himself no longer in the porno he had been watching but in a dimly-lit room, empty apart from himself and another tall, muscular, booted figure dressed in black combats and t-shirt, his face hidden in the darkness.

This is Damian's private online play space where he can tease and torment, in virtual space, anyone he fancies without being interrupted by porno trolls inserting their unsightly fuzzy webcam feeds.

A voice comes through the tinny speaker on Alex's phone, which startles him.

"Stand away from your cam, boy, I want to see all of you."

The unexpectedness of the commanding sound means he reacts instinctively.

"Yes, Sir," replies Alex, still assuming this is some sort of experimental feature where a film morphs into an adventure game.

Damian thinks the visitor's voice is sort of sexy in a strange way.

Alex props his phone up against an empty milk carton and stands back. He isn't sure what is happening but this is the most exciting and scary thing that has happened to him since he had his first wet dream. His heart pounds and his cock grows a little.

Damian scans over the sad dishevelled figure on-screen in front of him. The greasy long brown hair, the ragged t-shirt, the drab shapeless underpants with a sad limp dick hanging out of them, the stooped, sad posture are worse than most. And Damian moves to terminate the connection when he spots the guy's puppy-dog eyes again which, to his surprise, causes his cock to stir.

"I could work on this one," he thinks. The visitor doesn't look like he has any attachments or obligations. A partner or parent would insist he washes his hair and clean his clothes and he certainly can't have a job if he spends all his waking hours perusing porn.

And as it is a quiet Sunday evening he has time to explore this one a little further.

"You ever done any SM for real, boy?" Damian asks. "The sort you seem to like watching."

"No, Sir," replies Alex, his voice trembling with fear and excitement in equal measure.

"Want to try some?"

"Yes please, Sir," Alex replies, again assuming some sort of online role-play game would soon start like the war games he used to spend hours immersed in until his cock demanded something more adult.

Damian knows from the visitor's Internet address that he is in London and so, in a firm but friendly tone, he asks the visitor, "Where in London do you live, boy?"

Alex is confused. He'd assumed that this porno site, like so many others, was based in the USA. So when he replies "Paddington" he doesn't expect it to mean anything.

"That's not far from me," replies Damian. "Want to meet up for a coffee, boy?"

Alex is confused. Firstly, he'd assumed this person was computer-generated, not real. It's difficult to separate digital figures from real humans on the small screen on his phone. Secondly, no-one ever asked to meet him. He'd always done the futile chasing for a date. In fact so futile had this been that he'd given up some years ago.

And here he is, once again, being referred to as 'boy'. He didn't think there was any chance he was being confused with a child. And he'd watched enough SM porn to know the protocol.

"Can I ask a question first, Sir?" he asks tentatively.

"Sure, boy, ask away."

"Who are you?"

Damian's reply is succinct and to the point. "I'm the owner of this web site. That's how I was able to find you and control your activities here. Now do you want to meet or not, boy?"

"Yes please, Sir," Alex replies without hesitation. If nothing else he'd wrangle a free coffee and maybe a muffin out of it and he needed to go out anyway as it was rubbish collection night and his flat mate, Melissa, wasn't due back until after bin collection the next morning.

"Meet me outside Café Noir, corner of Edgware Road and Melchet Street, in an hour, boy."

"And before you leave, boy, have a shower and put on some clean clothes," Damian adds firmly, sighing and shaking his head.

Alex checks his loose change on the table and realises he will need to have a very quick shower and then walk there as he can't afford the bus. That will be easy as Café Noir is only 20 minutes away. Finding some clean clothes will be more difficult but he has some reasonably clean jeans and another t-shirt with only a few stains on it so that will have to do.

"How will I recognise you, Sir?" he asks, realising that he hadn't seen his inquisitor's face.

"I'll recognise you, boy. Wait for me outside. And you only get one chance. Understood?"

"Yes, Sir," Alex replies.

"Good boy. Now get on with it."

And with that the voice is gone and his phone's screen goes blank apart from a simple message: "Don't disappoint me, boy."

CHAPTER 2

Café Noir, West London. It's just before 9pm on this warm summer evening and Alex has arrived early for a change. Inside the place is pretty empty and he looks up and down the street looking for someone looking for him.

He's nervous. Very nervous. Not just because he's about to meet a stranger who seems to have aroused something inside him that thousands of hours of porn have failed to do, but also because he's not used to being around people at all, let alone talking to them.

Aside from with his supervisor at the job centre and Melissa, Alex has zero conversation with people in the real world. There is the cute youth on the checkout at his local convenience store where he buys his food who he tries to engage with, but he tends to grunt rather than talk while he swipes Alex's groceries across the scanner, so, coupled with Alex's shyness, their conversation is very limited.

Alex turns to look into the café and sees himself reflected in the window. His hair's clean but still hanging in disorganised clumps which Melissa's hairbrush failed to disentangle. And in the dim light, the stains on his t-shirt and jeans aren't very noticeable.

As he is about to turn back to the street, Alex spots a tall man dressed in black standing right behind him, reflected in the window. He tries to turn around and discovers that the man is closer than he realised and almost has him pinned against the window.

"Glad you made it, boy," the stranger whispers in his ear as he turns Alex around to face him and pushes him back against the window.

The stranger is older and much taller than Alex, shaved head, dark goatee beard flecked with grey and dressed in the same black t-shirt and combats he'd seen on his phone. He's too close for Alex to be able to look down and check on the boots.

Alex opens his mouth to speak but the stranger puts his finger to Alex's lips to indicate he should stay silent.

"Hands behind your back, boy, while I look you over," Damian orders.

Alex complies immediately, wondering nonetheless what any passer-by would make of this little scene being enacted in public. But once again, the commanding power of the stranger's voice washes away any doubts.

Damian steps back and looks over his prospect. Scruffy, unshaven, smelly clothes, flabby in places but nothing a new wardrobe, strict workout regime and diet couldn't fix. And there again are the shining puppy-dog eyes, hinting at some spirit trapped inside a distressed shell.

"You'll do for now, boy. Now let's get a coffee and I can get to know more about you."

Alex follows Damian into the coffee shop, hands

still behind his back which he thinks is probably the correct thing to do, though it feels strange, and requests a strong black coffee when asked. He also asks for a muffin when Damian says he can also have something to eat. Alex really wanted a sandwich but thought he'd better not push it too far.

Once they've been served, Damian leads Alex back out to a table and chairs on the street where they can be a bit more private while also being far more public.

The interview begins before Alex has drunk much of his coffee or even started on the muffin.

"I asked you online what you were looking for, boy, and you said you didn't know. Yet you're here clearly hoping for something. Any clearer about what it is?"

Alex isn't the most articulate of people and for him to be having a coffee with a very sexy man straight out of his wank fantasies makes him even more tongue tied.

"I suppose anything to make life worth living," Alex finds himself saying, though he'd intended to say he was looking for sex. This won't be the first time Alex's heart rather than his dick controls his mouth.

"That's very sad," Damian replies.

"Yup," Alex mutters, his head bowed with shame.

Damian frowns. Does this boy really know what's on offer?

"You spend hours inserting yourself into the SM dungeon scenes on my porno sites, always as the slave, the submissive one being tied up and beaten and servicing the tops. Have you ever done that for real, boy?"

"No", Alex answers softly, head bowed in embarrassment.

"Look at me when you're talking to me, boy. Do you want to?"

"Suppose so," Alex mumbles, still looking at his coffee and uneaten muffin.

"Then you'd better start learning fast, boy." And with that Damian moves his hand as if swatting away a fly but in fact deliberately knocking Alex's coffee over so it spills into his lap.

Alex jumps and makes to get up but Damian orders him to stay seated.

"Lesson number one, boy," Damian says firmly before Alex can say anything. "You always look me in the eye and call me 'Sir' when talking to me. If you don't you get punished."

Alex's crotch is on fire from the hot coffee. But that heat is nothing compared with the excitement swelling inside him as someone is starting to take control of his disastrous, chaotic life.

"Understood, Sir," Alex replies with a voice both assertive in its acceptance and submissive in its tone, looking Damian straight in the eye this time.

Damian is always prepared for any eventualities. It goes with being a control freak. He reaches into his backpack for a bottle of water which he hands to Alex.

"Pour this over your crotch to cool it down."

Alex reaches for the bottle and hesitates briefly before cooling his tender parts with its contents, making his jeans even wetter. Fortunately, it's a warm night and they'll dry soon enough, he thinks.

"Thank you, Sir."

"Tell me more about yourself, boy," Damian asks, continuing his interview. "Do you have a partner, a boyfriend, family, close friends?"

"I don't have any of those, Sir," Alex replies carefully, remembering to say 'Sir' and to look Damian in the eye when he's speaking, something that doesn't come naturally to him.

"Totally alone?" Damian queries.

"Well not totally, Sir. I suppose I feel alone. I live with a woman called Melissa – we're just a flat share, nothing more. I have a sofa bed in the living room of her place which is what you saw when we chatted earlier.

"As for family, my parents and older sister emigrated to Canada some years ago and I've lost touch with them. They sort of abandoned me and I didn't really cope well with being on my own. I sort of let everything slide."

"How did you meet Melissa?" Damian enquires wondering what sort of person would take Alex in.

"The first time was at the job centre. I was in there having an argument about my unemployment benefits and stormed out. Or rather tried to. But I tripped over her shopping bag and we had just a few words with each other.

"I expected her to be angry with me, especially as I almost stood on the packets of bizarrely-flavoured crisps that had fallen out of her bag, but she wasn't. Maybe she felt sorry for me."

Then Alex remembers something and adds "Sir."

Damian smiles and notices Alex's puppy-dog eyes again. He wonders if Melissa had seen them as well. "Go on, boy."

"It was a few weeks later that we bumped into each other again, at the bus stop outside the dog rescue centre near where she lives. She'd wanted to adopt a stray dog but had been rejected because her place wasn't suitable; it's on the 16th floor of a residential building with no green spaces visible even from that height.

"Melissa recognised me and jokingly asked if I was hoping to be offered a home there. I said I was looking for somewhere cheaper to live, though not in the dogs' home, and she said that as she couldn't adopt a dog I'd do instead as she could do with help with the rent.

"You must think me a very sad case, Sir, no better than a stray dog. So I won't be surprised if you decide to leave now."

"Not at all, boy," Damian replies. "I approve of taking in unloved puppies. Were you always such a mess?"

"No I wasn't, Sir," Alex replies, finding it strange that someone is interested in him and trying hard to follow Damian's rules by maintaining eye contact and dropping 'Sir' into his conversation when he remembers.

"I actually did very well at school and even got a decent job straight afterwards in a mobile phone shop. But, as I said, when my family left I never learned how to look after myself. I stopped going out and started consoling myself by watching porn and wanking all the time. It's interfered with me keeping a job as my mind's always on my next jerk off session."

Alex realises that in his excitement he's revealed his obsessional sex life to Damian and wonders if it will upset him, but it doesn't.

"So I noticed," Damian informs him. "I've seen how much time you spend on my porn sites so you must really enjoy watching porn and jacking off, boy."

"It's better than nothing, Sir. But that's a pretty poor standard to measure your life by. I wish I knew how to break out of it and take control of my life, but It's the only pleasure I get from anything."

"Do you want to take a risk and try turning your life around, boy? It might mean an end to watching porn and wanking and a start to getting pleasure from other equally exciting things."

Alex has never considered himself a risk taker, but there's something about the man in front of him that makes him feel warm inside in a way he hasn't felt for years. He even likes being called 'boy'. It hints at a relationship of some sort though he's not quite sure what that would be. And the idea of some new excitement sounds intriguing, though Damian's sales pitch sounds vaguely like an invitation to join a religious cult.

"How would I do that, Sir?" Alex replies, suspiciously.

"This is what's on offer, boy," Damian starts.

"I'm a sadist. I like controlling and tormenting other men, all safe, sane and consensual of course. You'll have seen some of my SM play in the porno films you seem never to tire of, and I'm looking for a personal slave. Someone whose life I can help change so they become proud of themselves and achieve something rather than being the sad wanker they are now.

"Those slaves portrayed in my films may seem submissive and gutless with no mind of their own. But in fact they're very proud of themselves and their achievements and have great self-worth."

Alex didn't realise this sort of thing happened for real. He'd hoped it would. But, even so, he'd never imagined it happening to him. And he is worried. Would he be injured? Would he be killed? Would he become a real slave with no freedom (though that bit didn't sound totally unwelcome as he was getting precious little pleasure from his freedom).

Damian knows from experience what Alex is thinking.

"Don't worry about your safety, boy. I may be

planning to control you, to hurt you in very pleasurable ways, as contradictory as that sounds, to own you. But I'm also there to ensure you're kept healthy, fit and happy and to help you grow as a human being. A sad, sick puppy is no fun at all. You'll learn new skills, both for work and for pleasure. You also seem to be something of a tech head so I may find you ways of helping my business with your knowledge.

"It won't be easy for you, boy. You'll make mistakes and be punished for them, as you've already discovered. But you'll gain self-esteem and pride in yourself, your abilities and your appearance, things clearly lacking at the moment. I want to be proud of you and your achievements. And I want you to be proud of yourself.

"Does that interest you, boy?"

Alex smiles, something he hardly ever does, and his puppy-dog eyes sparkle a little more than usual, making Damian's cock twitch again with anticipation of what he could make of Alex.

"Yes please, Sir," Alex replies, the shock of his hot coffee punishment now almost forgotten.

"You may ask me some questions, boy."

"Thank you, Sir," Alex replies.

Hundreds of questions race around in his head but he finds himself asking the only one that really matters.

"What happens next, Sir?" Alex asks, surprised at his own answer.

Damian is pleased and for the first time his stern expression changes and he smiles. "That's the correct question, boy."

Essential to this sort of relationship is trust. And Damian had succeeded in establishing enough for Alex not to bore him with endless worries about safety, money, limits and other things that he knew would be of no relevance. Things were looking good.

"Go home and think about our meeting, boy. Sleep on it. If you want to continue then be here tomorrow morning at 8am when we'll start your trial period. You don't need to bring anything with you, as I will provide for you from now on.

"If you need to tell Melissa where you're going here's my business card with my details on it. It's always good to make sure a friend knows where you're going when you go off with someone new for the first time."

Alex takes the card and reads the few details on it: Damian Hall, CEO, DH Productions and a phone number.

"Thank you, Sir," Alex replies, at last knowing the name of the man who is so successfully seducing him. "If I want to do it then I'll be here at 8am tomorrow."

"Good boy." Damian replies, smiling again.

"Oh, and one thing more, boy. Give me your phone. I don't want you distracted over the next ten hours while you consider my offer. If you don't turn up tomorrow then I'll leave it behind the counter here and you can collect it another time."

Alex's mind races again. Ten hours without porn? He'd not done that in years. Yet he knows this is a test. If he fails it then he may never get another chance like this. Nor would he have the nerve to return to Damian's porno sites which he had to admit were far more exciting than any of the others.

Alex hands over his phone which Damian switches off and puts in his pocket.

"Now go home, boy. I hope to see you again."

"Thank you, Sir," Alex replies as he gets up and leaves, still unsure if this was a wind up or a real opportunity. Whether he'd just been scammed of his precious smartphone or started an exciting new stage in his life.

As he walks off he turns back to see Damian calmly finishing his coffee and eating Alex's muffin, not even looking his way. Already Alex is missing his attention.

CHAPTER 3

Back at the flat, Melissa is in the kitchen devouring a bag of her favourite shrimp cocktail crisps and making some instant soup which she and Alex survive on. He didn't expect to find her home but apparently she and her latest boyfriend had an argument and went their separate ways.

"Hey there, where've you been?" she asks loudly, knowing that Alex never goes out.

"I went to meet a man off the Internet for a coffee."

Melissa looks Alex over and realises that there must be some truth in it as he's washed his hair.

"Either it was very exciting and you spunked loads in your pants or you had an accident," she observes, looking down at his damp crotch.

Even though Alex is used to Melissa's forthright bluntness and coarse language, he still blushes. He decides Melissa needn't know the whole truth. She is very dismissive of the Internet, thinking, fairly correctly, that many of the people on there needed to get out more. And as for hook-ups, she prefers the easy pickings of the ever-changing casual waiting staff at the hotel where she works behind the bar. Plus she doesn't know exactly how dark the porn is that is Alex's constant companion.

"I had an accident. Spilled my coffee," he says, uncharacteristically looking her straight in the eye in the hope it will make his explanation more believable.

"So what's he like?"

"Pretty ordinary really. Wants me to go stay with him for a while so we can get to know each other better while he assesses me for a job as his assistant."

"Whoa, hold on, Alex. One minute you're Johnny no-mates, the next you're shacking up with someone who's offering you a job. Who is this guy anyway?"

Alex shows her Damian's business card.

"This can't be for real," she exclaims. "He obviously can't want an ugly fucker like you to appear in his porno films. Not unless you're the gimp totally enclosed in leather like the one in the Pulp Fiction DVD I watched the other night."

Alex feels hurt. It's true he isn't attractive. But inside he still feels traces of the bright young attractive man he used to be. And Damian, who he is already thinking of as his future Sir, had maybe seen that.

"Have you called this number to see if it's legit?" Melissa asks.

Alex lies again.

"It seemed rude to check it while he was there and I left my phone at the coffee shop by mistake."

"Well I'll phone him and tell him not to mess with you," she replies, acting like someone whose pet dog has been borrowed by a stranger.

And before Alex can stop her, Melissa has rung the number.

Now back home, Damian's phone rings. He

doesn't usually accept calls from numbers he doesn't recognise but he has been expecting this call.

"This is Damian Hall," he answers.

"Hi there, this is Melissa, Alex's flat mate. Who are you and why are you messing him around?"

"Well hello Melissa, nice to hear from you. I'm glad you've called. I can assure you that this is all legitimate."

Damian decides to be cautious about what he reveals to Melissa as he isn't sure how much she knows about Alex, even if she knows he is gay, never mind his darker interests.

"I'm looking for a new assistant and really think I could make something of Alex. He's quite an expert on Internet porn as I'm sure you know, so I'd like to borrow him for a while if that's OK."

"Well I hope the pay is good and you treat him with respect," Melissa demands.

"You can be sure of that, Melissa. I think Alex has great potential but he needs cleaning up a bit and some training for his new role. Which is why I want him to come stay with me so we can spend lots of time together. But he'll certainly earn his stripes."

Damian is sure the last pun would go over Melissa's head but it amuses him anyway.

Melissa is a bit taken aback. She'd expected some anger at her interference. And instead she is talking to someone who not only claims to be a porn producer, but sounds like a porn star and is polite and respectful as well. And he seems to like Alex.

"Err, OK then. I suppose it's OK. But you can be sure that I'll be keeping track of Alex and if I think there's any funny business going on I'll call the police."

Damian finds Melissa's threat reassuring rather than intimidating. "I quite understand your concern, Melissa, and I'm glad he has someone looking out for him. I hope that when you speak to Alex after he's started his training you'll find him much happier and a bit more human. Do you have any more questions?"

"I suppose not," Melissa replies.

"Feel free to call me any time to check on how he is," Damian adds reassuringly. "And when Alex gets a new phone he'll be able to contact you himself."

"Thank you for looking after him," she adds as an afterthought. And with that she hangs up.

"He sounds legit," she tells Alex, who is feeling sad at not hearing Damian's commanding voice himself but happy that Damian hasn't been deterred by Melissa's interference.

"So when do you start?"

"In the morning," he says. "I'm to meet him at Café Noir down on the Edgware Road and go to his place. But I have to sleep on it and if I want the job (for Alex had guessed that Damian had been economical with the truth about the position) I guess I won't be back for a few days. Don't worry, I'll keep in touch."

Melissa is tired, too tired to have wondered how

Damian knew that Alex had lost his phone, and goes to bed.

Alex reaches into his jeans pocket for his phone so he can go online and maybe spot Damian in one of the porno films and then remembers he no longer has it. His craving for porn is now replaced with a craving for Damian, for his voice, for the firm grip of his arms as he turned him around outside the coffee shop.

Most of all he craves for someone who not only likes him for what he is but can see through the walking mess he is now to what he might become, even if that involved entering a world of harsh training. He hoped there'd be some love in there too, but Alex didn't really know about love, as there had been precious little of that from his parents when he grew up, so that was just an idle thought. But he knows he isn't happy now, far from it.

And if there is a chance of leaving his current life and starting afresh then what could he lose?

Alex goes to curl up on the sofa bed so wrapped up in the excitement of the past couple of hours that he almost forgets to take off his wet jeans.

He starts to think about what he is letting himself in for. What did Damian mean about him being Damian's 'slave'? How much pain was involved? What else would he be expected to do sexually?

As far as sex goes, Alex has never done anything other than wank, though occasionally he's copied some heavier stimulation he'd seen in porn films, slapping his balls once with a ruler, and even spending a whole ten minutes with clothes pegs on his nipples. These hadn't been too bad so how painful could it get?

But sex with another man? Would he get fucked? Would he have to suck cock? And what about the SM sex? Would there be flogging and caning and the like as he'd watched many times on his phone, finding what he saw both frightening and exciting? Would he have to drink piss (again copying a porno he'd tried his own once and realised that the tinned asparagus beforehand might not have been a good idea).

To a man who has never been touched, even the lick of a whip can feel like a kiss.

Back in West London, Damian is looking at his phone and thinking about the call he'd just taken from Melissa. Clearly Melissa cared about Alex, and the fact that she rang him was a good sign as it meant he wasn't alone in seeing something good in the boy. Maybe Melissa too had been taken in by his puppy-dog eyes.

CHAPTER 4

Alex doesn't sleep well that night. In fact he doesn't sleep at all, his mind racing with thoughts of the adventure he is about to embark on. Clips from his favourite Master/slave pornos flash by, always with Damian as the Master and him as the slave.

He knows he needs to make a change in his life. Spending all waking hours wanking to porn is actually really boring and not very satisfying.

Once he'd tried tuning his phone off for a few hours but his addiction was too strong. He even thought of giving his cock a rest and not wanking for a day. He lasted an hour.

What was there to fear? He didn't fear for his life. Melissa would make sure he was OK. And Damian seemed legit and he might even make enough money out of it to get a wide-screen laptop.

And so at 7am Alex rises from his bed, showers and prepares himself as best as he knows. He finds another pair of jeans and a t-shirt without too many holes in it, laces up his training shoes and leaves the flat, leaving a note for Melissa thanking her for her concern and saying he'd be in touch. She is fast asleep and her plan to turn up at Café Noir to spy on Alex and Damian backfires as it's 9am before she wakes up.

It is just before 8am and Alex is outside Café Noir scouring the passers-by for any sign of Damian when a large grey Mercedes with darkened rear windows pulls up to the kerb.

A tall black man in a smart grey suit, white shirt and black tie gets out of the driver's seat and comes over to Alex who he recognises instantly from Damian's description.

It isn't Damian and Alex's heart sinks wondering if he'd imagined the previous night or more probably been stood up again. "This guy's probably just lost and wants directions," he thinks, nonetheless admiring the man's handsome appearance with his shaved head, dark moustache and shiny black shoes.

"Hi, Alex," the driver says offering his hand. "I'm Jameson, Mr Hall's personal assistant. If you're ready, get in the back of the car."

With relief at not being stood up, Alex shakes his hand and mutters "Hi Jameson or should I call you 'Sir' as well?"

"Call me Mr Jameson, Alex."

Alex gets into the back of the car, expecting to find Damian there. But it's empty and his heart sinks again.

"Mr Hall is getting a few things ready for you, Alex, so he asked me to collect you," Jameson tells him as they set off.

"There's a note from Mr Hall there for you and some water if you need it."

Alex eagerly opens the envelope and reads the note.

"Glad you made the right decision, boy. I hoped you would. See you in a few minutes. XX SIR."

Alex heart speeds up as his adventure begins. And what's with the 'XX' at the end? This surprises him. And pleases him too. For the second time in twelve hours he smiles.

Damian's house is actually very close to Café Noir, so much so that by the time Alex has finished reading and re-reading the note they are there. Wide automatic doors open and the car enters an underground garage.

Jameson leads Alex up some stairs to a large hallway where Damian is waiting, dressed as ever in black combats and t-shirt and very shiny black boots.

"Welcome to my home, Alex. Hopefully it will become yours as well."

Alex stares around him at the expensive furnishings and paintings and feels somewhat intimidated. There are discreet small dark domes in the ceiling concealing CCTV cameras and Alex wonders if they're for security or so Damian can keep an eye on everyone and everything. Probably both.

"Well, Alex?"

"Thank you, Sir, glad to be here" Alex replies remembering to say 'Sir' as he doesn't want a repeat of the crotch scalding incident. And then remembers something else and puts his hands behind his back.

Damian smiles.

"Good boy, you're learning.

"First of all Jameson is going to get you all cleaned up. After that we'll have lunch and I'll show you your room. We can also discuss and start your training."

And with that Damian opens a door and enters what looks like an executive office. On the desk are three large computer screens and the only wall Alex can see is covered with shelves of DVDs.

"DHP Central" Alex guesses. The office door closes and Damian is gone.

Jameson presses a button hidden under a side table and a wall panel slides away to reveal a brightly lit corridor which he guides Alex through, pressing another button to close the panel. Alex notices the panel is very thick, probably soundproof he suspects.

Towards the end of the corridor on the left is a very large marble bathroom with more plumbing attachments than Alex knew existed, a shower, a chair and a massage table. Jameson puts his hand on the back of Alex's neck and steers him into the room.

"OK, Alex, you do exactly as I say and you'll be OK. If you don't you'll be punished. Understand?"

"Yes, Sir. Sorry, yes Mr Jameson."

Jameson smiles. "I don't do the punishing, Alex, but I am to report everything to Mr Hall who will reward or punish you as necessary."

"Understood, Mr Jameson."

"Now empty your pockets and take all of your clothes off and put them in this bag," Jameson commands, indicating a black bin liner. And with that he leaves the room.

Alex removes a few coins and his benefit card from

his pocket and places them on the massage table and quickly removes his t-shirt, jeans, underpants, socks and shoes and places them in the bag.

He is naked in a stranger's house, wondering what he's let himself in for.

He looks around the room but, before he can explore it, Jameson returns wearing black like Damian and picks up the bag.

"We're gonna have to incinerate this lot, Alex, for sanitary reasons," Jameson says peering into the bag then pulling away with a scowl as the smell hits him.

He puts Alex's money and benefit card in his pocket.

"We'll keep those safe for you, Alex, but hopefully you won't be needing them.

"And you'll get some new clothes in a minute. But first we have to clean you up, starting with your hair."

Jameson wheels over the chair and indicates for Alex to sit in it. "Hands behind the chair, Alex."

Alex's first shock is the cold plastic against his buttocks. The second comes when Jameson quickly secures his wrists together behind the chair with some handcuffs.

"What the fuck is going on?" Alex shouts, struggling against the handcuffs.

Jameson walks over to an electronic clipboard hanging on the wall behind him and makes a single black vertical stroke on it.

"Alex, no shouting, swearing or resistance is

allowed. You've just earned your first demerit."

Alex goes silent. This doesn't seem like fun.

"Don't worry, Alex, I'm sure you'll learn fast.

"This hair of yours is a disgusting mess. You'll have noticed that both Mr Hall and I have shaved heads. But for you I think a nice short military crop would look cute and go well with your sweet puppy-dog eyes."

"Gosh," thinks Alex. "This guy is sweet talking me while he's tying me up?"

And then he hears the clippers start and he watches his dark, mangled, greasy hair fall to the floor. Jameson takes his time, making sure to get the length right and even and then points to a mirror for Alex to see the result from his chair.

Alex has to admit the crop looks very cute. In fact it almost makes him look cute, were it not for his flabby body and stubbly face.

Jameson looks at Alex and can't ignore the fact that he hasn't had a shave in days. He goes off behind Alex to get some things and returns with a hot damp towel, shaving gel, a bowl full of water and some razors.

He wraps the towel around Alex's face. "There, just like they do in those swanky barbers in Jermyn Street," he laughs. "But they don't provide the added benefit of the handcuffs."

It takes two razors before Alex is properly clean-shaven.

"Now for the rest of your body hair. I don't have to

tie you down, but I will if you're going to be uncooperative or wriggle. I don't want to cut you when I'm doing your cock and balls."

"Shit!" thinks Alex, "he's going to remove ALL my body hair, even down there?"

And then he looks in the mirror again and thinks that maybe removing the random patches of hair scattered unevenly around his body might be a good thing. And already he's looking better – he'd forgotten how good-looking he used to be.

"I'll come quietly, Mr Jameson," Alex jokes, not being sure if jokes are allowed, but it helps him feel better.

Jameson smiles as he unlocks the handcuffs and Alex gets up from the chair and climbs onto the massage table. His first experience of bondage hadn't been that bad. In fact he found it quite exciting which was good as he expected more would follow soon.

As Alex lays still on the table, Jameson crops all the hair from his body. Alex has never had anyone else touch his cock and balls before. And being wankless for the last twelve hours, his stubby cut cock responds quickly when Jameson starts working on them.

Jameson seems unphased by the erection and handles Alex's stiffening cock like someone might a joystick, moving it out of the way when he needs access to more pubic hair, pulling Alex's balls out to get in the cracks.

Finally Alex is hairless apart from his short cropped head and Jameson tells him he needs a good clean out and then a shower.

Alex isn't sure what a 'clean out' is but soon finds out.

Jameson leads him into a wet area and tells Alex that he's obviously full of shit and there's no better remedy than a good few enemas.

Now enemas aren't something that Alex has ever tried, what with the bathroom in the flat being tiny and the water pressure very variable though he had seen some enema porn a long time ago and it got his cock stirring. Nor has he, as Jameson discovers, ever had anything larger than a small finger up his anus.

Undeterred, Jameson proceeds to give Alex a good internal clean out. And Alex admits that he feels a lot better afterwards, even though it is strange having all that water running in and out of him and a man he'd only just met stretching his arse hole with a gloved finger and then inserting a long metal tube up it.

Finally Alex is told to shower and clean his teeth. The shower is an odd experience. Alex isn't used to his body being so smooth and his cock and balls standing out so much, unsheltered by his pubic hair. He's tempted to give his cock a tug but thinks better of it, remembering the CCTV cameras everywhere.

After he has dried himself from the shower, he goes to the wash basin to brush his teeth. A new toothbrush, fresh tube of toothpaste and a bottle of mouthwash are waiting for him. Alex has never used mouthwash before and isn't sure whether to use it before or after brushing his teeth so plays safe and does both, fearing another demerit if he gets it wrong.

When he is finished, Jameson hands him a dustpan and brush and tells him to clean up all the hair and put it in the bag.

"This is your first job of the day, Alex. So do it properly. There's no hurry." And with that Jameson leaves, locking the door behind him.

Alex sweeps up the hair quickly and puts it in the bin bag. Then he notices there's more that he's missed and sweeps that up. The black streaks in the white marble floor aren't helping. And just when he thinks he's finished he realises there's hair on the massage table too. Cleaning this off puts more on the floor so that it takes a good twenty minutes before he's finished.

He feels strange walking and crawling around this room, naked and hairless. But kind of sexy. And just when thinks maybe he needn't try so hard to clean up every strand of his hair he remembers the electronic clipboard with its black mark on it (which he's sure Damian is monitoring) and decides he'd better not earn any more until he knows what the penalty is for earning them.

So he has one last crawl around, sweeping up the few remnants of his body hair.

Jameson returns and hands Alex a white t-shirt,

white cotton shorts with no pockets and short black lace-up boots with rubber soles. There's no underwear or socks.

"This is your uniform for now, Alex. You'll put on a clean t-shirt and shorts every day or more often if necessary. Be careful not to let Mr Hall see you dirty or you'll earn demerits. He doesn't want to see any stains anywhere on them, inside or out, or on you, as he's a real stickler for cleanliness as you've already discovered.

"Oh, and you'll find boot cleaning materials in your room to use every day. You'd better clean your boots naked so you don't get boot polish on your clothes."

Alex puts on the t-shirt and shorts and laces up the boots. The boots are new and a bit stiff and without socks a bit hard against his feet. But then there are so many holes in his own socks they don't offer much protection anyway.

Alex wonders what to do next as Jameson is just standing there, arms crossed, looking at him. Then one of the dim light bulbs in his brain glows brighter and he stands to attention, feet apart, hands behind his back and says "Ready, Mr Jameson." He's seen this sort of stance in the porn videos he watches and assumes it is expected of himself as well.

Jameson smiles. "Well done, Alex, you're learning fast." And with that he rubs Alex's head like one might a puppy. "Let's go see Mr Hall. He's ready for you now, and you're ready for him."

CHAPTER 5

Jameson leads Alex out of the secret corridor and back into the main entrance hall and stops outside Damian's office. He knocks once and a voice inside shouts "Enter".

Inside Damian is sitting at his desk.

"Gosh, you look almost human, Alex," he says, smiling.

Alex smiles too. He feels different. His body is clean and his clothes are clean, if a little skimpy. And the rough cotton of his white shorts is rubbing against his cock, making it twitch and grow a little. He wonders if Damian can see this and feels a little embarrassed.

Even so, he stands to attention, feet astride, hands behind his back and head up, remembering to look Damian straight in the eyes and hoping his erection will subside.

"Thank you, Sir."

Damian gets up from his chair and comes over behind Alex, massaging his shoulders with his strong hands.

"You even smell good for a change," Damian adds before kissing him lightly on the back of his neck and returning to his desk.

Alex feels warm. Feels accepted. Even slightly loved, a strange experience for him.

Damian's phone rings and Melissa's name and number appear on its screen. She's just woken up and panicked at missing the opportunity to secretly observe Alex at Café Noir and catch sight of the two of them.

"Good morning, Melissa," Damian answers, looking up and spotting Alex's erection.

"Yes Alex is here. He's looking quite good now, quite perky in fact. He's been cleaned up and got some clean clothes. He scrubs up quite well, actually, and he has a nice smile on his face."

Alex recognises Melissa's voice at the other end but can't tell exactly what she's saying.

Melissa had never seen Alex smile and doesn't know whether something creepy has happened or he's actually lucked out.

"That's OK, Melissa. He'll be in touch himself soon. Thanks for your call."

And with that he hangs up and looks at something on one of his computer screens.

"I see from your demerit board that there was a slight problem earlier. In fact I was watching on the CCTV so I know what happened."

"Sorry, Sir. I guess this is all new to me and I'm not very good at obeying orders."

"Never mind, boy, you'll learn fast. In fact I think it best that you pay off that demerit point straight away."

"Yes, Sir," Alex replies hesitantly, not sure what payment would involve and a shiver runs through him. His erection disappears.

"I'll go easy on you for now, boy, but you can be

sure the punishments will be more severe in future," Damian tells Alex, fixing him with a firm gaze as he gets up once again.

"Follow me."

Damian leaves the office and turns into the secret corridor, Alex following behind, hands still behind his back.

At the end of the corridor is a black door which Damian opens and indicates for Alex to go through.

Wide-eyed, Alex looks around the large room. It is a dungeon just like the ones he's seen in Damian's videos. Spotlights pick out bondage frames and tables, and leather whips and floggers hang from hooks on the wall. There are also numerous shelves of sex toys, most of which Alex has never seen before.

"Put your arms out straight in front of you, boy," Damian orders.

Alex complies. "Yes, Sir".

Once Damian has locked padded leather restraints on Alex's wrists and ankles he positions him in front of a leather-covered vaulting horse.

"Bend over and make yourself comfortable, boy."

Alex has seen this sort of equipment used before and fears for what will happen next. He knows it will be painful. And he doesn't know what will happen if he refuses. Nor does he know what real pain is like apart from that bad toothache last year. Oh, and busting his knee.

"Time to man up and take charge of myself," Alex

thinks to himself, trying hard to quell his nervousness.

Damian attaches the four restraints to the horse so Alex cannot move and then squats down by Alex's now downward-pointing face.

"Listen up, boy. You made a scene back there in the bathroom and you have to take the consequences. You'll be OK. Countless others have taken far worse than you are about to experience and they all lived and learned their lesson. This is going to hurt more than anything else you have ever experienced. But it's quick and then over with.

"Understood?"

"Yes, Sir," Alex mumbles.

"Can't hear you, boy."

"Yes, Sir," Alex says more clearly, his body trembling at the strain of being stretched over the horse and the fear of what will happen next.

"Good boy," Damian replies, tousling his cropped hair.

As he moves to stand up, Damian notices Alex's cock has once again started to grow in his shorts and smiles to himself.

Alex hears Damian move to the wall and remove something.

"Ready, boy?"

"Yes, Sir"

And then Alex experiences a pain across his buttocks like nothing else he's ever experienced. Damian was right. It feels like he's been cut or burned with a hot knife. He draws breath sharply at the shock, relaxes slightly and starts to cry.

Damian releases Alex from the horse, helps him stand up and encircles him with his strong arms, Alex's sobbing face resting on his shoulder.

"That was one stroke with one of my easiest canes, boy. And you had your shorts on which lessened the effect. You'll be OK. But if you don't do as you're told or make mistakes there will be more and not so easy. This is what I mean about training you to take control of your life, boy. Understand?"

"Yes, Sir," Alex whispers, still sobbing a bit and unable to speak properly.

Damian moves away from Alex and hands him a large black bandana.

"Wipe your eyes with this, boy."

Alex dries his eyes.

"And blow your nose as well, boy, you're snivelling."

Alex complies and hands the bandana back to Damian who wipes the remaining tears from Alex's face.

"There's no pockets in those shorts, boy, and for now this is your only possession. You'd better carry it with you always as I expect it will come in handy again." And with that Damian loops it around Alex's neck, cowboy-style, knotted at the back.

Damian undoes some fasteners and his black combats fall to the floor without him having to remove his boots. He is naked underneath and for the first time Alex sees Damian's large cut cock which is far from soft. Through the head of it is a metal PA ring going in through the front and out underneath.

"Come over here, boy," Damian orders and Alex follows him to a leather-padded chair. Damian indicates for Alex to kneel on the floor in front of the chair and fastens the wrists restraints together behind Alex's back before sitting down.

"You OK, boy?" he asks.

"I suppose so," Alex mumbles, his head looking down.

"I suppose, so, SIR" Damian reminds him. "You really must stop mumbling and show you really mean what you're saying."

"Sorry, Sir. I suppose so, Sir," Alex repeats more clearly, looking straight at Damian this time.

Damian softens a little at the sight of Alex's puppy-dog eyes and guides his head towards his erection. "You ever sucked a cock before, boy?"

"No, Sir."

"Well you'd better start now, boy. Take it slowly. Just use your tongue and lips for now. I'll train you slowly so that soon you will be able to take my cock all the way to the back of your throat."

Alex has always fantasised about sucking cock and the idea always gets him hard. And as he kneels there staring at Damian's cock, his own cock starts growing again under his shorts, something Damian notices of course. He wants Alex to be excited because he knows that sexual arousal and release is Alex's main driving force.

"What are you waiting for, boy?"

Alex leans forward and starts gently licking Damian's cock head, finding the PA ring something novel to move around and explore with his tongue.

Within a few minutes, Alex is taking a few inches of Damian's cock into his mouth, getting it nice and moist. It feels good having part of another man inside him. Damian encourages him to take it slowly as his cock has got bigger with the excitement of having his newly-owned boy sucking his cock.

Concentrating on not gagging on Damian's cock takes Alex's mind off his buttocks, which are still on fire from the caning, and he almost forgets his punishment.

"That's enough for now, boy. Thank you," Damian tells him.

Alex marvels at being thanked and, without planning to, finds himself saying "No, Sir, thank you, Sir."

"Good, boy" Damian replies and then holds Alex's head up and kisses him briefly on the lips.

It would be an understatement to say that Alex's brain goes into a tailspin. Here he is, restrained, buttocks on fire, his mouth and lips tingling from the cock sucking and his tormentor has just kissed him on the lips.

Alex has a lot to learn about the love and caring inherent in SM sex.

Damian continues talking.

"This is my world, boy, a world of control and pain and pleasure all mixed together. You can be part of it if you want. That was just a taster of what could be in store for you. The play will get heavier. And it is 'play'. It is fun. I'm not intending to damage you or degrade you. By learning to take heavier stuff you will get stronger and be proud of your achievements.

"And you will get pleasures way beyond what your feeble, porno-addicted, spunkless wanks on your own will ever achieve.

"But there are a few rules.

"Firstly you must trust me and obey me and do everything I say. And that goes for Jameson too. That way you will learn and experience things you would otherwise shy away from and you will avoid getting injured.

"Secondly, any disrespect to me or Jameson or anyone else, or any careless mistakes will be severely punished as you've just started to find out.

"And thirdly, remember you always have a choice. I didn't kidnap you. You chose to meet me the first time. You chose to return this morning. If at any time you want out then say so. But be sure you mean it. If you do ask to be released then I'll give you a cooling off period on your own, untouched by me, to reflect on what you really want. If you still want out 24 hours later, I will let you return to your sad world, free of any obligations. But there will be no second chance.

"In any case, there will be a trial period of three months. At the end of it we can decide whether this is working out for both of us.

"Understood, boy?"

"Yes, Sir."

Damian bends over and releases the wrist cuffs from each other but leaves them locked on Alex's wrists.

"Stand up, boy, it's time to show you to your room."

Alex complies without hesitation and stands to attention, his hands behind his back. He's tempted to feel where his buttocks are still burning but thinks better of it. He hopes there will be time for that later.

Damian fastens his combats back on and pulls a wide leather collar from a shelf which he locks around Alex's neck, loosening the black bandana a little so it doesn't get in the way. He reattaches the wrists cuffs to each other behind Alex's back and uses a chain dog lead attached to the collar to guide Alex out of the dungeon.

Alex's room is next to the dungeon, opposite the large bathroom, and Damian unlocks the door and leads Alex inside and shows him around.

The room is bare, with white painted walls and a small window high up covered with bars. Alex wonders if they are to stop people getting in or him getting out.

There's a metal-framed bed in one corner, which

seems to be bolted to the floor, covered in a mattress and blanket. Apart from that, the only furniture is a metal chair and a desk built into the wall. A back-lit digital clock high up over the door faces the bed.

Above the desk a computer screen with built-in speakers is attached to a wall-mounted swivel bracket and there's a keyboard and mouse on the desk, and a bottle of water. The screen seems to be showing one of Damian's videos and shouts and noises of leather hitting flesh resound through the speakers. Damian turns the volume down as he passes it.

A shelf to one side holds more white t-shirts and shorts and another has some boot cleaning materials on it.

Alex spots a bathroom off the bedroom with a bath and separate shower, a hand basin and a toilet bowl without a seat. On a shelf are a range of toiletries and there also appears to be another enema device hanging by the shower next to some white towels and a face cloth. A full-length mirror is mounted on the wall one side of the basin and a laundry basket on the other side.

"This is where you will sleep, boy, and spend time resting and maybe work at times. The door will be locked from the outside for now so no-one but Jameson and myself can get in and you can't go prowling around and startle my less-enlightened guests."

Alex takes it all in. It looks more like a prison cell,

even down to the CCTV camera in the corner of the ceiling, but he doesn't mind. It's spotlessly clean and clutter-free unlike where he lives with Melissa. And hey, the towels are clean and folded and there's a computer. He looks at it and wonders whether he can get access to the Internet on it. Maybe email Melissa. Send out an SOS if necessary.

Damian notices this and puts Alex straight.

"Boy, don't get carried away. That computer is locked down. At present you can view my porno sites but nothing else. When I think you're ready for more privileges or to communicate with Melissa I'll let you know."

"Thank you, Sir."

"Boy, do you need to piss?"

"Yes please, Sir."

Damian guides Alex into the bathroom and lowers and removes his shorts, something Alex can't do as his hands are still fastened behind his back.

Alex pisses into the bowl and is amused when Damian holds his cock and shakes off the last few drops of piss. He hopes the touch of a hand on his cock won't make it grow again.

"Thank you, Sir," Alex says with a smile.

"My pleasure, boy, any time," Damian replies also smiling.

As Alex turns around to return to the main room he spots the bright red stripe across his buttocks in the mirror. "Ouch", he thinks.

"Ouch, indeed," says Damian, reading his mind.

"Now it's time for you to rest and think about what's happened so far. Then we'll have lunch."

Damian releases Alex's wrists and tells him to lay face up on the bed.

"Now I've found you, boy, I don't want you to get lost," he says as he fastens Alex's wrists and ankles to the four corners of the bed and removes the chain lead which he hangs from his belt.

Alex notices the bulge of an erection in Damian's combats as he leans over fixing the restraints. He looks down at his own crotch and is thankful he hasn't started to get hard again.

"Jameson will come to collect you for lunch in a while, boy," Damian says as he walks over to the desk and picks up the bottle of water.

"Here, have a drink first," he adds. He opens the bottle, takes some in his mouth, then places his mouth over Alex's and slowly lets the water trickle in.

"Wow," thinks Alex. "That was cute. Maybe this guy isn't bad after all."

Damian leaves the room, turning up the volume on the computer as he passes it and angling the screen so that Alex can see it from the bed.

The door closes and Alex hears it being locked. Once again he's in bondage and he likes the security of it.

He looks around the room as best as he can spread-eagled on the bed. This could be his new home. Well, here, the dungeon and hopefully the rest of Damian's house.

From his restrained position, Alex can easily see the computer screen and the porno is reminding him of the endless hours he's spent getting turned on imagining being in just the situation is in. It's one of the better ones. Which is good as, being tied to the bed, he can't turn it off or adjust the volume.

His cock starts to grow but he can't reach it and he wonders if he'll ever be allowed to touch it again, given that he didn't even get to do that when he needed a piss.

Cum control and chastity had hardly ever figured in any of the pornos Alex had watched. And he was always amused and intrigued by the perverse notion of wanking about not being able to wank.

Still, Damian's world seemed full of perversity so Alex wouldn't be surprised if chastity was part of it, especially as Damian knew Alex was a chronic masturbator.

The pain from Alex's caning is subsiding slowly, though his bare buttocks rubbing against the rough blanket isn't helping.

"Still," Alex says smiling to himself, "at least I got my first kiss."

And with that he falls asleep to the soundtrack of his new life.

CHAPTER 6

Alex doesn't usually dream. Or if he does he never remembers them. But he dreams of Damian and Damian's cock in his mouth and being kissed and being caned and being tied up and more sexual scenes fuelled by the porno playing in the background.

His cock hardens many times as he sleeps and is still hard when he is awaked by Jameson's voice.

"Time for lunch, Alex."

Alex looks at Jameson and then with some embarrassment down at his cock.

"Don't worry about that, Alex, it'll go down soon."

Jameson releases the wrist and ankle cuffs from the bed but leaves them locked on.

"Go clean your teeth and then put your shorts back on."

Alex looks at himself in the bathroom mirror. He's almost unrecognisable from how he appeared the day before and he feels embarrassed at how he'd let things slide. He wonders how Damian saw through his protective dirty clothes and ragged appearance to what was underneath.

And then he remembers something and turns around to look at and feel the red stripe on his buttocks. The line is still there, bright red and slightly raised. He feels elated and proud to have taken his first step on a journey into an exciting unknown future.

Realising that Jameson is waiting, he quickly puts his shorts back on and is amused that his cock, though less erect, is still visible bulging through the white cotton fabric.

Alex puts his hands behind his back before returning to the bedroom and follows Jameson out of the secret area into the main house and then into a small dining room with open French doors leading to a sunny high-walled garden. Damian is sitting at a glass-topped table and rises to welcome Alex, noticing the bulge in his shorts.

"Sleep well, boy? Looks like you had some exciting dreams," he comments looking down at the bulge in Alex's shorts.

Alex blushes and replies succinctly and respectfully, "Yes, Sir, thank you, Sir. And I guess they must have been."

Damian motions for Alex to sit down opposite him and they eat lunch and talk. There's salad and cold meats and water to drink and Alex devours it all, having not eaten at all since the previous day. He tries not to bang his plate or the table with his wrist restraints and isn't always successful. And he notices Damian frown when he does. He also notices Damian keeping an eye on his shorts and noticing that the erection never quite disappears.

"Penny for your thoughts, boy?" Damian enquires.

Alex is careful not to speak with food in his mouth.

"Well this is all new to me, Sir, and my head is in a bit of a spin. But I'm feeling strangely happy, even about the punishment. I know I'm a bit of a mess and not very well disciplined so maybe you are just what I need right now in my life."

And then he remembers to add, "Sir".

"I think so too, boy," Damian replies noticing Alex's shining eyes once again. "And I think you're even finding it a bit exciting."

"Seems so, Sir. Though I didn't reckon on this being so obvious," he replies looking down through the glass table top at his shorts.

"That will be taken care of, boy. You won't be touching it for quite a while so you'll be storing up a decent amount of cum for when I'm ready."

Alex wonders about chastity again and then the thought passes as Jameson brings in some fruit for dessert.

"After lunch I'm going to add something to your simple wardrobe. Then I'll give you a book to read and you can go and sit in the garden for a while to let your food go down and get some sunshine. You're far too pale. The garden isn't overlooked so you can be naked.

"Then we'll play some more."

Alex never reads books and wonders what it will be. He also isn't sure what Damian's idea of 'play' is. Certainly not the sort of computer games he's used to. But he expects these new ones will be more satisfying and he won't get killed so often. Who knows, he might even get a decent orgasm for once.

After they have finished eating Damian attaches the

lead to Alex's collar and leads him into the playroom.

Alex is confused as he thought they weren't going to play until later.

"Take your shorts and t-shirt off and stand against that X-shaped frame on the wall, face out."

Alex does so and positions himself against the St Andrews cross, emulating what he'd seen in porno by placing his arms and legs at its corners.

Damian secures Alex's wrists and ankles to the cross and then retrieves a metal device from a box, holding it up for Alex to see.

It's a metal chastity device like one he'd seen in some of Damian's porno films. Alex's cock twitches. There's a metal waist band and hanging from the back of it is what looks like a flexible metal rod at the other end of which is a cock-shaped tube and a flat metal plate.

"I can't keep your hands secured behind you all the time, boy, and I need to make sure you don't play with yourself. You've probably had enough wanks for a dozen lifetimes. So this is going to keep your cock out of your reach. And it has other benefits."

Damian places the metal waist band around Alex's waist and then pulls the thin metal rod underneath his crotch. He puts some lube on Alex's cock and with a bit of effort pushes it into the tube.

Finally, the two ends of the waist band and the cock tube are attached to the metal plate and Damian produces a padlock which secures the whole thing together. The tight metal tube pushes Alex's balls to either side and they feel exposed and vulnerable.

"There now, all safe and secure."

Damian releases Alex and tells him to feel around.

"Don't worry, boy, there's drainage holes in the tube so you can still piss, though you'll need to sit down for that or it will go everywhere. When you need to shit or are giving your arse its daily wash out then that flexible rod at the back slides easily to one side."

The requirement of a daily enema is new to Alex but is soon forgotten as he starts to explore the stiff metal surrounding his waist and pubic area. There is no way he can touch his cock, which has grown more in the tube and is screaming for attention. And the flexible rod at the back seems to move easily enough.

"What do you think, boy?"

Alex has a question, namely how long he will be wearing it, but he thinks it best not to seem demanding or questioning.

"It's very secure, Sir, and I'll need to adjust to it. But to be honest, it will help me remember that you are in total control of me, even when you're not there."

Somehow, whatever the thoughts and questions uppermost in Alex's brain, his inner-most desires always push them aside. And he also realises that the chastity belt will put a stop to the addictive wanking that has probably ruined his life.

"That's the idea, boy. Now there's just one little addition and you're set for some sun bathing. Go bend over the horse. I don't think you need to be secured."

"I hope not, Sir," Alex laughs and does as he is told.

A few minutes later Alex feels something cool on his anus as Damian spreads some lube first around and then inside his arse hole.

"Relax and breathe deeply, boy. Jameson tells me you have a tight arse hole and I need to help relax it."

Alex feels something stretching his hole as a small butt plug is slowly pushed in. He has never had anything inside his arse before, not a cock nor any anal toys. So it's a bit painful at first, but he concentrates on his breathing and notices that Damian only pushes on the plug when he is breathing out and relaxing.

With one final firm push the plug slides in fully and Alex has two more new experiences in his life. One is his arse being plugged and anus stretched. The other is his prostate being massaged from the inside causing his cock to pulse in its tube.

Finally Damian adds a padlock to secure the plug to the metal rod so the plug won't come out, and so Alex himself can't remove it.

"There we are, your outfit is complete. Jameson will unlock the plug every morning so you can shit and wash out. Then it will be locked back in again.

When you're ready I'll replace it with something larger."

Once again Alex marvels at what he's experiencing and how fast fantasy is turning into reality. He wonders just how much larger the next plug will be as this one is certainly doing its job of stretching things and keeping his cock excited.

Damian watches his boy process what is happening and gives him a few minutes, not minding when Alex tests how secure the chastity belt and plug are.

"Right, boy, put your shorts and t-shirt on. I don't want you naked around the house, as the staff might get over excited and want you or one of those for themselves," Damian says pointing at the chastity belt. "But the garden is my private space so you won't be disturbed."

Damian removes the locked wrist and ankle cuffs as they won't be needed for a while.

Alex follows Damian out of the dungeon through the house and small dining room to the garden where a towel is laid out on the lawn, a bottle of water by its side and a very thick book, "Adventures in the dark side" by Damian Hall.

Walking through the house, Alex is aware that every movement is causing the chastity tube to slightly stimulate his cock and the butt plug to move about inside him. Though the plug is small, it bigger than anything that's ever been in there and a lot nicer than he expected. He's extremely turned on yet unable to do anything about it. Strangely, he finds it all very exciting. And he smiles to himself.

"Take your t-shirt and shorts off and rest in the sun, boy. I thought you might like to read some of my short stories to prepare you for what is in store for you. They're all true accounts. How many of them you get to experience depends on your progress. But you'll see that everyone in them has a great time and is very happy. No-one gets injured or killed. If you want that sort of thing I suggest we find you a Sherlock Holmes book instead."

And with that Damian returns to the house leaving Alex alone in the garden, naked apart from a locked leather collar and black bandana around his neck, his boots and his chastity belt to learn more about his Master's world and ponder on his future.

CHAPTER 7

For the next few hours Alex alternates between sunbathing, reading Damian's book, sleeping and exploring the garden. He thought this would be OK as Damian hadn't told him he had to stay on the towel.

The few stories in Damian's book are familiar to Alex and read like scripts for the DHP porno videos he'd been watching. Some get him quite excited and he feels his cock moving around inside its metal prison.

He decides to explore the garden, and as he does so he feels both naked and yet clothed, with his cock covered yet his balls fully exposed to the air. And as he walks the butt plug does its job of relaxing his anal sphincter and stimulating his prostate.

He's even starting to feel quite horny, physically, something that never used to happen as he dissipated his sexual energy as soon as it glimmered.

The garden is interesting and well maintained and stocked with exotic plants and Alex wonders who looks after it. He's never done any gardening himself and the one time he attempted keeping a houseplant in Melissa's flat it died within a few days.

After a few hours Damian returns to the garden and spots Alex at the far end bending down over some plants.

Alex sees Damian approaching and stands up straight, feet apart, hands behind his back and looks him straight in the eye.

"Hope it's OK that I looked around your garden, Sir," he asks.

"Of course, boy. And how are you doing in this?" Damian asks, cradling the cock tube in his hand and moving it up and down.

The movement causes the locked-in plug to slide around a bit, causing a shiver to run through Alex's body.

"I'm adjusting to it, Sir, and it feels very secure."

"It is, boy, and it seems to get you excited as well," Damian comments, noticing the drops of pre-cum from the end of the cock tube on his fingers.

"Open your mouth wide, boy, and stick your tongue out."

Alex does so and Damian slides his fingers into his mouth, letting him taste the pre-cum. He moves his fingers slowly back and forth along Alex's tongue and tells him to relax and learn to control his gag reflex, which proves difficult and Alex coughs and splutters.

Damian pulls a bottle of water out of a side pocket in his combats and wets his fingers.

"Let's try this some more, boy. You need to learn to have things moving towards the back of your throat if you're to satisfy my need to have my cock down there."

At the end of the garden the exercise continues for a while, Damian dressed in black, with the sun glinting on his shaved head, and Alex hairless and naked apart from his chastity belt, collar, bandana and boots, hands behind his back and mouth open.

"Let's go play some more, boy. Put your shorts and t-shirt on and follow me."

Damian and Alex return to the playroom, making a pit-stop in the marble bathroom as Alex indicates he needs to piss, something he hasn't yet done in his new metal underwear.

Damian watches as Alex gingerly sits down on the toilet bowl and relieves himself, amused at his piss streaming out from the numerous holes.

Damian warns Alex to give it a good shake afterwards and to wipe it dry with some toilet paper when he's done.

"I don't want to see or smell your piss dribbles on the floor or your clothes, boy," Damian warns him.

Alex seems a bit agitated by this unaccustomed attention to detail that is expected of him and Damian decides Alex needs to be more relaxed for his next experience.

"Take off your t-shirt and shorts and bandana and lay face down on the massage table."

Alex takes them off and drops them on the floor.

"You are a sloppy boy, aren't you. Fold them up neatly and put them on that table. Do that again and you'll be punished."

Alex quickly obeys, fearing a second more painful stripe on his now bare buttocks.

Alex lays face down on the massage bed, arms by his sides, while Damian massages his shoulders and back, feeling for any signs of injury or weakness.

No-one has ever done this to Alex and yet again his cock grows in its tube, wanting some attention.

When Damian is satisfied, he guides Alex into the dungeon and secures him to the cross, facing the wall this time, first by his wrists and ankles, then by leather straps around his upper arms and thighs and finally by a wide belt securing his waist to the cross. Alex cannot move his body at all.

"You're going to get your first flogging, boy. I'll start slow and soft and then see how far you can go. To help you focus on what you're experiencing I'm going to put a leather hood on you with a gag underneath it so you have something to bite on."

Alex is fearful but excited. "Thank you, Sir. I trust you to know what's best for me."

Damian unlocks Alex's leather collar and buckles on a leather gag before lacing on a heavy padded leather hood with only nose holes for breathing. Over this, he fastens a wider stiff leather collar which prevents him even moving his head.

Alex feels enclosed and controlled. Breathing is a little difficult and he learns to take it slowly. The gag too is a new experience and he bites into it, testing its strength and realising that it will prevent him making too much noise or involuntarily protesting, something he doesn't want to do.

He hears Damian move around and then return and he feels soft leather being rubbed slowly over his back.

"This is one of my favourite floggers, boy. It can start soft and caressing but also deliver quite a thud and sting when used harder."

Damian steps back and starts teasing Alex's back with soft flicks of the flogger, sometimes slowly, sometimes at a faster pace.

Alex's shoulders and back start tingling and he finds himself enjoying the impact of the flogger's soft leather tails on his skin.

Damian starts using a bit more force and Alex feels the heavier impact resonating through his body. It's quite unlike anything he's experienced before and the immobilising bondage and hood enable him to focus and submit to the sensations.

The strokes are getting stronger and the leather caresses are turning to sharper stings. He grunts and growls with each forceful stroke, sounds that excite Damian and spur him on.

"Now you're going to get ten really hard strokes, boy. Knowing how many will help you cope."

The flogger starts striking Alex's back really hard and he sees flashes of light before his eyes as he counts each one in his head. He is no longer able to make any sounds, the pain pushing him deep into a dark submissive space he's never visited before. His mind is still and he feels in touch with his body in a way he's never before experienced. For the first time he feels truly alive.

The ten strokes are done and Alex has survived. Even though his body is fully supported, he hangs limply, any resistance gone and his submission to Damian complete.

"Good, boy, you've done very well," Damian tells him softly, slowly massaging the bright red areas on Alex's back.

Damian removes the collar, hood and gag and releases Alex from the cross, carefully supporting him so he doesn't collapse, and turns him around to hold him tight in his arms, kissing him softly on the lips.

"Why are you crying, boy?" Damian asks.

"Because I'm happy, I think, Sir," Alex replies quietly, finding it hard to speak at all and adjusting to the unfamiliar feelings of exhilaration and happiness.

Damian motions for Alex to sit on the floor and offers him some water and the bandana he'd brought from the bathroom to dry his eyes.

"Thank you, Sir. That was wonderful," Alex mutters quietly, taking hold of the bandana and wiping his face and blowing his nose.

"You're very welcome, boy, and there's lots more to come. You're showing great promise and I'm very proud of you." Damian rubs Alex's head affectionately.

Alex's puppy-dog eyes seem to be sparkling even brighter than before and inside Alex feels very proud too. He's trusted Damian and allowed himself to leave his comfort zone and allow someone to break through his shell.

Damian removes his black combats and orders Alex to kneel in front of him. "Let's see what you learned this afternoon in the garden, boy."

Alex drops to his knees, hands behind his back, and takes Damian's hardening cock in his mouth, a little at first and them more until his nose is buried in Damian's warm pubic hair which smells wonderful. Damian allows Alex to set the pace, not moving his cock at all or forcing it further than Alex can take.

And there they remain for a while, Alex's back glowing from the flogging and Damian smiling as his new boy services his hungry cock, sucking on it like an equally hungry baby with a bottle at feed time.

Alex wonders if Damian will cum at all, maybe even cum in his mouth. But Damian does not have that on his agenda for today and after a while he tells Alex to stand up as it's time for some tea and a chat.

Alex puts his t-shirt and shorts back on and returns the black bandana to its place around his neck. Damian relocks Alex's leather collar on as well and then spots a damp patch in the crotch of Alex's shorts.

"I think you enjoyed that, boy."

"Yes, Sir, very much. Thank you, Sir."

"You can leave those shorts on for now but you'll need to put a clean t-shirt and shorts on before dinner. You're very sweaty. And there should be some clean black bandanas in your room as well. That one's been used enough I think."

Jameson serves them tea and biscuits in the garden and Alex answers Damian's questions about how he is finding things.

"Well, Sir, I didn't know what to expect. But I was willing to trust you. And so here I am, locked in a chastity device which is probably dealing immediately with the root cause of my problems. And I've learned to suck a cock and to take some pain.

"I didn't know that I wanted or needed these things, Sir. But clearly you did and I'm very grateful for you giving me this chance."

Damian smiles broadly. His hunch about Alex when he first spotted him in the porno appears to have been right. This boy did have potential. But there was more to do. And he needed to be put to work. There's a limit on how much time he could spend playing with Alex, much as he wanted to. He had his business to attend to and Alex needed to learn some new skills as well and make himself more than just sexually useful.

"I'm pleased you had the courage to take the first step, boy. Clearly you knew that you had a problem but I expect you didn't think submitting to the dark sexual desires of a man like me would be the solution.

"What do you think of the garden?" Damian continues, deliberately changing the subject and looking over Alex's shoulder.

"It's great, Sir. Who looks after it?"

"Jameson does but he has other work to do as well so he's going to train you as a gardener."

Alex smiles at this. He likes Jameson and while he'd never been an outdoor person, his solitary lifestyle being strictly an indoor one, the opportunity is a welcome one.

"I'd like that, Sir," Alex says, hoping he won't kill off the plants in Damian's garden like he did with his houseplant.

"You'll get some gardening overalls, work socks and sturdier boots. While the weather is warm you'll be wearing nothing underneath but your chastity belt, your collar and your black bandana.

"Come the winter I'll provide you with some warmer outdoor clothing."

Alex jumps back a bit. The mention of winter must mean Damian wanted him here that long. He'd been here less than a day and already his body was sore, his cock tamed and his head still processing all the new experiences he'd had. He wondered if the pace would stay the same. And what sort of person he would be in a couple of months.

"You seem surprised at something I said, boy," Damian observes.

"Sorry, Sir. You mentioned winter and I hadn't thought you'd want me here that long. It's not a problem, just a surprise. I hadn't reckoned on you accepting me so quickly."

"You've done well, boy and, until our play this afternoon, I still hadn't decided whether to keep you. But you did well, very well. I hope you're happy to stay here, at least through the trial period."

"Yes please, Sir."

"Any more questions?"

"None, Sir except that I would like to speak to Melissa at some point. I'm worried about getting money to her to pay my share of the bills."

"Don't worry, boy. You'll speak to her in good time. And don't worry about your rent and household bills. I'm covering those for the moment. If your stay here becomes permanent then Melissa can find a replacement for you, I'm sure."

Jameson appears in the garden to clear away the tea things and Damian issues some instructions.

"Jameson, we're done here now and I think Alex needs some time to rest. Take him back to his room and fill him in on his new daily routine and what you and I expect of him. Oh, and he'll be helping you in the garden. So sort him out some overalls, work boots and socks.

"He's done well today and earned a privilege so enable the TV channels on his computer screen."

Damian turns back to Alex.

"Pick up your book and follow Jameson, boy. I'm busy this evening so you will be eating with Jameson in the kitchen.

"Oh, are you any good at cooking?"

Alex shakes his head. "I can open a packet of soup and make a cup of tea but that's all, Sir."

"Jameson, something else for you to teach Alex. He

can start in the kitchen maybe helping prep vegetables or something. And make sure he doesn't break anything. If he does, make a note on the demerits board.

"And I need to change this," Damian says unlocking Alex's leather collar. "It doesn't do well getting wet in the shower and you need something more permanent."

He removes a short heavy steel chain from his pocket and wraps it around Alex's neck, securing the ends together with a large padlock which he snaps shut and lays on top of the bandana. Alex can already tell that he won't be able to slip the chain off over his head and it feels good knowing that he can't, not that he wants to.

And with that Damian goes back into the house. Alex feels sad that there wasn't a goodbye kiss but knows he has to be grateful for what he gets.

"OK, Alex, let's get on," Jameson tells him, and Alex picks up his book and puts it on the tea tray along with the mugs and plates and follows Jameson back into the house, carrying the tray carefully so he doesn't drop anything.

The kitchen is large, as Alex expected. In fact it's larger than Melissa's whole flat and he can't guess what most of the appliances are for.

"Leave those things there, Alex, and bring your book. We're going back to your room."

Alex follows Jameson back to his room, but not before he sees Jameson enter some codes on a digital panel on the kitchen wall.

In his room, the computer screen is now showing a daytime TV chat show and Jameson shows Alex how to switch between the direct feed of the DHP porn channels and the cable TV channels.

"We can monitor what you watch and how much, Alex, so remember that."

Jameson goes on to explain Alex's daily routine. He's to get up at 6am each day. The clock on the wall has a pre-set alarm to help him. And if he isn't awake and out of bed immediately there will be demerits.

"Each morning I will arrive just after the alarm goes off to unlock the butt plug and allow you to clean yourself out, shave, shower and be replugged before you put on fresh clothes. I'll show you how the bathroom equipment works tomorrow morning and how to keep your chastity belt clean.

"You'll usually have breakfast with me in the kitchen and then on gardening days you'll change into your work clothes and you can learn how to maintain the garden.

"There's a laundry room here and you are expected to wash and iron your own clothes and bedding. Be sure to keep those whites separate from the other stuff. You'll be able to move about the house freely but not leave it and you're not allowed to go above the ground floor. There's security on all the doors and windows and CCTV cameras everywhere.

"I expect Mr Hall will want some time with you

most days, some of it will be in the dungeon. But don't expect to play every day, he doesn't want to wear you or himself out. And sometimes the play will have effects that might take a few days for you to recover from.

"Any questions?"

Alex has lots but thinks it wise not to ask too many for fear of seeming anxious, which of course he is. He wonders if the "effects" would be physical or mental or both, being aware that his back has started to ache a little and his brain is still a bit mushy.

"If I am around the house and there are people there besides you and Sir, will they know who I am and what my position is?"

"Apart from when Mr Hall is entertaining family or straight friends, all the people you are likely to bump into work for him and will recognise you as his boy. They are unlikely to speak to you aside from maybe saying 'hello' and you should not speak to them unnecessarily. They know what a boy's position is and they will report any infractions to Mr Hall, and you know what the result of that will be."

"Understood, Mr Jameson."

"OK I'm going to leave you to rest and think about the experiences you've had. I'll come to collect you later on and you can help me make our dinner.

"If your back is feeling stiff, feel free to have a soak in the bath. Your chastity belt and collar and padlock won't rust so don't worry about them. In fact a soak in the bath is a good way of keeping your chastity tube clean."

And with that Jameson leaves, locking the door behind him.

Alex sits down on his bed thinking about the day and toying with his new steel collar and padlock. He remembers the wonderful sensation of the flogger on his back and the taste of Damian's cock in his mouth, making his own cock pulse in its cage, begging for attention. But it is so far from his reach.

Alex decides to have a piss and a bath before resting and goes to the bathroom, stopping by the mirror to check out his back and buttocks. His back is still very red, and the stripe on his buttocks is still visible though not raised up any more.

He spots something written on the padlock and laughs when he reads the words "Property of Master Damian" engraved on it. "I guess I'm owned, now," he thinks.

Alex stands back so he can see himself fully in the mirror, feet apart, hands behind his back, hairless apart from his short military crop, booted, chastity belted and collared with steel and a bandana.

"If you could see me now, Melissa, you wouldn't recognise me," he thinks and his whole body glows inside, even brighter than his back.

CHAPTER 8

Like Maggie Smith's Dowager Countess of Grantham in 'Downton Abbey', Alex wasn't used to there being any difference between a weekday and a weekend. For him every day had been the same, no work, just pathetic play with himself.

Now things are different as he is expected to work during the week and Damian has less time for him than he did on that first Monday. In fact they haven't played since then and Alex wonders if he has become an unpaid servant.

Still, while the weather is good he and Jameson work in the garden which he enjoys. Jameson is good company and entertains him with stories about his exploits with Damian as they do the weeding and pruning. Alex even learns how to use the petrol grass mower and produce a nice even finish with professional-looking stripes in straight lines.

"Who knows," he thinks, "I could always get a job in the city's parks department."

Alex has been given a dark navy boiler suit and heavy boots and socks to work in and likes the way the rough material of the suit rubs against his skin, specially his still-sensitive back and buttocks.

His chastity belt and plug keep him very aroused and he is learning that sexual arousal doesn't have to be quickly dissipated with a ten-second hand job whenever it appears. The horniness is something new, less intense but more persistent, and affecting more of his body than just his cock. In fact he wonders what playing with his cock would be like now.

But there are problems. The alarm going off in his room at 6am comes as something of a shock at first and for the first two days Alex isn't fully awake, washed and dressed by the time Jameson comes back for him at 7am.

Jameson tells him that each of those day's lateness has earned him a demerit point.

Alex fears for the punishment but knows that at least it will guarantee him some time with Damian.

On the Thursday, Jameson brings a wider longer dildo to his room at 7am to replace the butt plug he had got used to. Alex struggles to take it, But Jameson is patient and it is eventually locked in place before Alex puts on a clean pair of shorts and t-shirt and his very shiny, freshly polished, non-work boots.

He has been told to keep them well-polished and he is careful not to get any polish on his clothes so he does them naked. He'd made a special effort cleaning and polishing them that morning as he'd mistakenly gone out into the garden to work wearing them the previous day and the ground had been damp from an overnight rain shower.

As they walk out to the kitchen Alex feels himself being fucked by the dildo and it makes him slightly unsteady on his feet. Alex has never been fucked and wonders if Damian fucking him will feel like this.

Alex helps Jameson prepare breakfast for himself, Jameson and Damian. And today Alex is to take Damian's breakfast to him in the small dining room. Alex is pleased at this as he didn't see Damian at all the previous day.

With the dildo sliding in and out with every step he is careful not to drop the tray holding Damian's breakfast of coffee, toast and scrambled eggs.

He enters the dining room and places the items onto the table.

As he does so Damian frowns as he notices Alex's hands.

There's boot polish under his finger nails.

"That's bad, boy," he says in a stern voice pointing at the dirty finger nails. "I'm very disappointed in you."

"Sorry, Sir. Very sorry. It won't happen again, Sir," Alex says, genuinely hurt at displeasing Damian.

"You will be, boy. Now go back to your room and clean your hands properly and come back so I can see them."

When Alex returns Damian has finished his breakfast.

"Might as well serve the punishment close to the crime, boy, so you won't forget. And I believe there are two outstanding demerits as well because you can't get out of bed."

And with that Damian grabs Alex's chain collar and drags him to the dungeon.

Alex is sobbing inside as he hadn't intended to

upset Damian. But he's not used to paying attention to detailed things like his nails.

Inside the dungeon, Alex is told to remove his shorts and is strapped down over the leather horse and a gag put in his mouth. He knows what is coming and is dreading it. There will be punishment for his dirty hands and for his lateness as well. He braces himself by holding tight to the legs of the horse as Damian delivers three harsh strokes with the cane.

The pain is much more intense than before and he is glad he can't move or he'd have jerked himself out of the way after the first stroke. As the third stroke of the cane hits him he howls, as much to relieve his tension as anything. And then he goes quiet.

When the gag is removed he can barely speak but knows what is expected.

"Thank you, Sir. I'm sorry for my failings and won't let them happen again."

Damian releases Alex and stands him up, holding him tight while Alex sobs into his Master's black t-shirt.

"Here, dry yourself off," Damian soothes him, untying Alex's black bandana and putting it in his hands. "And it looks like I'll need my t-shirt drying off as well after your flood."

Alex laughs through the sobs and smiles. And Damian smiles back.

"Are you unhappy here or with the rules?"

"No, Sir, I know they're doing me good. It's just

hard to change my habits in such a short period of time."

"I understand, boy. You're doing well. Just a bit careless at times. And what's with the howling?"

"Well, Sir, it sort of just came out like there was an animal inside me needing some release."

"Well, puppy dogs don't howl. Maybe there's a bit of wolf inside there."

Alex laughs.

"The good news, boy, is that I have no meetings this afternoon so we can play."

Alex hopes that the play will be more pleasant. "Thank you, Sir."

In the middle of the afternoon Damian collects Alex from the kitchen where he has been helping Jameson prepare for a big dinner Damian is hosting that evening. Jameson warns Alex that these will be some banking friends and so he will be kept out of the way.

Alex follows Damian through to the dungeon, the dildo sliding in and out and his buttocks still very painful from that morning's punishment. He hasn't had a chance to check the marks from the caning yet as he had only used the toilet off the kitchen since leaving his room that morning, but he expects that there will be three new bright red lines to replace the fading original.

"Today you're going to experience something new, boy. You've had your dose of pure pain today. Now take your t-shirt and shorts off and let me look at your arse."

There are indeed three bright red lines there and a fading yellow one from the first caning.

"You'll live," Damian jokes and pats Alex on the buttocks playfully.

Alex smiles and says "Thank you, Sir. I never doubted it."

Damian points to a leather sling suspended from the ceiling hanging out from one wall of the room.

"Sit on the edge of that and then let me guide you into it."

With some adjustments of position Alex is laying in the leather sling, wrists restrained behind his head and ankles raised up on the bottom supporting chains. A rigid rod between his ankles keeps his legs spread out so he can't wriggle or move, and a wide leather belt around his stomach and under the sling further immobilises him.

Alex wonders what will happen next and is surprised when Damian unlocks the dildo and chastity belt and removes the dildo and frees his cock from its cage.

With difficulty Alex looks down at his cock, which he hasn't seen for days. "Hello, old friend," he silently whispers to it. "Been missing me?"

Damian gives the cock tube a quick sniff and tells Alex that he is doing a good job of flushing it out each morning before letting it hang down on its securing rod.

"Thank you, Sir, I do it as well as I can as I know

you like things clean, including me."

"Clean inside and out," Damian replies examining the dildo which is covered in lube and nothing else.

Damian gets a warm wet face cloth and gives Alex's cock a wipe down, the rough sensation causing it to swell quickly in response. Alex is amazed at how much more sensitive it now is.

The heavy padded leather hood is on Alex once again, but no gag this time, and in the darkness he has no way of knowing what is in store for him. All he knows is that Damian had told him it wouldn't be painful.

Damian picks a shiny ribbed metal butt plug from a box on the shelf. It is slightly larger than the dildo which he had just removed. He gives it a good coating of thick viscous lube and warns Alex to relax and breathe deeply.

Alex feels the cold tip against his anus and then the repeated bumps as the ridges of the plug slowly slip past his sphincter and inside him.

Damian gives the plug one last push and then rotates it around a few times to make sure the lube is well distributed inside and out.

Alex feels Damian coating his cock with something cold. More lube he assumes. And then he feels some rubber straps being tightened around his cock, one just under his cock head and one at the base.

Somewhere in the past Alex had seen something like this being set up on a porno film. But at the point at which the cock straps had gone on he'd cum, stopped the film and fallen asleep in his chair so he didn't find out what happened next. It must have been his eighth wank that day and his body couldn't take any more.

Alex is aware of Damian moving around and seeming to attach something to the plug and straps. There's a vague noise of some switches being flicked but it's difficult to hear as the thick leather hood muffles a lot of the external sound.

Then he feels something in his arse. It's as if he's being tickled on the inside. Alex is wired into Damian's electro stimulation box.

He experiences a sort of fizzing sensation that rises and falls rhythmically and causes him to involuntarily suck the plug in and out in unison with it.

Seeing this, Damian knows he has reached the lower level of effectiveness and raises the output level a bit. Next he adjusts the output to the cock straps.

Alex barely notices as a tingling starts to run up and down his cock but then it gets stronger and he feels like he's being crawled over by a million ants.

His cock gets harder and starts pulsing.

"Not so fast, boy," Damian thinks to himself while observing Alex's cock, and he turns the cock level down a bit while raising the arse one. Alex is a long way from being allowed to cum.

Alex is in ecstasy. His cock and arse are being stimulated like never before. It's intense and pleasurable to the point of almost being unbearable. He tries to writhe around but can't move a muscle. Nor can he just lay back and relax as the electro pulses keep him on edge, tensing up every muscle in his body.

Damian moves to Alex's head and speaks to him. "What do you think, boy?"

"It's amazing, Sir," Alex says as clearly as he can inside the constricting hood which is holding his jaw quite still. "I never knew this sort of thing was possible."

"Well there's no hurry and there's plenty more power still available. You're going to endure this for as long as it pleases me, boy."

Alex moans softly.

Damian moves back to the electro control box and adjusts the program and levels. Now the sensations are a little less pleasurable and a bit more spikey and painful.

Alex groans as sharp pulses and peaks break the more pleasurable tingling.

Damian returns to Alex's head end of the sling so he can be sure he can hear him through the padded hood.

"You're cooking nicely, boy. An hour of this and you should be well done. I don't need to do anything now but sit back and watch and get my cock warmed up. The box has pre-set programmes which will change the patterns from time to time, never repeating and slowly increasing bit by bit."

A brief thought of protest crosses Alex's mind and disappears as quickly. He has no choice. Damian owns him and he is now Damian's remote-controlled toy.

Over the hour, the changing electro patterns produce different levels of intensity, sensation and frequency of stimulation. Alex feels like the lights at a rock concert, rising and falling, flashing and strobing, changing colour and swivelling about. Throughout, his cock stays hard and on the edge of cumming, but never close enough to that edge to go over it. For this he is thankful as he suspects any unauthorised orgasm would lead to even more painful red stripes and maybe even longer in his chastity belt before being released again.

Alex is at Damian's mercy, struggling to remain focused on his Master as his cock and arse are relentlessly stimulated. And when the box is finally switched off he is drained of any will of his own.

Damian removes the cock bands and plug and hood and gently helps Alex out of the sling and onto the floor. Alex gratefully accepts the bottle of water as his mouth is dry from the being in the hood, dribbling as he takes refreshment.

In front of Alex's face, Damian's cock is large and hard and Damian guides it into Alex's mouth. There's no resistance and it slides easily all the way in, the PA ring reaching the back of Alex's throat.

Alex sucks eagerly, wanting to please the Master who has given him such an overwhelming experience.

Damian gently holds and fondles Alex's head, grabbing the black bandana around his neck to hold it in place as he slowly moves his cock in and out, finally cumming. Damian's cum tastes salty and bitter and quite unlike what he expected. And he relishes this gift from his Master.

"You're a good boy, Alex, getting better every day."

Alex feels his life, at last, has a purpose: to be Damian's play thing, to be moulded into submission and to serve his desires.

He is happy.

"You've done well, boy, and deserve a break. The chastity belt is going back on, of course, as I can't be sure you won't quickly revert to your previous obsessive habits. But you will have a spell with your arse free."

"Thank you, Sir, that was amazing."

"There's lots more where that came from boy. More of the same, and other things we can explore together. Now just sit there and rest for a few minutes."

When Alex has recovered, Damian locks him back in his chastity belt and sends him back to his room to rest.

Alex hasn't cum but his cock and arse are still tingling and pulsing from the electro and, as his body settles down, he is once more aware of the slight burning on his buttocks from his punishment.

He turns off the porno film on the computer

screen. What's on there, he realises, is not important any more. Not compared to what he is now experiencing.

Alex sleeps long and deep into the next morning, a happy boy.

CHAPTER 9

During the following weeks Alex settles into his daily routine. He usually awakes before the alarm goes off and is ready, cleaned out, shaved, showered and dressed when Jameson collects him at 7am. They do gardening and kitchen work together and when not working they sometimes watch movies together in Damian's home cinema or Alex reads.

His computer is still restricted to Damian's porno channels and cable TV so he has no access to the Internet or email. And no way of communicating with Melissa. But he suspects (and hopes) she may have phoned Damian to check up on him.

His arse remains unplugged apart from the nights before Damian intends to use it and most days he sees Damian for lunch or tea at least.

They play on some of the days. More flogging, more electro and some amusing impact play involving just Damian's powerful hands and a surprisingly painful wooden spoon that leaves interestingly-shaped red marks on Alex's upper arms and thighs.

There's more cock sucking too, with Alex getting more relaxed and taking Damian's cock deeper inside him.

Damian decides that Alex's nipples need working on, but they're pretty small and undeveloped, so he gives Alex a suction pump and nipple tubes and instructs him to pump them every night for 20 minutes.

After breakfast one day, Damian asks how Alex is getting on with his book and Alex tells him he's just finished it.

"What did you think of it?" Damian asks.

"Really well written, Sir, and I recognised some of the plots from stuff I've seen in your videos or what I've done with you."

Damian is about to reply when he notices that Alex's nipples are now standing prouder and clearly visible poking up the white t-shirt.

He gets up and walks behind Alex, reaching over and slowly massaging them between his strong fingers.

Alex moans gently, "I like that, Sir."

"Good, I'll have some more fun with them later. But for now come into my library and choose a new book."

The library is a small room off the main hallway with floor to ceiling bookshelves. The books seem arranged very neatly and Alex reminds himself to replace any he removes in exactly the same place.

"Apart from times when I have visitors and you're confined to your room, you can come in here any time to change your book."

Damian sits down in one of the high-backed leather armchairs and watches as Alex removes and replaces a number of books.

The boy looks good in his white t-shirt and shorts and boots, though Damian thinks maybe he should now be given some white socks to wear. Alex has given him a lot of pleasure and he is proud of his achievements.

However his body is still a bit too flabby and lacking in definition and he resolves to get Alex working out in his fitness room off the secret corridor.

Alex continues browsing the shelves of books. He used to read a lot until porn took over his life. Back then, he spent many hours in the local public library as it was warmer than his flat and gave out free coffee if you were unemployed. He worked out that if he started a book and made it to the third page then it was probably worth borrowing.

Ten minutes later Alex is still reading the same book and Damian interrupts him.

"Found what you wanted, boy?"

Alex spins around and apologises.

"Sorry, Sir. You mentioned Sherlock Holmes when we had our first discussions and I just came across this complete works. Is it OK if I take this, Sir? I really enjoyed watching the new TV series with Mr Jameson the other night"

"Of course, boy. But be sure to put it back where you found it when you've finished it."

Alex turns around and realises that he can't remember where the book came from, so he'll have to work out if there is any order to the books when he tries to replace it.

Sadly, the book proves to be the cause of Alex's

next punishment.

As the weather has started getting colder there's been little work to do in the garden, so Alex spends much of the next two days engrossed in his new book, sometimes in his room, sometimes in the kitchen keeping Jameson company as it's now too cold to sit in the garden.

Come Thursday morning, he realises, after shaving and showering, that he'd been so engrossed in the adventures of Holmes and Watson that he'd forgotten to do his laundry the day before. And he's run out of clean t-shirts and shorts.

He sorts through his already-worn clothes in the laundry basket and finds a t-shirt and shorts that aren't too crumpled or dirty, puts them on and goes to help prepare breakfast with Jameson, hoping he won't run into Damian until he's done his laundry.

"Alex, I have more stuff to do here so will you take the breakfast tray through to Mr Hall in the small dining room?"

Alex gulps, braces himself and prepares the tray to serve Damian his breakfast. He can't avoid Damian now.

Damian seems in a grumpy mood but appears pleased to see Alex is serving him his breakfast.

"This is a nice surprise, boy, I wasn't expecting such a sexy waiter this morning."

After Alex has laid the table, Damian gets up and comes over to give Alex a hug.

As his arms encircle Alex he notices an unfamiliar

smell.

"Didn't you shower this morning, boy?" he demands standing back.

"Sorry, Sir, I was so wrapped up in my book I forgot to do my laundry yesterday."

"Boy, I don't know what to do with you. We provide you with plenty of clean clothes, access to a laundry, plenty of free time to take care of things and your former sloppy habits start emerging. You'll get a punishment of course."

"Yes, Sir. Sorry, Sir. I won't let it happen again."

"I suspect you won't, boy. When you've finished in the kitchen clearing up after breakfast go do your washing and ironing. And report to me in my office at 5pm."

"Yes, Sir."

A despondent Alex leaves the room. He does try, he thinks to himself. And he is upset to have failed Damian again, the man who has given him a new home, fed him and introduced him to some wonderful sex.

Alex washes, dries and irons all his whites apart from the ones he's wearing. He decides to give his work clothes a wash as well, even though they don't all need it.

When he's finished he returns to reading his book in his room, always careful to look at the clock regularly as he knows he must not be late.

At 5pm, in clean clothes, he reports to Damian in his office. He seems grumpier than that morning.

"Come, boy," Damian commands and pulls Alex by his chain collar to the dungeon.

Alex is ordered to strip to his boots and sit on a hard armless chair with his feet astride and his hands behind the chair's back. Damian secures Alex's wrists and also ties his ankles to the chair legs.

"There's no pleasure for you today, boy. This will be a timely reminder that you are getting complacent."

Alex's face is sunken and his head is hanging down as he mutters a despondent "Yes, Sir.".

"You need to remember to look at me when I'm talking to you, boy." And with that Damian removes the padlocked chain collar and bandana from around Alex's neck and replaces them with a wide lockable leather posture collar so Alex has to look straight ahead and cannot even move his head from side to side.

Damian stands behind Alex and starts massaging his tits, until they are firmer and standing prouder than before. Then the punishment starts.

From a box behind him Damian retrieves some sharp-toothed nipple clamps joined by a metal chain. As the teeth bite in Alex screams in pain. "Please, Sir, I'm not sure I can take them."

Damian isn't used to or happy that Alex is refusing things and ignores his plea. "You don't have a choice, boy, they're staying on," he barks.

Alex wonders if Damian means forever or just for now, and he is frightened of Damian's anger. But the thought is brief as Damian is pulling on the chain, increasing the pain.

Alex grits his teeth and closes his eyes as tears start forming.

"Books, like television and films, your freedom to walk around the house and garden, the meals you get, even the chance to leave your room are privileges you earn by learning and obeying, boy. And they can be taken away if you take them for granted or in enjoying them you forget your duties."

"I'm sorry, Sir," Alex replies, opening his eyes briefly to be sure he is looking at Damian when he speaks to him.

"You will be, boy," Damian replies as he tugs again on the chain connecting the nipple clamps. Alex's mouth opens as he breathes in deeply from the pain, eyes clenched tight once more and tears flowing faster.

Damian lets the chain drop which causes fresh pain in Alex's now very tender nipples, and he walks across the room, returning with a cane in his hand.

"Look at this, boy, and you'll learn something."

Alex examines the cane. It seems darker and less springy than the one Damian had used previously.

"It's called a dragon and is more severe than the one I have used on you so far. The wood is denser and the impact penetrates deeper. So you may not see the full bruises and marks until tomorrow. And you can be sure there will be some."

And with that he steps back and delivers a single

strong blow straight across the top of Alex's thighs.

Alex screams and jumps so much he almost tips over in his chair.

"That's done now, boy. I hope you won't forget today and I won't need to punish you again like this." And with that Damian removes the nipple clamps which causes new waves of pain to run through Alex's chest and Alex screams again.

Damian crouches down in front of the still-bound Alex. "Keep quiet, boy, and look at me while I sort these out," he says sternly.

Alex looks into Damian's eyes and then feels fresh pain as Damian's strong fingers massage his nipples back into shape.

For the first time Alex sees the real sadist in Damian when he looks into his eyes while his nipples are being tortured even more. He feels no warmth there and he hates what has just happened between them.

Alex is silent which doesn't surprise Damian who hadn't intended this experience to be pleasant or arousing for Alex.

But he is troubled that his own cock had seemed aroused by what had just happened. He'd always believed that SM pain and play should never be used in anger. Yet perhaps just now he had broken his own cardinal rule.

Alex's notices that Damian is silent too and assumes this is part of the punishment which makes him even more unhappy.

After a few minutes Damian snaps out of his thoughts. "Let's get you sorted, boy," he says, almost forcing himself to give Alex a playful rub on the head. But he still feels angry.

Damian wipes away Alex's tears with a bandana and then unties him.

"Follow me to your room," Damian orders Alex, his voice lacking any emotion.

Inside his room Alex notices that his book has gone and the computer is turned off. All his clothes are gone as well, apart from his work boots.

"You're to stay here until the morning, boy, just you and your thoughts. The door will be locked and you'll get no dinner."

And with that Damian is gone, leaving a distraught Alex more alone than he ever has been. He's naked apart from his chastity belt and posture collar, both inescapably locked on.

He looks at the clock and it is just 6pm. He realises it's far too early to go to sleep, and if he did, he risked waking up in the middle of the night and then maybe falling asleep again and not waking up in time for his morning routine.

He decides he might as well make himself useful and takes off and cleans his black everyday boots. In fact he polishes them twice just to be sure they pass muster. Then he washes the mud off his work boots and gives them a good waterproofing.

The posture collar is starting to become uncomfortable but he can't take it off and it makes it difficult for him to look down at the boots while he's cleaning them so he ends up holding them in front of his face.

Alex thinks about what has just happened. He has seen a cruel side of Damian for the first time. And he is frightened.

It's true he deserved the punishment. But he sensed that in carrying it out Damian had forgotten the caring ownership he had of Alex. What if this resurfaced and Damian ended up really injuring him?

An unhappy, hungry and troubled Alex goes to bed at 10pm but does not sleep well. He cries often. Damian has removed the chain collar and padlock, a sign of ownership which Alex is always proud of. And doesn't even have his black bandana to mop up his tears.

At 5am he awakes, still troubled. He decides to give his room a clean after his morning bathroom duties. As he's wiping down the surfaces, polishing the taps and mopping the floor he wonders whether he should leave. In the bathroom mirror he looks at the angry red welt across his thighs from the caning and cries some more.

Maybe the fun is over now and his world will become one of work and pain with no pleasure. The sort of slavery he feared when Damian first proposed he moved in.

He'd still not been allowed to talk to Melissa, whom he misses, and he finds the constant presence of the chastity belt annoying at times. His horniness, though totally absent right now, has often raged inside him leading to tears of frustration and he fears Damian will never allow him any release. He resolves to talk to Jameson about it at breakfast this morning and is considering telling Damian that he wants to be released.

So it is a very unhappy Alex who looks up from his bed when he hears his door being unlocked at 6am. And an astonished one who sees Damian walk in followed by Jameson carrying his clothes and black bandanas which he puts back on their shelf before leaving.

Alex stands to attention immediately. Even more to attention than usual because the posture collar is still locked on. He isn't sure what sort of mood Damian is in.

"Good morning, boy," Damian says tentatively smiling.

"After yesterday afternoon I thought I should be the first person you saw this morning. And I wanted to see you first as well before I bumped into anyone else besides Jameson.

"You know, boy, that I'm very fond of you. And it may seem trite to say it, but punishing you yesterday afternoon really hurt me. Maybe not as much as it hurt you. But it hurt me nonetheless and I was sorry that it upset you so much.

"We need to talk more, boy. Here are your clothes and bandanas back. join me for breakfast when you're dressed.

"And I think this has served its purpose."

And with that Damian unlocks the posture collar around Alex's neck and replaces it with a bandana and the chain collar and padlock which he gives a playful flip as he snaps it shut.

Damian leaves.

Alex is both dismayed and delighted by what has just happened. He thought he knew what he wanted. He'd pretty much decided he wanted out. And then Damian comes in and confuses him.

He wonders if the previous day was a temporary lapse or the beginning of a dark downward path.

He goes to the bathroom to check his clothes look OK and spots the bright red mark around his neck where the bottom edge of the posture collar had been pressing against him. He decides not to hide this and loosens his black bandana a lot so that Damian will be sure to see it.

For the first time Alex is fighting his own corner.

CHAPTER 10

Alex prepares breakfast for himself and Damian in the kitchen and then joins Damian in the small dining room. There's no sign of Jameson.

The atmosphere is a little tense and Damian and Alex say little while eating. Alex notices Damian looking concerned at the red mark around his neck occasionally, which gives him a little satisfaction, but he says nothing about it.

When they have finished eating Damian breaks the uncomfortable silence.

"I'm sorry about that mark around your neck, boy. It will go soon. Any marks on you should be deliberate and not incidental."

Damian is apologising again and Alex guesses that maybe not everything had gone according to plan the previous day.

"That's OK, Sir, I was getting sloppy and deserved to be punished."

"How are your nipples, boy?"

"Still very sore, Sir, and a little crusty this morning."

"Ask Jameson for some moisturiser to rub into them. That will help.

"Next time I start working on them I hope it will be in better circumstances," Damian adds.

"Thank you, Sir, I'd like that."

"And your thighs?"

"Also very sore, this morning, Sir, Especially when

the hot water in the shower got onto them. And you were right, the marks are darker and more noticeable than yesterday."

"Yesterday wasn't good for me, boy. I was in a bad mood from some work problems and I forgot myself a little so I was harsher on you than maybe you deserved.

"Those marks will be there for a few more days, boy, a reminder to both of us."

Alex wonders what Damian needs reminding of, but decides it is better not to ask. He is starting to see a faint crack in Damian's otherwise self-controlled, confident, totally in-charge exterior. And he's not sure he wants Damian to be human and fallible. On the other hand he doesn't want to be abused.

"Anyway," Damian continues, "you might be able to help me with these work problems which made me so angry yesterday. We're having some difficulties with our interactive porno films – like the one where we met."

Alex listens attentively, fascinated by this rare insight into the workings of Damian's business.

"There's a guy turning up and being destructive. Not physically – after all it's totally virtual so he can't cause other people any actual harm. But he's throwing stuff around, trying to break the dungeon equipment, being violent to people and so on. We want the rooms to be a safe place for people to play in and feel good about exploring and enjoying their kinks. As it is, he's pissing people off and we risk losing customers."

Alex had never thought of himself as a customer. For him the ecommerce side of the web had passed him by and he'd never paid for anything on the Internet.

"If you're willing," Damian continues, "I'd like you to help us identify who this person is. Maybe some of your Sherlock Holmes reading with help with your sleuthing, though I don't know what Holmes would have made of the Internet. He had to make do with his 'Baker Street Irregulars' instead of the web for his research."

Alex relaxes some more and laughs a little, noticing a change in Damian's tone. He's not being told what to do but is being invited to.

"Yes, Sir, I'll do what I can. How would I find out who he is?"

"Well our usual monitors don't have time for much more than hitting the 'ban' button. And as he's using some internet trickery he appears as a different person each time he visits. So we can't find out where he is or recognise him when he returns until someone spots his tantrums and throws him off.

"But you have time to engage with him. You'll have access to that private messaging system I used when I first got your attention, and maybe some other facilities. I'll get one of my staff to walk you through how it works. You can do it in your room."

Alex smiles. "I'd like that, Sir. Those functions are

responsible for me being here now. So I'd like to repay the debt and help others maybe meet up with someone like you."

"Good boy. Thank you. Is there anything else you'd like to discuss? Yesterday afternoon was a bit of a watershed and we're overdue for a review."

Alex hesitates, not wishing to push his luck and take too much advantage of Damian's contrite manner.

"There is something, Sir. It's about this chastity belt. I've adjusted to not being able to wank and cum whenever I want. And I like feeling horny much of the time. I even enjoy it being used to lock a plug in occasionally.

"But I've never gone so long without cumming, Sir. I get raging almost unbearable surges of horniness from time to time. My cock just aches for attention which of course I can't give it, and I'd like to know more about how to cope with it as I'm sure you don't plan to let me touch it any time soon. I've been too embarrassed to ask you about it, thinking it's been brought on by my previous bad habits.

"As you know I've never played with anyone before you," Alex continues. "And with my obsession with looking at porn and playing with myself, wearing a chastity device was the last thing I'd have thought of doing, though I have come across guys who seemed to get a contradictory thrill by wanking over not being able to wank."

Alex stops short of asking when Damian will let

him cum, feeling that he should take it one step at a time.

"Don't be embarrassed, boy. I know you will have those bouts of horniness and frustration and the fact that I can cause them in you excites me. You should get some advice and it's better coming from other guys who are locked than from a keyholder like me.

"There's a really great web site for locked guys and their keyholders. We'll give you access to it and you can read about how other guys cope. You'll discover that there are thousands of guys locked up like you, some of them not cumming for a year or longer. Imagine how horny and frustrated they must get."

Alex gulps. Not cumming for a year? He think's he'd go mad. Or else lose interest completely.

Damian knows what's on Alex's mind.

"Don't worry about not cumming, boy. You will when I'm ready, and it won't be a year before it happens. But you can be sure that when it happens I will be in control and your hands will be secured well away from your cock."

Alex smiles. "Thank you, Sir. It really helps that you seem to know what I'm thinking and feeling and take account of it."

"You're very welcome, boy. I really do have your best interests at heart," Damian replies. "Feel free to discuss your situation here with guys on the chastity site. It'll be good for you to get some perspective on it. But you mustn't reveal who or where you are or reveal anything identifiable about me or the other people in this house."

"Understood, Sir."

Damian picks up his phone and makes a call. "Lars, Alex is going to learn more about how our interactive films work. Can you set up a junior moderator log-in on his computer? And while you're at it, Alex is ready for some contact with the outside world. Add a link to that chastity site to the web browser on his machine and give him limited web access. Thanks." And with that the call ends.

Damian returns to Alex. "After you've finished clearing up the breakfast things go back to your room and Lars will be there waiting for you. He'll give you a lesson in how moderator mode works on our porno sites. And you can explore the chastity community as well.

"Oh, and keep it to yourself why I'm giving you access to the system. You heard how little information I just gave Lars. I don't want my staff to think I don't trust them to handle things."

"Thank you again, Sir," Alex says feeling much better about everything and his thoughts of quitting now firmly out of his mind.

Back at his room, Alex meets Lars, a young Scandinavian guy who seems to know all about him. He's the same size as Alex but muscular rather than flabby, short blonde hair and piercing olive-coloured eyes that hold Alex's gaze when he looks at him. He's wearing nothing special, DHP-branded polo shirt, tan chinos and black work boots.

"Mr Hall asked me to show you how junior moderator mode works on our sites. Are you ready for me to go through it now with you?" Lars asks him.

Alex agrees and he spends the next hour learning and practising the special commands that let him send private messages to visitors and other management functions. There's now a pad of paper and some pencils on his desk and he takes copious notes, fearing that if he makes mistakes he'll get punished. And he doesn't want that to happen in case Damian is once again in a bad mood.

Lars shows Alex how to access a control panel and insert himself into one of a long list of interactive porno films, and Alex sees an animated version of himself there, his virtual avatar character dressed in his familiar white t-shirt and shorts, black bandana and padlocked chain collar around his neck and black boots.

The surroundings in this film are sparse, just a bondage table, some rope and some floggers. Alex wonders if he could try them and Lars suggests he has a go.

Lars laughs loudly when Alex's avatar tries to wield a flogger against a wall and manages to hit himself more often than the wall.

"Better ask Mr Hall to give you some lessons," Lars says. And then realises how inappropriate that is. "Sorry, Alex, I forgot your position here. But feel free to tell Mr Hall I'd said that. None of us has any secrets here. After all our business is about helping people explore and own their deepest sexual desires. And what good would we be if we couldn't share those things with each other here in this house. We're all really close to Mr Hall."

Alex smiles. "I'm sure if Mr Hall thinks I should learn how to flog he would arrange it," Alex says, feeling it right to refer to Damian as "Mr Hall" when discussing him with a work colleague. He asks how much Lars knows about what has gone on between himself and Damian.

"Well I don't know what goes on in Mr Hall's play area. That's out of bounds for his employees apart from Jameson. All I know is that you're his boy.

"Anyway I have other work to do. But if you need any help you can send me a message via that control panel in the system."

And with that he shakes Alex's hand, once again looking straight into him with his piercing olive eyes.

Lars leaves and Alex clicks around the system. It feels very strange to be back in the same porno videos he used to be obsessed with before his life changed. He is no longer looking for a quick thrill. He is here to work and it makes him feel important, somehow superior to the visitors to the site, and superior to his former self.

Nonetheless he finds some of the videos very exciting and his cock stirs in its cage begging for attention.

"Damn," Alex shouts, looking down at his crotch.

"Not now. Don't you know I have work to do." Then he remembers the chastity community Damian mentioned. He looks around and finds a web browser shortcut on his computer screen and clicks on it.

On the browser's toolbar a few sites have been bookmarked but there's no address bar. So he can't browse wherever he wants. He also discovers, after reading some stories on a news site he's allowed to visit, that he can't follow links to any sites not in the toolbar. "So this is what limited web access means," Alex thinks.

There's a bookmark for a site called LockedMEN which Alex clicks on, assuming this is the chastity site Damian had mentioned.

"Welcome back, MasterDamiansboy," it says. Alex likes the nickname Damian had chosen for him.

He wonders if Damian had already created a profile for him and clicks on his own nickname in the list of recent visitors.

The page has few details on it:

Location: London, UK

Age: 27

Role: Locked boy

Locked status: Locked indefinitely

Keyholder: MasterDamian.

Last visit: today

There's a picture of him in his chastity belt which Alex realises must have been taken when he was hooded in the dungeon as he doesn't remember

Damian ever taking any photographs.

Alex spots that his account was created just two days after he arrived. "Damian sure plans everything well in advance," he thinks.

Underneath the summary are a few words. "I am the boy of Master Damian who controls me and monitors this profile. I am locked in chastity and Master Damian has yet to tell me when I will next cum so my lock-up is indefinite."

Alex clicks on the link to Damian's profile which appears on his own and sees it has fewer details:

Location: London, UK

Age: 42

Role: Keyholder

Last visit: yesterday

Underneath it just says "I am the proud Master and keyholder of MasterDamiansboy" with a link back to his own profile.

Alex feels warm inside and his left hand moves to hold onto the bandana and padlocked chain around his neck while he clicks around the chastity site with his right hand.

The web site seems to have thousands of profiles and photos of guys locked in chastity. There's also a busy message area and he starts reading some of the discussions. But a tingling across his thighs reminds Alex of what happened last time he forgot his duties and got too immersed in something recreational so he decides to visit the site only in the evenings.

Alex is at last organising his own life.

CHAPTER 11

It is two days before Alex comes across the "vandal", as Damian refers to him, when he inserts himself into a video Alex is watching and starts kicking out at everything.

Alex can't tell much about the guy as the visitor hasn't enabled his webcam feed, so his entire appearance is computer-generated. Alex decides to try to engage with him rather than ban him.

A couple of keyboard commands takes Alex to his on-screen control panel where he can send private messages to the vandal. But then he stops and notices something.

Lars has either been sloppy or mischievous because Alex is listed not as a junior moderator but as a senior one. And this gives him more options, including being able to change the appearance of his online character and make use of a private dungeon like Damian's, something Lars never mentioned.

Alex wonders whether to take advantage of this and decides that his white clothing looks a bit out of place in the dungeon. So he overlays himself with a black and white camo-patterned t-shirt and matching combat trousers. This has the effect of covering his collar and bandana as well. And he changes his nickname, taking his cue from the computer screen in front of him.

Alex likes his new look and wishes he was in a position to ask Damian for some clothes like that.

The next challenge is how to lure the vandal into his private dungeon. And then has an idea, remembering something he'd seen in one of the DHP pornos. He sends a private message to the vandal.

"Hey there, SIR," he types. "I'm one of the senior slaves here. Would you like to go somewhere private and use those boots to kick me instead of the furniture?"

Alex's first thought was merely to extract the vandal from the video so that other people could enjoy it. That would buy him time because if the vandal was left there one of the supervisors would ban him and Alex would have to wait for him to return. He hopes with time he can get the guy to reveal more about himself.

"Why not, slave" the vandal replies.

Alex types in a few commands and he and the vandal enter Alex's private dungeon.

"Hey, this is great, slave. I didn't know these spaces existed," the vandal says.

Alex isn't sure how to explain the private dungeon, and doesn't want to risk getting Lars into trouble for setting his privileges wrong. But he has an idea. "I'm a computer hacker, SIR, and I managed to link the main site to my own site where this private space is."

Alex isn't sure if this will work and quickly changes the subject to divert the vandal. "Now about this kicking, SIR."

"What's your name, slave?" the vandal asks.

"I'm Delboy, SIR" Alex types.

"That's right, slave, I'm your 'SIR', the vandal replies. "Now go lay on the floor, slave, so I can kick the shit out of you."

"Whoa," Alex thinks," this is getting out of hand too quickly." And then he remembers back to his recent punishment session with Damian.

"Yes, SIR. But before that could I respectfully ask that you turn on your webcam. I always find it easier to obey and take pain if I can see the sadistic look in my Master's eyes," he types.

"Put yours on first, slave" comes the reply.

"I'm sorry, SIR, but my Master doesn't allow me a webcam. But I'm really keen for a good kicking. I love the look of the bruises afterwards."

There is a brief pause. The vandal knows he needs to act quickly or he'll be banned again and have to start afresh. Plus he's never been invited to a private dungeon on this site and is intrigued about how far he can go.

The head of the vandal's figure changes and is replaced with a cam feed of the vandal's head. He's wearing a leather hood, but the eyes are visible. As Alex prepares to move his own character onto the floor he spots something and thinks, "It can't be."

He adjusts the brightness and contrast on his computer screen and zooms in. Through the eyeholes in the hood, Lars' piercing distinctive olive eyes are clearly visible.

Alex doesn't know what to do. Should he tell

Damian immediately? Perhaps not until he has more proof. He doesn't want to seem to be badmouthing Damian's staff without having the evidence to back it up.

He resolves to discuss it with Jameson first before quickly pressing the "ban" button and terminating the session.

Alex's heart races but he sees from the clock in his room that it's nearly lunchtime so he gets his chance very quickly.

Fortunately Damian is out of the house so it's just Jameson and Alex having lunch together in the kitchen.

"I met a guy called Lars the other day," Alex mentions as casually as he can, his heart pounding with nervousness. "He showed me how the moderator system works as Sir has asked me to help identify someone who's vandalising the interactive porn films."

Alex decides not to tell Jameson about the mistake Lars made in setting up his access but assumes that Jameson knows about the job he's been assigned as he seems to know everything.

"He seems nice enough," Jameson replies. "Been here quite a while. He works in one of the offices upstairs though I haven't seen him around today. Maybe he's sick."

"Sick is the word," thinks Alex.

Alex takes a deep breath and decides to confide in Jameson.

"Well here's the thing, Mr Jameson. The vandal entered an interactive porno film I was in today and I'm sure it's Lars."

"Hold on a minute, Alex. Lars is one of Mr Hall's most trusted members of staff. How can you be sure? Did it look like Lars? After all, as I understand it visitors just appear as animated graphic figures in these films, like in a computer game."

"Well, I managed to get the vandal to turn on his web cam. He had a leather hood on but I'd recognise those piercing olive-coloured eyes anywhere."

"You still can't make accusations like that without more proof, Alex. After all lots of people have olive-coloured eyes. And you didn't see his face or anything."

"I know that, Mr Jameson. Will you help me find out if it is Lars?"

For a moment, Alex sees himself as Sherlock Holmes and Jameson as his trusty Watson.

"What can I do, Alex? I don't go into those films. I have my own work to do."

"How about this," suggests Alex. "I'll keep looking out for the vandal and note down the dates and times when he's in there. If it is Lars, then he can't be doing it in the office as he had that leather hood on in his web cam feed. If you could make a note each day whether Lars is in the office then maybe after a week we could compare notes and see if they match."

"Good idea, Alex," Jameson replies, though he

worries that maybe Alex has been reading too many detective stories.

"Thanks, Watson, sorry Mr Jameson," Alex says, laughing with embarrassment at his mistake.

Jameson laughs too and takes delight in hearing how Alex narrowly avoided a good kicking. He doesn't understand how the porno system works and so doesn't question why, if it was Lars, he didn't recognise Alex and leave immediately.

"But before anything else we need to clean you up a bit," he tells Alex. "You're overdue for a haircut and a body shave. I don't think Sherlock Holmes ever went around looking scruffy."

They both laugh and finish their lunch.

Even so, Alex is nervous. What if he's wrong? Will Jameson tell Damian what's going on and maybe anger him? Alex rubs his hands on his still recovering thighs and hopes not.

Alex is laying on the massage bed trying to relax and not get too aroused while Jameson shaves off his pubic hair. As he's working, Jameson decides to tell Alex a bit more about Lars as he has started to wonder if there's some truth in what Alex is suggesting.

"You wouldn't know this but Lars, like you, was spotted by Mr Hall in one of the interactive porn films. There were some technical difficulties with the system and Mr Hall was looking for someone who seemed to know the system really well and could possibly be paid to help sort them out.

"I remember Mr Hall mentioning Lars at the time and saying that he had found this guy who was really interested in playing with him to the point of almost stalking him. But Mr Hall found him far too pushy. Even so, Lars seemed to have a good technical background and had some good suggestions for improving the system. So Mr Hall offered him a job.

"I wonder if Lars' destructive behaviour is him getting back at Mr Hall for rejecting his sexual advances. But that's speculation. You need to get to know this guy better. Alex. And be sure of your facts. After all, Lars's eye colour isn't unique. He might be quite innocent."

Then Alex remembers something that's been niggling at the back of his mind.

"You remember I told you that Sir phoned Lars and asked him to show me how to be a junior moderator. Well it occurred to me afterwards that he didn't tell Lars why this was being done besides just helping out. And when Lars was showing me how to work the system he didn't ask. Nor did the topic of the vandal come up at all in our conversations. Is it a case of the dog that didn't bark in the night?"

"Sorry, Alex, I don't understand, we don't have a dog," replies a puzzled Jameson.

"It's a Sherlock Holmes reference. What can be a vital clue isn't what does happen, but what doesn't.

"After all Lars told me that staff in Sir's business don't have any secrets from each other. So why did Sir ask me to keep my assignment under my hat? Was it really because he didn't want his staff to think he didn't think them capable?"

"You may have a point there, Alex. Maybe Mr Hall isn't ruling out that it may be an inside job. But remember, lots of people have olive eyes."

Alex looks up at Jameson, checking the colour of his eyes just in case. They're brown. At least he knows there's one person he can still trust, he hopes. Especially when they have a razor in one hand and your bollocks in the other.

CHAPTER 12

That evening after dinner Jameson informs Alex that Damian wants to play with him the next morning and he is to sleep plugged. They go to Alex's room and Jameson locks the larger dildo in for the night.

Alex is excited, as he and Damian haven't played for a few days. But he is worried about whether Damian will ask too many questions about his vandal hunting. But this is soon forgotten as the dildo does its work of stimulating his prostate and it is a very horny, frustrated, chastity-locked Alex who wakes up the next morning when Jameson comes to unlock the dildo so he can clean himself up and get himself ready.

At breakfast, Damian confirms that they are to play that morning when Alex's food has settled.

"And how is your sleuthing going, boy?" Damian asks him.

"Slowly, Sir. I've only come across the vandal once but he knows I'm interested in him, from an online play point of view, not an investigative one."

"Find out anything about him?"

"Not really except that, as well as dungeon furniture, he seems to like kicking men as well. So I'm going to use that as bait."

"Sounds good, boy. Keep me posted. I'll see you in the playroom at 11am."

And that's all that Damian asks which makes Alex feel better. He doesn't want to risk upsetting Damian by mentioning Lars just yet. If Jameson has mentioned anything to Damian about Lars, then Damian isn't letting on which is good as it means he's trusting Alex to raise it when he's ready.

So Alex gets himself ready for his play session without any worries. Clean white t-shirt and shorts, freshly polished boots and a clean black bandana around his neck though he hopes it won't be needed to mop up any tears. The chain collar, with its padlock engraved with Damian's name, is of course always there.

At 11am Alex enters the playroom to find Damian busy making preparations. On the bondage table is what looks like a leather and canvas body bag, all covered in straps and fixing rings.

"Take all your clothes off, boy, including your boots."

Alex carefully folds up his clothes on a chair and stands to attention, waiting his next instruction. Damian removes Alex's chastity belt and lubes up and inserts the ribbed electro plug inside his arsehole before attaching the cables and helping Alex climb onto the table and into the bag.

"What is this, Sir," Alex asks. "Looks like one of those things they use to remove dead bodies from crime scenes."

"It's called a sleepsack and it'll keep you nice and secure while I play with you. And very much alive I can assure you."

Alex looks at the sleepsack and thinks that it

doesn't provide much opportunity for the more painful things Damian has done to him, which he feels happier about.

He knows that the painful impact play, aside from the punishments, has been Damian's way of helping him understand his position and the control he has over him. And, to his surprise, he finds the thuds and stings invigorating while at the same time making him feel very relaxed and calm. And very much controlled and submissive.

Damian shows Alex how to insert his arms into the internal sleeves of the sleepsack so that, when Damian then zips it up, he is totally enclosed from the neck down and unable to move more than wriggling his fingers and feet. There are in fact two zips along the front which meet in the middle and Damian pulls Alex's cock and balls out between them so they are easily accessible.

He then adds a leather hood, but unlike previous ones, the lower half of the face is open.

Alex's play with Damian hasn't involved much intricate bondage so far, so he is looking forward to something new.

With some lengths of thick rope Damian cinches the sides of the sleepsack together, making it much more constricting, and then starts attaching some haulage straps from the various fixing points along its side to a frame overhead. He also adds some to the fixings on the hood to support Alex's head.

Slowly Damian shortens the straps in turn,

repeating the process until the sleepsack is suspended horizontally above the bondage table which he then rolls out of the way. Damian starts playfully rocking the sleepsack back and forth.

"Did you like the swings when you were a kid, boy?" he asks mischievously.

"I did, Sir," Alex laughs. "But they were never as exciting as this one."

A few minutes later Damian has added to the arrangement, connecting the electro plug to the control box and adding some conductive rubber tubing electrodes, one around the head of Alex's cock and the other around his cock and balls like a cock ring.

Damian turns on the electro box and Alex feels the familiar tingling in his arse and up and down his cock as the stimulating electrical patterns make their moves.

Alex then discovers that there is more to the sleepsack when Damian opens up two small flaps, one above each of his nipples. Alex squeezes his eyes shut fearing the very painful sharp clamps that he'd suffered from the previous week.

"Don't worry, boy," Damian reassures him, spotting Alex's face tighten. And with that he massages each of Alex's nipples in turn to swell them up a bit and then attaches a clover clamp with ridged but not sharp rubber pads to each one. Alex thinks they're not too bad, and starts to enjoy them but is distracted by the increasing stimulation from the electrical symphony playing out lower down his body.

His enjoyment of the nipple clamps is short lived as Damian attaches the clamps to the overhead frame so that, when he rocks the sleepsack, they are pulled in unison. "But still," he thinks as his nipples are squeezed and pulled in different directions, "at least they're not biting."

Damian has orchestrated this play scene in great detail. He knows he has been harsh on Alex at times. And he senses that Alex has some worries about his work assignment but decides not to probe too far today. Today is going to be pure, if intense and frustrating, pleasure for Alex. And pure evil pleasure for himself.

He loosens the straps supporting Alex's head so that it drops down and allows him to slide his erect cock easily into Alex's mouth.

Alex is in heaven. His cock, balls and arse are pulsing in time with the electrical patterns; his nipples are being squeezed and pulled by the movement of the sleepsack and he has Damian's cock in his mouth.

Damian has positioned the electro control box so that he can adjust the patterns and levels without removing his cock from Alex's mouth and he increases the intensity of the settings higher than Alex has been subject to before.

As the peaks of electric energy get stronger and spikier Alex opens his mouth wide and he lets out a deep ecstatic moan which is what Damian has been waiting for and his cock slides right to the back of Alex's throat so he almost swallows the PA ring.

"Bliss," Damian thinks. He stands still and rocks the sleepsack back and forth on its supporting straps to move Alex's mouth and throat up and down his cock until he cums.

When he removes it, Alex is grinning broadly. "Thank you, Sir. That was amazing."

"It's not over yet, boy," he says as he supports Alex's head once more in the straps.

Damian turns off the current to the cock bands and removes them from Alex's now very hard cock.

Alex feels Damian apply a thick layer of lube to his cock. It feels cold but then feels very hot at the same time.

Damian moves to Alex's head and shows him something.

"Hmm, Icy Hot, Sir," says Alex. "I've seen that before but never knew what it was like."

"You're going to find out," Damian tells him as he returns to attend to Alex's cock, changing the programme on the electro box stimulating the plug in his arse to a different one called "Orgasm".

He starts edging Alex's cock, stroking slowly, then faster and harder, then more slowly again, always ensuring Alex's cock stays hard, always ensuring Alex gets close to cumming but never gets there.

This goes on for half an hour, leaving Alex more aroused and desperate to cum than ever. But he is not in control and Damian seems to know exactly when to stop so that he doesn't actually cum. It's the most frustrating time Alex has had since he met Damian.

Satisfied he has brought Alex as close to climaxing as he dares without going too far, Damian stops the edging and gets a hot damp cloth to wipe the Icy Hot off Alex's cock.

"You're not cumming today, boy. But you will soon I can assure you," Damian tells him.

Alex feels Damian putting a metal cock ring around his cock and balls and wonders if this is to restore his erection as his cock has softened.

Then he feels some cold lube applied to his cock and what feels like a metal tube being slid over it. The end of his now-soft cock hits the end of the tube and then he senses a key being inserted in a lock.

Damian's hands are no longer holding any of the metal and Alex realises that the cock ring and tube are now locked on to him. This must be a different electro device, he thinks.

Damian rolls the bondage table back under the sleepsack and carefully lowers Alex onto it. After a few minutes Alex is free and standing up, as he does without any prompting now, looking straight at Damian, hands behind his back, feet apart, not daring to look down at his cock and balls.

Alex feels extremely aroused and deep inside his lower body something feels like it's ready to explode. But on the other hand the intensity of the session also leaves him somewhat drained.

Damian tells him to look in the mirror. "Go check out your new chastity cage."

Alex looks at his cock's new prison. There's a metal cock ring and locked to it by a rigid fixing is a metal tube with cage bars at the end. His cock is soft and is already filling the cage and touching the end of it.

Alex wonders what it will be like when his cock tries to get hard again.

"I thought maybe that other belt was getting a bit boring for you, boy. So I decided to lock you in something which you'd find more exciting," Damian tells him, adding just to himself "and more frustrating".

That night Alex finds out soon enough. As soon as his cock tries to get hard the tip of it pushes the cage forward a little and the attached cock ring pulls his balls away painfully from his body. So he wakes up many times in the night.

His cock seems more accessible in this new device as he can see his cock head through the bars at the end. But it feels as far away as ever. He can't get anywhere near as hard in it as he could in the full belt. And every time he starts to get hard it gets painful.

Desperate for a solution, Alex logs into the chastity community and discovers his experience is not unique. The solution, it seems, is to have a piss which helps tremendously.

Alex isn't sure whether or not he's happy with the

new chastity device. But he knows he has no choice; coping with it will be a new challenge and one that clearly Damian has set for him. And that morning's play session was so extraordinarily exciting that he knows that meeting the challenge is the price he has to pay for those wonderful experiences.

Upstairs in the house Damian is in bed trying to get to sleep. But he is still very aroused by that morning's play with his boy. So he has his own cock problem. It is erect and demanding attention as well. But he knows to save himself for the next time he plays with Alex. He doesn't need a chastity device to control when he cums.

And next time he does, Alex may get to cum as well.

CHAPTER 13

Next morning Alex has breakfast with Damian.

"Sleep well, boy?"

"Not at all, Sir," Alex replies, laughing. He knows exactly why Damian is asking.

"In my previous chastity belt my cock could grow a bit. But in this one there's no room for growth at all. And after yesterday's really exciting play session I was left feeling really horny and frustrated all night as I was so turned on by it all. Every time my cock tried to grow it pushed the cage out and pulled on my balls."

Through the glass table top Alex spots Damian's cock growing under his combat trousers. "Lucky bugger," Alex thinks.

"I told you I thought your previous belt was getting a bit boring, boy," Damian replies with a broad grin on his face.

"Fortunately, Sir, you've given me access to that chastity community and I found a way of solving it when it happens – go have a piss. That doesn't stop it happening, but at least I am able to relieve the pressure so my cock goes down and I can get back to sleep."

"What's on your agenda for today, boy? I don't really have any time for play I'm afraid," Damian asks thinking that Alex probably still needs to calm down from being so aroused and frustrated the day before.

"Well, Sir, the garden's pretty much done for now,

so I'm going to have a determined effort to track down the vandal.

"I realised that I needed to look for him at different times of the day and evening, even during the night if my cock wakes me up. And I've worked out how to be in more than one interactive porno film at once. So I can increase my chance of being in the same place as him."

"You're a lot smarter than you first appeared, boy, I didn't know that moderators could do that. I hope you succeed because we're getting quite a few complaints. He's started attacking other visitors as well. If you need any help with the system ask Lars."

Alex thinks to himself that will be the last thing he does but says "Yes, Sir, I will, but I think I've got the hang of everything now."

He's still puzzled about many things, though. If Lars is a system manager why didn't he know that the person he talked to the other day was Alex? Maybe system manager tools can only be used in the office for security reasons. So when he's at home being a vandal he has no more information than any other visitor. And didn't he know about the private dungeons? Maybe they are only available to Damian. But then, if he encountered a hacker on the site, wouldn't he have alerted Damian? Maybe he had.

And what's his reason for being destructive? Is it purely the vengeance of a jilted playmate? Or is he acting for one of Damian's competitors? Alex discounts this. If an organisation wanted to destroy a competitor they'd hire a bunch of hackers to flood the site or infiltrate and corrupt its software.

The vandal clearly isn't that clever or he'd use these more sophisticated methods himself to upset things.

That Thursday afternoon Alex spots the vandal in one of the interactive films he's watching and has another go at engaging with him. He dresses his online figure in the black and white camo t-shirt and combats again so that, if it is Lars, he won't be recognised. He realises how lucky it is that he'd done that before their first encounter.

He sends the vandal a private message just as he is about to rip a flogging frame off the wall along with a visitor's avatar still strapped to it.

"Sorry about last time, SIR, but just as I was getting on the floor for you to kick me you disappeared. Maybe someone blocked my access to the site," Alex types innocently. "Want to have another go?"

"Sure, slave, it's pretty boring in here."

Alex is relieved that the vandal doesn't seem to have got suspicious after their previous encounter and activates his private dungeon and invites the vandal in.

"OK, slave, on the floor, you're gonna get your head kicked in."

"Can I see your eyes again, SIR, it really does make a difference?"

The vandal turns on his web cam and once again there's the leather hood pierced by the olive-coloured eyes, all lit up by the vandal's computer screen.

Alex doesn't think he can delay much more and places his character on the floor of the online dungeon. A virtual kick hits his character on its head and the animated figure spins around on the floor.

"Ouch, SIR, my head's spinning," Alex types. Of course it isn't as this is all on-screen and virtual. In fact Alex's head is in very good shape and he continues typing.

"Next time, SIR, could I see your real boots. The ones on here are a bit lame, they look like ballet shoes."

Alex is being deliberately provocative. He expects that if the vandal is into kicking he will be wearing some pretty strong boots and will be insulted by the suggestion he's wearing ballet shoes. He's hoping to goad the vandal into expanding his web cam view to include his whole body. There might be some more clues such as how tall the vandal is, or his body shape.

The vandal rises to the insult and a few seconds later Alex can see the vandal's full body. He's dressed in black leather shirt and jeans and a long black leather coat which ends just above his boots. The boots look like pretty standard steel toe-capped black biker boots. There are no distinctive characteristics on any of the clothing.

Alex scans the web cam feed hoping for some clues in the background but the room behind the vandal is very dark so he can't see any distinctive furniture or anything on the walls.

"Damn," thinks Alex, but decides to let his character get another kicking in case something else shows up. Alex moves his online figure's head back in position on the floor and again and watches his screen as the vandal kicks him in the head. As the boot connects there are flashes of green light and Alex wonders if these are some online pyrotechnic features he'd not spotted before like the "pow" splashes they used to have in those old Batman TV shows.

Just as the vandal prepares to kick him again the leather-clad figure disappears. Alex assumes someone else is watching the room and has banned him. This isn't surprising as kicking someone in the head isn't good at the best of times and doesn't have a place in safe SM play which is what these films and play spaces are about.

Alex wonders if Lars comes to work in a long black leather coat. In Damian's SM world such leather fetish clothing wouldn't seem out of place and he expects that any staff member coming to work in one wouldn't look out of place. But he has only met Lars once and he didn't have his coat on.

It is dinner the next day before Alex has a chance to catch up with Jameson and discuss his investigations.

"I met the vandal again yesterday," Alex tells him. "I got a look at his whole body though it was difficult to tell much about him except he has a long black leather coat."

"The vandal and loads of other people, Alex. The weather has got colder and those coats seem to be really popular at the moment. I see them on the street all the time."

"Was Lars in work yesterday?" Alex asks Jameson.

"I don't think so. But not seeing him isn't proof he wasn't here. The only thing I can tell you for certain is when I do see him and know he is here and not kicking you or the dungeon furniture."

Alex feels a bit despondent and helps Jameson clear up their dinner things. Suddenly the lights go out and the fire alarm sounds.

"What the fuck," shouts Jameson. "We're not due a drill so this might be real. Follow me."

Alex follows Jameson through the passage from the kitchen to the main hall, their way lit dimly by emergency lights. A number of people from the offices upstairs are also moving quickly through the dingy main hall, using the front door as their exit.

Alex doesn't recognise many of these people and he anxiously scans the crowd for Damian as he follows Jameson towards the front door. Then he stops suddenly. Ahead of him, low down in the gloom, he sees flashes of green light as the heels of one of the men ahead of him pound on the floor.

And just as suddenly the fire alarm stops and the lights come on. The hall fills up again as people return from the street and go upstairs to their offices. But the hall is now brightly-lit and any green flash is impossible to spot.

Damian enters the house last and shuts the front door and Alex breathes a sigh of relief.

"Wow, boy, that was a bit of excitement we could have done without. Seems like someone put some really thick pieces of bread in a toaster upstairs. It got jammed and caught alight. The smoke detectors set the fire alarm off and then the main fuses all went as the toaster caught fire as well."

"I'm glad you're OK, Sir, and it wasn't anything more serious."

"I need a cup of tea. Jameson, will you bring me one while I have a quick chat with Alex."

Once they're in his office, Damian asks Alex how he's getting on with his vandal hunting.

"I came across him again yesterday, Sir. Got a better look at him. But nothing distinctive. Head to toe in black leather, which could be anyone. I'll keep trying, Sir"

"Your new computer skills working well enough for you, then?"

"Yes, Sir, though I could have done with a bit of help yesterday. I messaged Lars but never got a reply and by this morning I'd solved it myself so I didn't follow it up," Alex says, hoping Damian doesn't spot that he is lying or check with Lars.

"Lars wasn't around the office yesterday, something about a sick puppy he was looking for or something," Damian tells him. "But he was in the office today I'm sure, as I saw him out in the street just now."

Alex tries very hard not to break out in a very broad grin. "Bingo", he thinks. He has three bits of evidence: the olive eyes, the matching absences from work and the green flashing boots.

"Thanks, Sir. I'm off to bed soon if that's OK."

"Yes of course, boy. And when I've finished my cup of tea I need to go see how much damage the toaster has done."

Alex doesn't sleep well that night. Not because of his balls aching but because his mind is racing with ideas of how and when to present his evidence to Damian. "Jameson will know," he thinks. And for the first time since he got his new chastity device he sleeps through the night.

CHAPTER 14

When Jameson arrives in the kitchen, Alex is already there making breakfast for the two of them and Damian. "You're up bright and early, Alex. Couldn't sleep?"

"On the contrary, Mr Jameson, I slept wonderfully. I think I now have enough evidence to convince Sir that the vandal is Lars. I just don't know how to present it to him."

"OK, spill the beans, Holmes," Jameson replies not realising how unlike Watson and Holmes' formal Victorian English he sounds.

Alex goes through the events of the past day and Jameson agrees that the evidence is pretty strong. But he also adds that Damian considers Lars to be one of his best employees.

"Even so, Alex," Jameson continues. "If you add your evidence to the fact that Mr Hall, we think, suspects it might be an inside job then you may find it not so hard.

"I'll take Mr Hall his breakfast and ask if he has time for the two of us to have a meeting with him and deliver your conclusions. I won't tell him any more than that. You've done all the hard work and should get the credit for it."

At 11am Alex and Jameson are in Damian's office. Jameson sitting on a chair by Damian's desk and Alex standing to attention in front of them. He feels comfortable in this position and it also feels more formal and gives him confidence.

Alex tells Damian how early on he found he was a senior moderator and so could change his appearance and make use of a private dungeon. "I don't know how that happened, Sir, but it sure was useful."

"I did it," Damian reveals. "As you may have worked out, I wondered if it was one of my staff with a grudge. I'm not sure why they should. I pay them well and look after them. And I knew that, with your white t-shirt and shorts and locked collar and bandana they'd recognise you immediately.

"Also those private dungeons are actually only available to me. None of my staff know about them. But I gave you access as well as I thought they might be useful.

"And you made good use of those extra facilities I made available to you. You're really smart, boy, which is why I never understood how your life ended up in such a mess."

No-one has said that to Alex before and his heart swells with pride.

"Thank you, Sir. Maybe this chastity stuff is really helping. And I must apologise for lying to you. I never sent a message to Lars asking for help. But I wanted to find out if he was in the office when the vandal was kicking his way around."

"I knew what you were doing, boy, and as with the moderator thing, I was happy to let you work out your own strategy and help in any way I could without making it obvious what I was doing."

Alex goes through the recent days' events, detailing how he lured the vandal into his room, the match of the olive eyes and the green flashing boots.

"It's time I confronted Lars," Damian tells him. "Go back to your room, boy, and get changed. You'll find some new clothes there. Then come back here."

Alex goes to his room and can barely believe what he sees. There's a black and white camo-patterned t-shirt and matching combats, a new pair of black boots and some thick white socks. Alex starts laughing. "Boy, Damian sure was keeping an eye on me."

He takes off his white t-shirt and shorts and puts on his new clothes, leaving his bandana and locked chain collar visible for once. The new boots feel great and it's wonderful having thicker socks at last.

When he returns to Damian's office Lars is there too and Alex gulps. He's not sure he has the confidence to confront Lars himself and waits to see what Damian says.

"Lars, I think you may recognise Alex better like this. Or maybe he needs to lie down on the ground to convince you."

"I'm not sure what you mean, Mr Hall. I've never seen Alex dressed like this."

Damian looks down at the floor and sees that Lars is wearing a very solid pair of black boots. "Well he's certainly seen you and your vandalising of our interactive videos. Let's settle it right now. Take your boots off, Lars."

Lars continues to protest his innocence but nonetheless obeys Damian's order.

Damian walks around to the front of his desk and picks up the boots and examines them closely. Along the upper edge of each heel is a clear plastic strip like you find on some kids' shoes. He bangs the heels together and even in the daylight, green flashes can be seen.

"I thought these sort of gimmicks were meant to be for kids," Damian scowls. "And clearly you're just a juvenile delinquent."

Lars is flustered and speaks incoherently. "I was only having a bit of fun, Mr Hall. I was bored and still angry that you didn't want to play with me. If you decide to punish me then I accept it."

"Well I don't know what you're thinking of, Lars, but floggers and canes and the like are for play and fun and nurturing. Not for revenge. Obviously your employment here is terminated immediately. And you and I will never speak again. I didn't want to play with you when we first met and I certainly don't want you anywhere near my playrooms now, real or virtual.

"Jameson, escort Lars out of the building. If there's anything of his own in his desk we can post it to him."

Lars starts to protest but Damian ignores him and returns to his desk, quickly removing Lars access to the company's servers before he can do any more damage.

"Let's go, Lars," Jameson tells him and Lars turns and leaves the room with Jameson following close behind him.

"You did an excellent job there, boy. I'm very pleased and proud of you; you helped my business immensely with your investigation. Of course, I'd love to offer you a proper job here but I don't believe in mixing work and play, as you know, And play with you is far more important. You're not easily replaced in my life or my heart.

"On the other hand, people like Lars are easily replaced and I must remember in future not to use our porno sites like a recruiting centre."

"Thank you, Sir. I learned a lot and I'm glad to have been able to give you something back. And thank you for watching over me and protecting me while I found my own way to solve the problem."

Damian gets up from his desk and gives Alex a big hug, before putting his mouth over Alex's and giving him a deep kiss.

"I need to find you some new skills to learn, boy, both in the playroom and outside it. Maybe Jameson can teach you how to drive. It's about time you got out of this house and I'd love to have my collared and locked boy driving me around.

"And as I may need to get hold of you when I have more jobs for you, you'll need this."

Damian hands Alex a mobile phone. Alex can't believe this is happening.

"It's restricted, as you'll expect, but you'll find some numbers already programmed in there."

Alex turns on the phone and checks the address book. There's just three people in it, Damian, Jameson and Melissa.

Grinning from ear to ear, Alex steps forward and wraps his arms around Damian, something he's never felt he could initiate in the past. "Thank you, Sir, that's wonderful."

"Oh, and as a final thank you, boy, I think you're owed an orgasm."

"I hope it isn't an anti-climax Sir," Alex replies, laughing at his own joke. "It's been a long time and hopefully worth waiting for."

CHAPTER 15

For the next few days Damian needs to spend time with the rest of his staff finding out how much other damage Lars has possibly done to his business. So it seems a good time to give Alex a new challenge to keep him occupied.

In his room, Alex answers a call on his mobile phone from Damian.

"I tried you a few times, boy, but you were engaged. How's Melissa?"

With his phone only being able to call Damian, Jameson and Melissa, it wasn't hard for Alex to work out how Damian knew who he had been talking to.

"I just wanted to have a brief chat with her, Sir, just to tell her that I was fine and happy. But she rabbited on about how worried she'd been about me and about her latest waiter boyfriend. I said I hoped to be able to meet up with her at some point, if that's OK, Sir."

"That will be soon, boy. But for now there's someone I want you to meet. Come to my office when you're ready."

A few minutes later Alex goes to Damian's office and finds him talking to a tall muscular man wearing a blue track suit and training shoes.

"This is Gordon Brakes. He is going to be your personal trainer."

Gordon shakes Alex's hand. "Good to meet you, Mr Brakes," Alex says, feeling unsure how he should address him and decides on a middle ground between "Gordon" and "Sir".

Gordon's handshake is very strong and Alex regrets how feeble his own is.

"Good to meet you, Alex, I've heard a lot about you," Gordon replies in a deep Scots accent.

A wave of sadness also comes over Alex as he wonders if "personal trainer" meant that Gordon would be his new Master. So maybe he should have called Gordon "Sir".

"What sort of trainer, Sir," Alex asks, hesitantly, not knowing which one of them he should be addressing in that way.

"Well you have the basis of a good body, boy, but it needs to be exercised properly and developed. So you will be working out under Mr Brakes' direction," Damian tells him, confirming how Alex should address Gordon in future.

Damian had considered allowing Alex to call him "Gordon" but thought that might not generate the respect Alex needed to show for someone who wasn't going to give him an easy ride and would be pushing him hard in his workouts.

Alex relaxes, now sure that Damian wasn't passing him on to another Master.

"Off the hall is a fitness room you've not seen yet. You and Mr Brakes can go off there now and he can explain what the equipment is and assess what needs to be done.

"He'll put you through your paces to see where

your strengths and weaknesses are. Then he'll work out a fitness training schedule for you and supervise it. I'll be keeping track of your progress, of course, and hopefully notice the results soon.

"I think your white t-shirt and shorts will do for today though Mr Brakes may suggest some other clothing for me to get you. To start with you'll find a new pair of training shoes in your size in the fitness room. Those boots aren't suitable."

Alex marvels yet again at how Damian manages to measure him up for clothes or footwear or even chastity devices without him noticing.

Inside the large brightly-lit fitness room, two of its walls covered with mirrors, Alex discovers some impressive equipment. There's a complicated captive weights machine, a rowing machine and a treadmill in the middle, and some exercise mats and a padded bench with horizontal bars in another.

"I'm also Mr Hall's personal trainer," Gordon tells him. "He spends too much of his time sitting behind that desk. So he works out with me here a few times a week and the exercise helps relax his muscles and maintain his physical strength."

Alex knows from the way Damian has man-handled him around the playroom and the force with which he can wield his floggers that Damian is indeed strong.

Alex changes from his boots to the white and blue trainers that are there. They're a perfect fit, of course.

"Let's start with you running on the spot and doing some press ups for a while to warm you up and then move on to some stretching exercises to help relax your muscles," Gordon tells Alex.

"And then we'll try you with some weights to see how strong your arms and legs are."

Finally Gordon gets Alex doing some time on the treadmill while he monitors his heart rate. All the time he's taking notes on a clipboard.

When Alex is done, Gordon weighs Alex and frowns.

"You're carrying too much weight, Alex, and it's the wrong sort and in the wrong places. It's fat not muscle. But together we can change that."

Alex is sweating and breathing hard and realises from just a little exercise how out of shape he is. He fears the physical training won't be easy and will be yet another challenge set by Damian. He also wonders if Damian has set him some weight-loss targets and what the penalty would be for not meeting them.

But Gordon's use of the word "together" eases his fears as he hopes that Gordon is also included in the challenge.

"We need to build up your stamina as well," Gordon continues. "Mr Hall tells me there's a lot of digging to do in the garden come the spring and you need to be strong and fit for that or you'll strain yourself."

Gordon looks at the scales again.

"I'll have a word with Mr Hall and Jameson about making some adjustments to your diet."

Alex realises that he has eaten far better since arriving than he did when he and Melissa survived on packet soup and chips and it shows in his flabby body and excess weight.

"You need a loose tank top to give you more freedom to move your upper body and some looser shorts so you don't put pressure on your balls when exercising. I don't want one of your balls slipping through the cock ring of that interesting device in your shorts. I'll ask Mr Hall to organise them."

Alex blushes, not realising that Gordon knew about his chastity device.

"Understood, Mr Brakes."

"You'll work out here three times a week, Alex, starting tomorrow at 5pm. It's not going to be easy but I'm sure you'll be pleased with the results."

Alex looks at himself in one of the mirrors and realises how much work there is to do.

"See you then, Alex," Gordon says, shaking his hand again very firmly as they leave. Alex hopes his own hands get stronger soon or he'll have a very sore hand after many more of Gordon's handshakes.

Alex calls in on the library for a new book on his way back to the room as he feels tired from just this brief exertion and he needs something relaxing and none-physical to do. There's too many to choose from and it takes him a while. In the end he settles on a biography of Charles Atlas, hoping to pick up some body building tips.

When he finally gets back to his room Alex discovers some white tank tops and shorts and a set of weighing scales have appeared.

"This is going to be a whole new world of pain," he thinks to himself.

CHAPTER 16

Before getting dressed for his workout the next afternoon Alex weighs himself. He reckons that, if Damian and Gordon are keeping track of his weight, then he had better do so as well. He doesn't want any nasty surprises when Gordon does his weekly weight check. But he also reckons skipping a second piece of toast at breakfast and having salad for lunch aren't going to have made much difference from the day before.

Alex doesn't know what Damian and Gordon think his weight should be, but he's certain that it should be less than it is now. So he just writes the figure down and puts on his new tank top, looser shorts and training shoes and sets off, grabbing a bottle of water from the kitchen and a clean towel from the laundry on the way.

When he arrives at the fitness room he hears some voices inside so he knocks rather than just going in, and a very sweaty Damian opens the door and invites him in.

The room is warm and smells of Damian's body. Clearly Damian has just had his own strenuous workout and Alex hopes that Gordon has lower expectations for his own performance. Alex's cock tries to grow in its chastity cage and he realises how much Damian's muscular body and its smell excite him.

"Have fun, boy" Damian tells Alex, ruffling his hair

as he goes off for a shower. Alex has never seen Damian in his shorts and he notices the muscular legs usually hidden under his black combats.

"Right, let's get started, Alex," Gordon tells him with a smile.

"Yes, Mr Brakes."

"Let me explain something of what we're going to achieve here, Alex. Your body is made up of lots of muscles which, in your case, haven't been exercised and developed as much as they could. Now I'm not going to turn you into world class body builder. I may succeed in achieving the impossible with you, but the miraculous is beyond me."

Alex laughs and remembers the Charles Atlas biography he took from Damian's library but hadn't yet started.

"What I've drawn up for you is a list of routines for you to do three times a week."

Alex looks at the piece of paper on the clipboard Gordon is holding. Listed on it are about ten different exercises labelled with the muscles they're targeted at. In the next column is a space to put the weight used, while the third column is labelled "reps", whatever that is, he thinks.

"Most of those exercises you'll be doing on the captive weights machine," Gordon explains.

Over at the machine Gordon explains to Alex that it is designed to develop a wide range of muscle groups and points at an instruction sheet on the wall which shows which levers and handles to adjust.

Alex notices it's headed "Brakes Multigym"

"Did you invent this, Mr Brakes?" Alex asks.

"Actually I did, Alex. I used to work out in a professional gym where they had separate machines for each muscle group. But of course that's impractical in people's homes so I got together with an engineer and invented this. It combines the functions of about ten different machines and is sold around the world."

Alex marvels at how both Gordon and Damian managed to turn their hobbies into successful businesses while his own more personal hobby lost him any employment he managed to get.

Gordon adjusts the seat on the machine and moves a pin in the stack of weights at its rear to use only a few kilos, and then tells Alex to sit down. Alex notices it has a seat belt which Gordon tightens across his thighs.

"This looks more like something that belongs in the playroom," Alex says. "What's the seat belt for, Mr Brakes?"

"Well Mr Hall has used it for bondage at times in the past," Gordon tells him, laughing. "The belt is actually to keep you steady when you're pulling against the weights. So you don't need to worry about that. It's not to stop you getting away."

Gordon shows Alex the different routines that can be done on the machine, demonstrating how to adjust levers at the back of the device so the weights are attached to the correct part of the machine.

And for each exercise Gordon adjusts the weights so that Alex has to use some effort to move the bars or pads, but not so much that he will strain himself. He makes a note of the weights on the clipboard.

"I've noted down on this work sheet what weight you will start at. After a few sessions you'll find that it doesn't take much effort to complete the reps and we can then increase the weight for that exercise."

"What are reps, Mr Brakes?" Alex asks.

Gordon laughs. "Sorry, Alex, they're repetitions. You do each exercise ten times, so pull down on the bar and ease it back up ten times. Then you rest a little and do another exercise. And then you do the whole cycle twice more."

Alex pulls down on the bar and feels the tension in his arm muscles. He lets the weights pull the bar back up until he hears the metal blocks behind him clank as they drop onto the heavier ones below them.

"Alex, you need to control the up stroke as well as the down one. So control the weight as the bar goes back up and stop just before it hits the other weights. That way you're doing the work and not the machine.

"And pay attention to your breathing. Your muscles are doing a lot of work and so need more oxygen than usual. Be sure to breathe in at the start so your lungs are full when you pull on the weight, then exhale slowly as you lift the weight. That way you'll have more stamina."

Alex has another go and his face tightens as he tries to slowly control the weight in both directions. Concentrating on that and getting his breathing right takes a few goes before he has everything in sync.

"You're getting the hang of this, Alex. Well done."

By the end of the afternoon Gordon has supervised Alex working through the exercises on the machine as well as doing some time on the treadmill and rowing machine. After the last one, Alex has new found admiration for the rowers he's seen on the river and understands why they have a cox shouting encouragement. He's sure he wouldn't get through the exercises if Gordon wasn't there urging him on and making him work hard.

"Your body will ache tomorrow, Alex, which is good just so long as it's not painful. If it is painful then you've been straining too hard or not positioning yourself correctly for each exercise."

Sure enough, the next morning Alex's body is aching in places he didn't know he had muscles and he has a soak in the bath to help ease things and he thinks about the previous day.

He's not sure if he will enjoy the workouts. To his surprise, he felt quite elated after the previous day's session with Gordon. But making sure to do all the routines correctly was going to take attention to detail and he is glad Gordon will always be there to urge him on and make sure he doesn't break the machine or get things wrong and injure himself.

Alex also wonders about why Damian is putting him through this. He knows Damian likes controlling him and making him his plaything. But changing his body so that it becomes fitter and more muscular isn't something he'd expected. Body builders were the men he got turned on by. He'd never thought about becoming one of them.

"Still," Alex thinks looking down at his belly sticking out of the bath water, "I've nothing to lose but a load of flab."

A few weeks later Gordon informs Alex that he will be away for the next week. He has to go to the USA to a trade show where they are promoting his multigym machine.

"You'll have to do your workouts on your own next week, Alex. But you know how to use the machine and the work sheet will remind you what weights to use for each exercise."

The slowly developing optimistic streak in Alex thinks he should cope OK. But his old lazy habits prove to be stronger.

At the last session before the USA trip, Gordon had slightly increased the weights used for some of the exercises and Alex had found himself having to make more effort once again. So without Gordon checking up on him he misses his next workout completely.

Two days later he thinks he'd better get back to the fitness room or he'll be completely unable to match what he'd achieved when he and Gordon were last together.

He starts his next workout routine but he doesn't do all the exercises. In fact, he barely completes ten reps of any of the exercises he attempts, skips the rowing machine and does only a few minutes on the treadmill which he always finds boring.

"Still," Alex thinks to himself, "at least I tried and there's one more opportunity before Gordon gets back."

He's just about to go have a shower when the fitness room door opens and Damian comes in, carrying a small bag.

Alex's heart sinks and he remembers the CCTV camera in the ceiling.

"Oh, shit," he thinks. And he stands to attention, hands behind his back, knowing he is in trouble.

"I don't know, boy," Damian tells him, solemn faced. "You've been doing really well with Mr Brakes and I can see the benefits already. But as soon as he's gone you miss a session and do this one half-heartedly."

"I'm sorry, Sir. I guess it's hard work and I'm not sure why I'm doing all this," Alex explains gesturing at the equipment with his hand.

"You're doing it for two reasons, boy. Firstly because I want it and you agreed to obey me. Remember the first rule?"

"Yes, Sir."

"Secondly because I want you to be fit and healthy. And you should want that for yourself as well."

"I guess I'm not used to thinking about the second

part, Sir."

"Well let's check some things out, boy," Damian tells him as he grabs the ring binder which holds a record of Alex's progress over the weeks.

"Look at this. When you started you could barely lift any weights. Now you can do 10 kilos. On the treadmill you were a panting wreck after only a few minutes. Now you can do longer and on a steeper incline."

"I guess I forget those things, Sir."

"I can fix that, in two ways, boy, one easy and one hard. When we're done here go ask Jameson to find you some large sheets of paper and some marker pens and a ruler. Draw up some graphs of your weights and times and the settings for each of the exercises you've done on the multigym since you started working out. Then we can put them on the wall and when you're working out in here you'll have a visible reminder of your progress. And I think you'll get some satisfaction at updating them each week."

"And the hard one, Sir?" Alex asks already guessing what's in store.

"You're going to complete your workout in here today under my supervision. And you won't want to repeat it that way."

"Yes, Sir," Alex replies grimly.

"Let's start with the treadmill," Damian tells him. When Alex is in position Damian attaches some sharp weighted clamps to his nipples. They bite and swing around as he runs on the rubber belt. But he continues to the end of the pre-set time when Damian removes them and holds Alex tight with one arm while he massages his nipples back into shape with his free hand.

Alex screws his eyes up tight as the pain runs through his chest.

But his cock stirs in its cage as well as he enjoys Damian's tight grip and complete control over him.

"Now for the weights machine, boy. Let's see how you do without any painful encouragement. You have 300 reps to do in total. For every one you don't do you'll get a stroke with this." And with that Damian removes a wooden paddle with holes drilled in it from his bag.

Alex manages most of the exercises but they are hard as his nipples are still sore and his chest muscles ache from the weight of the clamps. And on occasions he clumsily lets the weights drop back noisily onto their rest rather than stopping before they get that far.

"I make that 27 missed reps in total, boy. Now take your shorts off and lay down on that bench.

Alex complies, knowing he has to take his punishment. In fact he is strangely eager for it, knowing deep down that it will help with his inner struggle against his former self.

The strokes of the paddle are strong and well-aimed. And the holes in it mean it stings like hell. By the end Alex is sobbing but he knows he needs and deserves what he is getting.

Damian stands back admiring the bright red glow on his boy's buttocks with the distinctive circles from the holes in the paddle.

"Stand up, boy, dry your face and listen to me."

Alex stands up and wipes his eyes with his black bandana as he assumes his position.

"That's a lesson for you, boy. It's a reminder to you that you need to do your workouts properly because I want it. Working out in here is good for you both as a lesson in obedience and as a way of reminding you to look after yourself."

"Understood, Sir. And thank you."

Damian puts away the paddle and gives Alex a warm hug and kiss.

"There's a good person inside there, boy. It just needs to be made stronger mentally and physically. When you've showered and got dressed go get that stuff from Jameson and make those charts. And be sure to include the missing session and the reps you did before I made you finish them. I think having a dip in the graphs will serve as a reminder to you."

Not long afterwards, Alex is kneeling on the fitness room floor, sheets of paper scattered around him and a marker pen and ruler in his hands. He goes through his work sheets and draws the graphs, seeing for himself how he's getting stronger week by week and feeling embarrassed by the gap and downward slant for today's effort which will, of course, be noticed by Gordon when he returns.

He looks around the room at the equipment.

"I guess I need to make friends with you," he thinks. "This should be a room where I learn to control of my bad habits and take pride in myself. Pain and pleasure should be reserved for the playroom."

CHAPTER 17

After having lunch with Jameson the following week, Alex returns to his room and sits at his desk, reading a celebrity gossip web site. Since things eased up on his restrictions and he has been allowed to walk freely around the house, he has tended to leave his room door open a little. It makes him feel less of a captive and more part of the household. And, as no-one but himself, Damian and Jameson enter the secret corridor there's never any disturbance.

However, this afternoon he is startled to hear someone opening the door to the playroom, next to his own room. He's been so intent on reading that he never spotted anyone walking past his door. Then he hears two voices and realises that it's Damian and Gordon, and they're coming out of the playroom.

He sits back, puzzled. Was Damian showing Gordon around, maybe telling him more about what he and Alex get up to in there? Then he hears Damian speak.

"Thanks, Gordon, that was great. It's been a while since I had a session like that and my back feels wonderful. You sure know how to use that rubber flogger."

"Any time Mr Hall," Gordon replies in his distinctive Scots accent.

Alex tries to make sense of what he has just heard. Could it really be that Gordon had been flogging Damian's back? If so, he wouldn't have heard it anyway as the playroom door is well soundproofed, as are the walls.

Surely Gordon can't be Damian's Master, Alex thinks. And if he is then, whatever he calls him in public, shouldn't Damian have called him "Sir" when there was supposedly no-one else around. It can't be true.

Alex is trying to find reasons to avoid the idea that Gordon has been topping his Master. But before he can think much more one of two men outside seems to have noticed Alex's door is open and they go silent. The door opens fully and Damian, dressed in just black shorts and boots, enters the room, telling Gordon he'll catch up with him later.

Gordon, in his usual blue tracksuit top and bottom, says "See you at the next workout" to Alex and walks off.

"How you doing, boy," Damian says. "What you up to?"

"Just catching up on some gossip sites, Sir. Then I have work to do with Jameson later putting away some deliveries."

There's an awkward silence. Alex wants to ask Damian what he and Gordon have been doing. He can't believe that his Master has been submissive to another man and be flogged by him. But he doesn't want to appear to be intruding into Damian's heavily controlled external persona.

Damian breaks the silence. "I think we need to have a chat, boy. If you have time before helping

Jameson later on we can do it now if you want."

"Yes, Sir, I'd like that very much," Alex replies trying to smile but in fact deeply troubled inside.

"Me too, boy. I'm just going to shower and get changed and I'll be right back," Damian replies, ruffling his boy's hair and kissing him on the head before crossing the hall to shower in the marble bathroom opposite.

Alex notices how red Damian's back is with a lot of what look like dark red cuts.

Fifteen minutes later Damian returns in his usual black t-shirt and combats and he and Alex sit cross-legged on Alex's bed facing each other, Damian holding Alex's hands in his own.

"I guess what you just heard between Mr Brakes and myself outside your door must have confused you, boy, maybe even upset you."

"Yes, Sir, it did. It sounded like you and Mr Brakes had been having a session in the playroom. And that Mr Brakes had been flogging you or something and that confused me. I've always thought of you as a Master and that Mr Brakes was just your personal trainer. But now it seems that he's your Master."

"Well, boy, I can see how you might find it confusing. You're new to the realities of SM relationships and I hate to break it to you but they're not the stereotypes you see in even my own porno films.

"Not everyone into SM is either 100% top or 100% bottom. It's more of a sliding scale with, hopefully, everyone finding their own mix of top and bottom. For myself, I'm probably 90% top. But there's a side of me that does like the feel of a flogger or a whip on my back.

"For me, having a man work on my back isn't about power and submission but about the sheer physical sensation. And there's very few people I would trust to do it well and not believe that, because they're on the handle end of the flogger, they're somehow in control of me.

"So between Mr Brakes and myself it's more an extension of his being my personal trainer for physical fitness. He's not my Master in any sense. Does that help?"

"Not really, Sir. I know when we have really painful play it makes me feel very submissive and controlled. Doesn't it you?"

"I wouldn't say 'very submissive' but it does help me keep in touch with the submissive side of myself from time to time. That's important for me. Because if I'm to understand how you're feeling I strongly believe I need to have had some of the same experiences. That way I can know something of what it feels like when I use the full force of my arm wielding the flogger on your back. And you'll be pleased to know I also know what it's like to have a stroke from the dragon cane on the top of the thighs. It hurts like hell."

Alex smiles. Rather than diminishing his respect for Damian, what he's just learned has enhanced it.

Damian is a man confident enough of his own will and self-worth that he can relinquish control on occasions and not be damaged by the experience. And he clearly has thought a lot about what it takes to be a good Master.

"I even spent 48 hours in a chastity device to find out what it's like. It really helped me understand how they work and what effect they have. I felt incredibly horny and frustrated."

Alex's hand moves to his crotch and he moves his chastity cage around a bit, getting aroused at the thought of Damian's cock being locked up. He finds himself smiling.

"What are you smiling at, boy?"

"Somehow the idea of your cock being locked up has got me a bit excited, Sir."

"See, boy, there seems to be a bit of a dominant streak in you that you never realised. Maybe one day you'll have a boy of your own and let him experience the things you've enjoyed."

"Do all Masters start off as slaves, Sir?"

"Not at all, boy. Some even start as Masters and end up as slaves. But as I said there are many who play both ways, even in parallel.

"Since you arrived here I haven't played with anyone else but you apart from this one time today with Mr Brakes. I enjoy our time together so much I haven't wanted to play with anyone else. But before that I regularly had a number of slaves in my playroom.

"And just so there are no unpleasant surprises, boy, you should know that there may be times in the future when I play with other slaves as well. But you'd still be my number one. You might even be invited to join them in the session.

"Beyond that, there may be SM activities that I don't have enough expertise in which I think you should experience. And I may suggest you go play with other tops who can do those things better than I can. They won't be your Master and you will have a choice. And I'll always be in control of what happens.

"Who knows, you might even want to try a bit of topping yourself at some point. And as long as I approve of who they are and am sure you know what you're doing I'd be happy with that."

By now Alex's head is spinning. He's not sure he likes the idea of Damian lending him out to other Masters or sharing Damian's attention with other boys. And aside from the brief excitement he felt when thinking of Damian's cock being locked up, he's never thought of himself as being in control of anyone else. He hasn't even been able to control himself.

"That's a lot to take in, Sir. What sort of experiences?"

"Well there are things like fisting, for example. I have really large hands and there's not many guys can take them, so it's not an activity I have much experience of. But you might like to try it."

Alex looks down at Damian's large hands encircling his own. "I have enough difficulty with those larger dildoes, Sir, so I think I may be very old before that happens. And I see what you mean about your hands"

They both laugh and the tension eases a little. But Alex is still troubled.

"As for you playing with other boys, Sir. That does worry me. What if you like another boy better than me?"

"You can't legislate for those sorts of things, boy. I've come across too many couples trapped in loveless, sexless relationships. Been in them myself in the past. It's much better to be honest all the time and keep talking. As I've always said to you, you have a choice about whether you stay here or not.

"We never stop growing up and developing. And our interests, sexual desires and needs change. And if you deny this then you end up in a very different world of pain. And not a good one.

"As long as you're honest with me about how you're feeling and we keep talking then I hope we won't have any nasty surprises. And I intend to be totally honest with you as well, boy.

"Of course sometimes I may not tell you the whole truth, as happened with the vandal. But I won't lie to you and I don't expect you to be dishonest to me either. Though I think you also realise that sometimes it's better not to speak all of your mind. You didn't tell me about Lars until you were sure of your facts, for example."

Alex smiles and nods his head. "Yes, Sir."

"And I suppose I should have told you about what I get up to with Mr Brakes before you discovered it for yourself. I'm sorry about that," Damian adds.

"Maybe I should keep my door closed in future, Sir."

"No need for that, boy, unless that makes you feel more comfortable. But I'd rather you spoke up when you heard or saw things that troubled you rather than hiding in here hoping the problem will disappear. Your neck's not long enough for you to make a good ostrich, even with my posture collar on."

"Understood, Sir. I agree," Alex laughs.

"Now boy, I'm feeling a bit tired. What do you say to a bit of indulgence and we sneak in an afternoon nap? I'm sure we could both fit on this bed if we snuggle up tight. But be careful with my back, it's quite sore as you can imagine."

"I'd like that very much, Sir," Alex grins, once more feeling Damian's warmth. "And I'll be careful."

Alex continues to process what he has just learned and wonders if the relationship side of his journey with Damian is going to be harder to navigate than the physical one.

"Better a bumpy road to excitement than a boring one to nowhere," he thinks to himself.

A little while later Jameson walks past Alex's open door on his way to check supplies in the playroom and he spots the two of them wrapped around each other, fast asleep on Alex's bed. He realises their relationship has just moved up a notch.

"You're doing well, boy," Jameson thinks, looking not at Alex but at Damian.

CHAPTER 18

It is a few days before Alex and Damian play again.

The night before, he sleeps plugged and in the morning Jameson gives him a haircut and body shave, paying particular attention to make sure his pubic area is completely smooth and hairless.

Once in the playroom with Damian, there's plenty of flogging, including some surprisingly painful hits with a flogger made from a loop of thick hessian rope. It leaves wonderful braided rope marks on Alex's back and buttocks.

When Damian orders Alex into the sling and restrains him there tightly, Alex hopes he will get to cum at last.

The electro plug is inserted and after his chastity cage has been removed, Alex's cock and balls are wired up too.

Following his previous routine, Damian plays with the electro patterns and levels, causing Alex to writhe around and moan in ecstasy. And as before, Damian spends much time at the head of the sling fucking Alex's throat which Alex is now well-practised in coping with.

When Damian has cum he removes the electro bands from Alex's cock and edges him for what seems like hours, always stopping just short of Alex cumming and keeping the electro plug pulsing away stimulating Alex's prostate. Alex is desperate to cum but suspects he will be punished if he cums too soon. Damian seems to be pretty good at spotting when Alex is getting close and then removing his hand which makes it extra frustrating for Alex.

Part way through the edging session, Damian attaches tight chain-linked clamps to Alex's nipples and pulls on the chain to rock the sling back and forth while he edges Alex further. Finally he decides it's time for Alex to get his reward and be allowed to cum.

Damian turns up the level on the electro plug and grips Alex's cock tighter in his hand, getting Alex closer and closer. Just when he knows Alex is about to cum he pulls hard on the chain so the clamps rip off Alex's nipples and Alex's cock explodes with a fountain of thick dark cum that has been building up over the past weeks.

Alex's expression is a mixture of contradictory emotions. His eyes are screwed up from the pain of the nipple clamps being ripped off but his mouth is grinning widely from the brilliance of the orgasm he's just had.

"There boy," Damian tells Alex as he switches off the electro box, "I hope that was worth waiting for".

"Yes, Sir. Thank you, Sir. Wow!."

"I'm not done with you yet, boy," Damian says as he releases Alex from the sling. "Go have a piss and wash that spunk off your cock and chest, then come back here.

"And check in the mirror, boy, I think there's some on your chin as well," Damian adds laughing loudly.

When Alex returns there's another man in the playroom.

"Boy, this is Simon. As well as building up your physique with the gym routines, there's a couple more changes I want to make to your body. I think you'll like them."

By now Alex trusts Damian totally so the idea of having his body further controlled and shaped by Damian doesn't frighten him too much. And he's used to Damian's mischievous surprises which he enjoys tremendously. Alex can certainly say his time with Damian hasn't been boring.

"Simon here is the man with the expertise to do what I want. I'm not an expert in everything, you know, boy.

"The whole thing won't take long and might hurt a bit. But nothing like the pain you've already learned to enjoy. Now get back in the sling."

Alex realises that whatever changes Damian is going to make to his body, they will happen now in this room.

Once more he is restrained in the sling, and he's blindfolded as well. Damian stands at the head of the sling holding his boy's hands.

Alex hears Simon put on some surgical gloves and then feels him holding his cock and wiping it down with something. Then a sharp pain as if a needle was being pushed through his cock head followed by a strange sensation of something else being pushed through.

Damian's own cock grows as he feels Alex's hands tightly gripping his own as he reacts to the pain and he humps the top of Alex's head playfully with his bulge.

"Congratulations, boy, you now have a PA ring in the head of your dick to match mine. Of course yours is quite small to start with but I'll stretch it over time and then I can the use the PA piercing to make your chastity more secure."

Alex relaxes, feeling proud that Damian is transforming him into a copy of himself in some ways. The idea of his new piercing somehow becoming part of his chastity hardware excites him too, but his cock is too spent to respond.

"Now for the second modification," Damian whispers to him.

Alex feels a bit scared. He can't think what it will be. Damian would hardly castrate him. He enjoys slapping his balls around too much to have them removed.

Then Alex feels Simon wiping his freshly-shaved pubic area and hears a buzzing sound. Suddenly his crotch feels like it's on fire, the pain alternating with the sensation of his pubic skin being wiped some more. This lasts for maybe thirty minutes and then it stops and Alex feels Simon give a final wipe to his skin.

"What do you think, Mr Hall?" Simon asks, taking off his gloves and putting away his equipment while he's speaking.

Damian removes his hands from Alex's and walks around to the foot of the sling.

"Excellent, Simon. He's now ten times the boy he was half an hour ago"

Damian removes the blindfold and releases Alex from the sling.

"Go look in the mirror, boy," Damian says with a big grin on his face.

Alex walks over to the mirror. His cock now sports a shiny PA ring through its head. And above it, tattooed on his pubic area, are the words "PROPERTY OF MASTER DAMIAN" in bold black letters.

"Wow," thinks Alex, "that was unexpected. I guess I'm properly owned now." And despite being totally drained, his cock now manages to grow a little with excitement.

In the mirror, Alex sees Damian come to stand behind him and watches as his Master encircles him with his arms and kisses him on the neck. "What do you think, boy?"

"It's a total surprise, Sir. I guess I now have a permanent reminder that you own me."

Alex's puppy-dog eyes, more sparkling than ever, almost bring tears to Damian's eyes.

"Well, boy, that tattoo is temporary at the moment. But it's still a reminder to me that I own you and need to care for and protect you."

Alex thinks back to the subtle ways Damian watched over him when he was investigating the vandal and smiles. The memory of the unfortunate time when Damian let his anger about the vandal get in the way of that caring now seems very distant.

"I know that, Sir, even if it isn't always visible to me."

"You know I love you, boy, and always want the best for you, even if I may seem harsh and over-controlling at times."

"I know that too, Sir, and I wouldn't want to change anything. And I love you too."

Alex ponders how easily those unfamiliar words came out of his mouth. He knows that, unlike the tattoo which he expects Damian will make permanent at some point, there's no guarantee his relationship with Damian will last forever. But he also knows that the tattoo will always speak the truth. That the better, stronger person he is becoming will always be because of Damian.

"That PA piercing will take a few weeks to heal," Damian continues. "And you need to take care of that tattoo while it heals as well. Simon will put a sterile dressing on it for you to keep there today and give you some instructions for what to do after that.

"Of course I had all this planned for you from the start so your chastity cage will fit over your new PA ring quite easily and won't snag on it while it heals.

And with that Alex's chastity cage is carefully locked on again and Damian leaves him to admire his newly-modified body in the mirror while he and Simon chat in the background, Damian occasionally looking over, smiling proudly, as he admires his boy.

Alex feels wonderful and happy with himself and his place in the world. He reflects on what has happened to him over the past few weeks. It feels like another world when he was a sad bedraggled porn addict with no useful skills and no sexual experience at all.

And now here he is, pierced, tattooed, locked in chastity and with interesting marks on his back from activity that, in his previous life, he would have run a mile from.

He has a Master who loves and cares for him and who he loves too. He's learned to do gardening and uncovered an Internet vandal, and he is confident Damian has more adventures planned for him, inside and outside the playroom.

Simon leaves and Damian tells Alex he is free for the rest of the day.

Back in his room, Alex once again admires his new marks of ownership in the bathroom mirror.

Damian has told him that it will be some weeks before his PA is fully healed and stretched and then the PA ring will be replaced with a custom padlock which will go through the PA piercing hole and back out through his piss slit, securing his cock head to the bars at the front of the chastity cage.

"Absolutely no chance of getting out on my own then," Alex realises, not that he ever thinks he would want to. And with that he falls into a long, deep and contented sleep.

CHAPTER 19

There is no sign of Alex at breakfast the next day so Damian and Jameson are alone.

"Should I go wake him, Sir?" Jameson asks.

"No, let him sleep in," Damian replies. "The boy had a pretty eventful and momentous day yesterday and anyway it'll give us time for a catch up.

"What do you make of Alex, now he's been here a while?" Damian asks.

"We'll to be honest, Sir, when I first went to collect him outside Café Noir I thought I must have got the wrong guy. All that was missing was a cardboard sign, a dog on a string and a dirty blanket and he would have looked indistinguishable from the homeless young people you see in shop doorways at night. But then I recognised his face from the video you showed me."

"Yes, I'm not surprised," Damian replies, laughing. "It was a risk, but something about his puppy-dog eyes made me think he might be worth a try."

"Good judgement as always, Sir" Jameson says admiringly.

Damian and Jameson compare notes on Alex's adventures and what the future might hold for him.

"You know," Damian ponders aloud, "Alex seemed to cope well with discovering that Gordon flogs me sometimes. Maybe you should fill him in on the nature of our relationship. It might make things easier for the two of us when he's around as well. I assume you haven't told him already."

"No, I haven't and you're probably right, but he seems a much more confident and resilient boy now than when he arrived. I'll take it slowly."

"Let me know how it goes," Damian replies as he leaves for his office.

Just as Jameson is starting to prepare lunch for the two of them, a sleepy-eyed Alex surfaces in the kitchen.

"Sorry I slept in, Mr Jameson. Don't know what happened."

"I do, Alex," Jameson replies. "After all that you experienced yesterday you've got an endorphin hangover."

For Alex, whose only experience of hangovers were from drinking too much cheap cider, Jameson's answer wasn't helping.

"Endor-what?" he asks.

"Endorphins are chemicals your body releases in response to pain, excitement, exercise and even orgasms. And you've had all of those over the past few days. So you probably had a backlog to process," Jameson explains knowingly.

"I'll take your word for it, Mr Jameson," Alex concedes as he makes himself and Jameson a cup of tea while Jameson finishes making them lunch.

"So what do you think of your new body art, Alex?" Jameson asks as they start eating. He thinks this might be a good starting point for his own revelations.

"Well they were a complete surprise. Actually, the PA wasn't a total surprise. I'd wondered, from the fact that Sir has one, whether he liked other men to have them too, though I also wondered if they were something only tops had. Obviously not.

"But the tattoo was totally unexpected," Alex continues.

"And how do you feel about having the tattoo?"

"It's very strange. It made a part of me inside very happy, a part I didn't know existed. I know the tattoo is only temporary but I'm not scared of it becoming permanent. In fact I think I want it to as a permanent reminder of what's happening here."

"I think it's called contentment, Alex. It's something I discovered during my time with Mr Hall."

Alex senses that Jameson is loosening up a bit and decides this might be a good time to fill in some gaps in what Jameson has told him about his life, especially as Jameson's use of the phrase "my time" suggested something in the past but not the present.

"How did you and Mr Hall meet? Did he find you through an employment agency?"

"Not at all, Alex," Jameson laughs. "Mr Hall and I met in a leather bar down by the river."

"Gosh, I didn't know you were into this SM stuff," Alex asks.

"Yes I am, or rather was, Alex. And in some ways I still am though I don't do the heavy dungeon play you and Mr Hall get up to anymore."

"So Sir picked you up in a bar and you were his slave?"

"Actually, no, it was the other way around."

Alex's fork drops noisily onto his plate as he stares wide-eyed at Jameson. "Sir is your slave?"

"Not now, Alex, but he was at one time.

"I used to be a heavy Master like Mr Hall is now. He was young and learning about SM from more experienced guys like me by being their slave or submissive or just one-off bottom. We met in this bar and got on well both in the playroom and as friends. It carried on for quite a few years with both of us playing with other guys as well. And throughout this I was the top and Mr Hall was the sub."

"Wow," Alex responds. "Of all the things I might have guessed since coming here, Sir having been your slave is not one of them. In fact had it not been for my catching him and Gordon after they'd been playing I'd never have thought of Sir as having a submissive side at all."

"Actually he's always had a bit of both in him," Jameson tells him. "But the sub side emerged first."

"So when did he stop being your slave?" Alex asks.

"As you haven't been out on the SM scene you may not realise that there's about ten bottoms for every top. And as a top I was in constant demand from guys wanting to be played with. I made the mistake of thinking that any sex was better than no sex until a friend pointed out that I'd become what he called a 'service top' – basically satisfying other guys' sexual needs and ignoring my own. I was actually being controlled by them.

"The funny thing is that I realised I actually enjoyed the service side of it more than the sex side. I liked making other guys happy and my own sexual needs were really quite small.

"At about the same time, Mr Hall started enjoying being top in his play with others more than when he was subbing to me and other men. He knew what the subs were experiencing and how to do things like impact play well. In fact, part of what spurred him on was how incompetent some of the other guys were who topped him.

"He used to tell me how being tied up was no fun when all he could think about was how loose the knots were or how bad the aim or how feeble the strokes were of the guys who topped him."

Jameson continues. "Mr Hall is one of those people who believes that if you can do a job better than the next guy then you should do it. And so Master Damian was born."

"And how did you get to be his slave then?" Alex asks. "You were now both tops."

"As I've already said, as a top I enjoyed providing service to other guys. And Mr Hall was the man I enjoyed servicing the most. So when he suggested switching roles with him I jumped at it."

Alex continues his questioning. "So you became his sex slave and his personal assistant?"

"Not his personal assistant to start with as the

business was much smaller then. And not a slave in the SM sense, though he did enjoy fucking me a lot which is why my tattoo is on my..."

Jameson stops, realising he'd not intended to reveal quite so much so soon, and is brought out of his temporary shock by Alex dropping his fork again.

"Well I suppose that cat's out of the bag, Alex," Jameson laughs. "I have a tattoo like yours but it's in the small of my back."

"And do you have a PA and are you locked?" Alex asks seizing on this unforeseen opportunity.

"Yes I do have a PA and Mr Hall locked me in a chastity device. He would only unlock me and let me cum once for every ten times he fucked me. But our sexual relationship stopped some years ago and I then became more of his personal assistant than a slave.

"In fact I still wear my chastity cage. It's more a reminder of our past relationship rather than actual cum control as I have the keys, so my cage is more like sentimental jewellery."

"Boy, they sure kept that well hidden," Alex thinks to himself. He wants to know more about why they stopped having sex but decides that's a detail he can explore another time.

For now he's coping with the fact that the two men he has got closest to and who have got closest to him have each been both top and bottom to the other.

"I'm not sure what to say, Mr Jameson, except to say a very big thank you for sharing all this with me.

I assume Sir said it was OK for you to tell me."

"Well he did suggest you were right for some more information though I don't think he intended for you to find out as much detail as I let slip."

"Will he punish you for it?" Alex asks.

"Oh no, that sort of thing is behind us now in our particular relationship, Alex. We'll just have a good laugh about it.

"And another thing, Alex. Now you know the truth of my relationship with Mr Hall you'll understand when I call him 'Sir' too. I've not done that so far when you were present as he and I both felt you had enough to cope with."

Alex leans back, looking intently at Jameson with admiration.

"Well, Mr Jameson, if I can turn out to be even one-tenth as good as you in making Sir happy then I will be very content. There, I've understood what that word means."

With that, Alex stands up and gives Jameson a big hug. "Thank you for looking after me and Sir."

And as Jameson hugs Alex closer, Alex feels their chastity cages bump into each other.

"Cheers," Jameson says, laughing.

Damian hears the laughter as he is passing the kitchen door and calls in.

"I guess I ended up telling Alex more than I should have, Sir," Jameson tells him.

"What did you learn, boy," Damian asks Alex.

"I learned that you two have had some wonderful

adventures together and that I have a lot to learn from both of you.

"Knowing that you used to be slave and Master and have now reversed those roles gives me huge respect for you both and also a glimpse of what I might become in the future, not that I think I'd ever be anything but your slave and boy, Sir," Alex says addressing Damian directly.

"We'll see, boy. But I'm glad it's all out in the open now so we can all be more relaxed with each other.

"Oh, and it's about time you got out a bit, boy. Why not call Melissa and arrange to meet her soon. I'll organise some street clothes for you. And call by my office some time. I have a travel card for you."

Sometime later Jameson comes to Alex's room carrying some jeans and a black hooded sweatshirt for him to wear when he leaves the house. Though the brand is a bit retro now, the word "BOY" printed in white on the front makes Alex shudder a little with pride.

He tries his new clothes on, deciding it probably best to keep the padlocked collar hidden underneath when he meets Melissa. But his black bandana will be definitely be on top. He can't imagine going out into the world without some visible sign and reminder of his relationship with his Master.

Alex phones Melissa and arranges to meet her at Café Noir early the following week. He's looking forward to telling her of his adventures and wants her to see what a smart, sexy, confident man he is becoming.

More than this, he wants to thank her for caring for him and for letting Damian know that she was keeping tabs on him.

At the back of Alex's mind is the thought that Melissa's concern had persuaded Damian to take him in. He's not sure, but he wouldn't be surprised if that wasn't somehow very important.

CHAPTER 20

A month later Damian and Alex are having breakfast and Damian has a surprise for his boy.

"Tell me, boy," have you ever been to the USA?"

"No, Sir," Alex replies immediately, looking up from his scrambled eggs. "The only time I've been out of the country was when my parents took myself and my sister on holiday abroad a few times when I was growing up. But then they all moved to Canada and I never went on holiday again."

Damian looks over at Alex and thinks back to when Alex first arrived. He had no self-confidence, mumbled when he spoke to people and never looked them in the eye. On top of that he was far too overweight and had never had sex with another person. He'd forgotten that Alex had been abandoned by his parents and now understood better why Alex was so ready to accept his offer of moving in and being his slave. He needed to belong somewhere.

"Well I think it's about time you did, boy," Damian continues. "You've done well over the past months in lots of ways. You're really enjoying the serious flogging, whipping, and electro work I've done with you in the playroom. And that mouth of yours sure knows how to make my cock happy. Even the chastity device I have your cock locked in has done its job. You seem to have lost your obsession with pornography and wanking."

"I don't have much choice about the second one, Sir," Alex replies, smiling as he affectionately strokes his crotch and the metal cage surrounding his cock underneath his shorts. He can feel the special chastity padlock that has now replaced a standard ball-closure ring in his PA.

"Where are we going?" Alex asks.

"I think it's time to show you off to some of my SM friends, boy, and let you meet some other Masters and slaves," Damian tells him proudly. "You'll also see and maybe want to try out some play stuff we haven't done."

"Does that mean you'll be playing with other boys, Sir?" Alex asks nervously, this worry never having left him.

"I told you that would happen at some point, boy. I also said that one day you would get to play with others and maybe even top them. And where we're going is the best place I know for you to start."

"I remember when you said that, Sir," Alex replies. "I felt very insecure, worried that maybe you would prefer other boys to me or that you would hand me over to another Master. But now I think I'm ready for it. Well, maybe playing with some other tops you have selected for me. As for me topping someone, that seems very strange."

"Why's that, boy?"

"I'm only just learning to be in control of myself, Sir. So controlling someone else might be tricky," Alex continues. "Like Mr Jameson, I get a real inner satisfaction from serving you. So I can't see myself dominating someone else or getting any pleasure from it."

"I'm not so sure of that, boy. I remember you saying how excited your cock got when I told you that I'd tried locking myself in a chastity device for a few days to see how it felt."

"I'd forgotten that, Sir. And it looks like maybe it still does," Alex laughs looking down at his crotch again where his cock is trying to grow in its metal prison.

Damian laughs as well. "Then where we're going might be just the place for you, although it won't be my cock that you'll be locking up, I can assure you. But there are always plenty of guys into chastity there."

"Where that, Sir?" Alex asks.

"To Camp Hickoryswitch, boy. It's an SM summer camp I used to go to every year near Washington DC. But as the business took off, I couldn't spare the time. Now everything is running well, with no little thanks to your sleuthing efforts, and I have you to show off, I think it's time I returned and took you with me."

Alex is intrigued. As a child, he sometimes went to summer camp with his school. But he expects that the games played at Camp Hickoryswitch will be more adult than the ones he played when he was young. And then he remembers his favourite game at kids' camp.

"Funny you should mention summer camp, Sir. I was just remembering how much I enjoyed a game I often played with some friends when I was a kid that involved some of us being tied to trees and others pretending to torture them.

"I always got a very strange thrill when playing cowboys and Indians as a kid," Alex explains. "I always loved being tied up and gagged with a bandana and being tortured, which was usually no more than having nettles pushed down our shorts.

"I guess deep down SM play has always excited me but I was a child then and I didn't think of it as sexual."

Damian grins broadly. "You know, boy, those old westerns on television have a lot to answer for. It's interesting how many people had their first taste of SM through them."

"If it's not too disrespectful, Sir, can I ask if playing cowboys and Indians was your introduction as well?" Alex asks, though he thinks the fact that Damian has him always wear a black bandana around his neck and has lots of rope and bandanas in his playroom might make the answer obvious.

"Yes it was, boy. Like you, I got very excited by those TV westerns and kids' tying-up games and often other films. Somehow, my favourite cowboy heroes were always being ambushed by bandana-masked outlaws and being tied up and gagged.

"I even remember my first erection though it wasn't a western I was watching. It was at a Saturday morning kids' cinema club and Flash Gordon was standing in a torture chamber, spread-eagled by heavy chains with an all-enclosing metal box on his head, being zapped with electrical shocks.

"There was this very strange movement in my shorts which I'd not experienced before. Much later on I realised it was sexual arousal. But at the time I hadn't a clue what was going on and felt too embarrassed to mention it to anyone."

"Sounds like that's where you got your taste for electro toys as well, Sir," Alex observes.

"I'd never thought of that, boy, but maybe you're right," Damian laughs.

"When are we going, Sir," Alex asks, trying not to seem too pushy.

"Here's the plan, boy. We leave in three weeks for Washington DC. There's an apartment there that belongs to a friend who runs a porno business in the USA but he doesn't use it often. So we can stay there and have a couple of days sightseeing and getting over our jetlag first before going to Hickoryswitch.

"Then on the Thursday we drive down to the camp to help set up the dungeon equipment. There are not many guys there on that day as the camp officially opens on the Friday. Setup is a good way to get to know the layout of the camp and meet just a few new people at first. And if there's time, I can give you your first experience of the camp's play spaces.

"But we'll need to get you a passport first as I assume you don't have one. You and Jameson can go down to the post office later to arrange that."

Alex has masses of questions and for once isn't supressing them for fear of forgetting his position as Damian's boy. Things are good between them and Damian is in a very good mood.

"Is this a camp with tents and camp fires?"

Damian laughs. "Not at all, it's very civilised. It has cabins with a bathroom and maybe ten beds in each, and a proper catering kitchen and dining room. And the play spaces are huge industrial barns with masses of frames and dungeon equipment."

"How many people go to this camp?" Alex asks further.

"About 200 or so, mainly from the USA, but guys fly in from all over the world."

Alex's eyes widen. "200! Wow I hope I don't lose you in the crowds, Sir."

"It's not crowded at all, boy," Damian continues. "The campgrounds are massive and there's a swimming pool and basketball courts and lots of open spaces to play in as well. I've seen guys tied to trees, staked out on hillsides and covered in mud in the swamp. It's all very sheltered so there's no fear of anything being seen or overheard by the neighbours."

Alex hasn't seen Damian so animated for a long time. And he himself is already so excited by this new adventure that he forgets Damian having reminded him that he will be playing with others there and that he himself may as well.

Jameson enters the small dining room where Damian and Alex are eating to clear away the breakfast things.

"I guess you just told Alex about Hickoryswitch, Sir," Jameson says seeing the big grin on Alex's face.

"Sure did, Jameson. It's about time I went back and I'm confident you and my business crew upstairs will look after things while we're away. It might be a good time to get Alex's room decorated while we're gone. And you and Alex need to go down to the post office to get him a passport."

"We can organise Alex's passport after lunch when Alex has found some clothes more suitable for a passport photograph," Jameson replies laughing.

"I'll arrange the decorating tomorrow, Sir. Will basic white still do?"

"What do you think, boy?" Damian asks tuning to Alex.

Alex likes his almost cell-like sparse room because it's all clean and orderly, unlike the cramped chaotic flat he shared with Melissa. And the lack of too much furniture and possessions helps him avoid slipping back into his former sloppy ways.

"White is fine, Sir, though maybe once it's decorated you could find some pictures for the walls."

As with all things to do with Alex, Damian makes all the decisions – about his clothes, his haircut, his lack of body hair, his schedule, his fitness regime and at times his diet. So Alex does not usually get to make decisions on his own.

"Of course, boy. When we're back from the US, Jameson can drive us to the shopping centre. One of the department stores there has a good selection of pictures and we can choose some together. That is unless you want something more hard-core in which case I'm sure my designers upstairs could rustle up something."

"I think something a little less arousing might be preferable, Sir," Alex replies and starts thinking about the trickle-feed of independence that Damian has allowed him.

When he first arrived at Damian's house, Damian kept him away from any distraction to the point of him having no contact with the outside world for a while and no possessions. This meant he stayed focussed on pleasing Damian, learning obedience and taking nothing for granted, including his freedom.

Now he has a mobile phone, unrestricted television and internet access, and the option to leave the house when he is not required for other things. When he arrived, he was allowed none of these. He had to earn them through changing his behaviour and attitude, learning to be respectful and obedient.

These days Damian allowed Alex much more say in his life, and choosing the décor for his room was another step forward.

Damian has another thought. "I haven't finalised

our flights yet, boy. Do you want to go via Toronto and maybe see your family? You can tell them you're coming over for work with your employer. I suspect our actual relationship might be a bit much for them."

Alex hasn't thought about his family for years. After they moved away and his life started its destructive downward path, he stopped replying to their emails.

"I think that chapter in my life is closed now, Sir. The time between when they left and when I met you isn't one I'm proud of. And what I am proud of, being here with you, isn't something I think they'd understand.

"Even when I was growing up they seemed to be very disapproving of anything they didn't understand. In fact, when they discovered I was gay there were huge arguments and they almost threw me out of the house. I really should have hidden that porn better.

"My older sister, Roxanne, was very supportive of me, and she seemed to get on well enough with them, even though they didn't seem to approve of her, for reasons I never learned. She thought that moving to a big city in Canada with them might give her a fresh start, as she was never comfortable around people in the small country town where we lived. After the three of them emigrated, I moved to London where I knew being gay would be much easier.

"I'm sure I could find them via the internet if I

Jacob Morrison

wanted, Sir. My mother was always a big Facebook fan as was my sister. But it's so long ago and I wouldn't know where to start explaining things to them. So the short answer is thank you but no thanks."

"OK, boy. Jameson can book our tickets this morning," Damian concludes.

Damian had never known much about Alex's background and these further revelations helped him understand why Alex was so keen to find some security in his life. While he wasn't old enough to be Alex's parent, he recognised that in some ways he was standing in as Alex's father.

"You know, boy, families are strange. We don't choose our parents and they don't always match who we become as we grow up. Many people move away from them and create their own version of a family with people they love and care for and who accept them for who they are."

Damian looks at the two men beside him and smiles to himself. He too came from a family that didn't understand his sexuality. But in his case, they came to accept it, as he was articulate and able to discuss it with them. They even invited Jameson over at Christmas when they were an item. And though he is still on good terms with his parents, his real family is the one he is with now, Alex and Jameson.

Back in his room after breakfast, Alex turns on his computer and immediately goes to Facebook. He used to have a Facebook profile but stopped using it

190

when his sexual urges drove all his online activity elsewhere.

He searches for Mary-Ann Jenkins and finds his mother's page. It's full of the usual photos of cute pets and cupcakes and silly road signs. And there's a photo of his mother and father at Niagara Falls taken a few months earlier. They look a lot older than he imagined and he feels a little sad. But then he remembers the arguments and their lack of love and acceptance. There's no mention or photos of his sister on his mother's page, which saddens him much more.

"Maybe you moved on as well, sis," Alex thinks. "I wonder where you went."

He searches Facebook and then Google for Roxanne Jenkins and doesn't find her anywhere. He assumes she must have got married and changed her name.

Alex sits back and a few tears start welling up in his eyes. For all that his parents were so bad to him, he still misses them a bit. And deep down he really would like to find out what happened to his sister who he now realises he misses a lot.

Still, he thinks, I have Damian and Jameson as my family now.

Remembering the business of the afternoon, he searches the passport site for any guidelines on clothing and is pleased that there's nothing banning jewellery around the neck. So he is pleased he can keep his collar and bandana on for the photograph and wonders whether the immigration officers would understand their significance. Wearing his "BOY" hooded sweatshirt will be good as well, he thinks, until he realises the photograph will be only head and shoulders.

"But I will know it's there," he says to himself, laughing.

CHAPTER 21

The weeks until Damian and Alex depart for the USA pass quickly. Alex's new passport arrives and it makes him feel grown up at last. He laughs, realising that unseen in the photograph he is wearing his BOY hoodie and, underneath it, Damian's padlocked chain collar.

Damian buys him a suitcase and backpack for the trip and some new clothes. And as he has plans for using Alex's arse while they are away he buys him a portable douche so he can continue his wash-outs.

Damian had told him that the weather would be warm and sunny during the day at camp but might get chilly in the autumn evening, and sometimes activities went on late into the night. And it might rain, so he gets a new waterproof jacket as well.

Alex looks over his growing collection of clothes and marvels at how his wardrobe has changed. In his previous life, his clothes were dull and creased and full of holes and usually covered in stains. When he came to Damian's house, they were replaced with white t-shirts and shorts and outdoor work clothes. Now the shelves in his room are filled with colour and he feels like he's re-joined the human race.

The day before they are due to leave for the US Alex starts selecting the clothes he will take, keeping an eye on the size of his suitcase and trying not to take too much. He knows that much of the time at camp Damian will want him wearing his whites or his new grey camo combats. But for their days in Washington, he selects some things less obviously sexual. Who knows, Damian might even take him out to a restaurant. And if they go to a leather bar then his boy clothes will work well there as well as at camp.

But packing a suitcase properly is not something Alex has any experience of, as his parents used to do it for him. And he is concerned not to make a mess of his new clothes by folding them badly and so incur Damian's anger and possibly a punishment. So he asks Jameson to help him, which gives him a chance to ask Jameson more about Camp Hickoryswitch.

"Have you been to this camp, Mr Jameson?" he asks.

"I haven't, actually, though Sir told me lots about it after each trip he made there."

Alex has just about got used to Jameson also referring to Damian as "Sir" unlike when they first met when it was "Mr Hall". But he still finds it hard to reconcile his experience of Damian as his controlling, confident and very skilled Master with the fact that he used to be Jameson's slave before they swapped roles.

"Was Sir your slave when he used to go?"

"No, Alex, that started after we switched. He started going there to learn more about how to be a proficient Master. They run demonstrations and workshops and whenever he came back he was always excited about the fresh skills he'd acquired, usually followed soon after by new equipment and toys appearing in the playroom. Of course by then we'd stopped playing so I didn't get the benefit of those new skills myself."

"Do you feel sad that you and Sir don't play any more?" Alex asks hesitantly.

"Not at all. For me the warmth and love was always the most important. I don't miss the sex much. We had a great time while it lasted and it sort of came to a natural end."

Alex wonders if this will happen between himself and Damian but realises he's getting ahead of himself. But he still worries a little about how he will feel when he sees Damian playing with others at the camp and how he will cope with being topped by someone else.

"Are the guys at this camp the same age as Sir and myself? I assume it's just men."

Jameson shakes his head. "What's amazing is how wide the age span is. You have young guys in their early twenties right through to men in their seventies and maybe older. And who is top and who is bottom has nothing to do with their relative ages. What matters for them is the play and the feeling of belonging and acceptance, not the age of the person. They're not there looking for a partner, though that does sometimes happen through meeting at the camp. And yes, it is just men, though some of the camp's staff are women. But they know what goes on and don't seem to mind. Maybe they even get a few ideas to try out with their partners."

It doesn't take long for Jameson to help Alex pack his suitcase and get the right items for his backpack. He reminds Alex that he will have to go through the security at the airport without his chain collar and padlock and chastity cage or they will set off the metal detector.

"What about my PA padlock?" Alex asks.

"That should be OK," Jameson assures him. "Sir flies all the time with his PA piercing ring in and that's made of steel. Your PA lock is titanium which is less likely to set off any alarms. But I expect Sir will replace the chastity device once you've gone through security and are in the airport lounge."

Alex has visions of himself standing in a crowded airport departure lounge with his jeans around his ankles as Damian locks him up again.

"Shouldn't that be done somewhere private?" Alex asks nervously.

Jameson laughs. "You'll be travelling business class with Sir, of course. So there should be somewhere quiet and private in the business lounge at the airport. It won't be happening in public I can assure you, Alex."

Alex laughs at his own naivety and gets excited at the thought of travelling business class, sitting there locked and collared with the smart business people around him unaware of the interesting hardware under his clothes. He feels special and cared for and important.

Alex is used to getting up at six every morning so he's dressed and ready in the main hallway early the next morning, suitcase and backpack by his side, when Damian comes downstairs a few minutes later.

"Come into my office, boy, while I make you travel-ready," Damian tells him.

Inside his office, Damian unlocks Alex's chain collar and padlock and the chastity cage and puts the padlock and chain in one of his suitcases and the chastity device in his own backpack. Alex guesses that Damian's second, smaller bag is probably full of sex toys and restraints and he feels excited at the prospect of playing somewhere new. He realises that there will probably be others watching and hopes he doesn't embarrass Damian with his grunts and the occasional scream.

Damian relocks the PA padlock through Alex's cock, as he doesn't want the piercing hole to start closing up. "I thought about putting your chain collar and padlock in my backpack as well, boy, so I could lock it back on when we've gone through airport security. But they might think I'm planning to chain myself to the cockpit or something. So that will have to wait until we land."

Alex feels strange. He's worn Damian's metal since he arrived and he almost feels naked. He reaches for where his padlock and chain usually are around his neck and feels incomplete.

"You look uncomfortable, boy."

"Yes, Sir, almost like a dog that's been let off the leash for the first time on a busy road."

"Well, boy, I don't have any fear that you are about to run off into the traffic. And as soon as we're through security and in the business lounge I'll lock your cock up again."

"Thank you, Sir. Mr Jameson thought you would."

Alex gets dressed again and feels his now very sensitive cock head rubbing against his underwear and growing a little as it discovers its unaccustomed freedom. He hopes he won't spend the next few hours with an obvious erection in his jeans.

Jameson knocks on the door to tell them that the car is ready.

The drive to the airport is quick, as is check-in and it isn't long before Alex is following Damian through airport security.

Alex finds the process a bit nerve-wracking. Despite Jameson's reassurance, he still fears that the PA padlock through his cock will set off the metal detector arch and is surprised that it doesn't. And he gets anxious again as he watches the operator puzzle over the x-rays of their hand baggage. He wonders what she makes of his metal chastity cage, which is bound to show up in Damian's backpack, and whether he will be asked to explain it. But it all passes through without any demand for an inspection of its contents. Alex wonders if she recognised it, even had one locked on her husband which makes him feel much better.

"They've seen it all before, boy. If they ask what the chastity cage is, I'll say it's an erotic paperweight I'm taking as a rude present for my brother-in-law who's meeting us at the airport."

Alex laughs at Damian's ingenuity and brazen attitude and follows him to the business lounge, which is almost empty.

Damian beckons Alex to follow him to a corridor at the far end where there are some large washroom cubicles. When he is sure there is no one around to disturb them and no CCTV cameras watching, he ushers them both into one and he orders Alex to lower his jeans and Damian unlocks the PA padlock. It only takes a few minutes for Alex's cock to be locked in its chastity cage once again with the PA lock making it extra secure. Alex feels a lot better but still misses his chain collar, though he knows that will be back around his neck in a few hours.

Soon they are boarding the plane and settled in their business-class seats.

The eight-hour flight to Washington is boring at times. Alex has seen most of the in-flight movies already and doesn't want to read too much of his book in case he needs it later on. So he starts thinking about what he'd like to do at camp and compiles a mental checklist.

But this doesn't take long and Damian senses Alex's boredom.

"Go for a walk around the plane. It's good for your circulation. Plus you can look at the other passengers and see if you can guess which ones might have the person next to them locked in chastity. When I worked at a bank, I had to go to these really boring cocktail parties where we entertained big clients. I found that guessing game a great way of livening up an otherwise dull event. Sadly, I never got a chance to find out if my guesses were right. But there might be one or two guys on this plane also going to Hickoryswitch. You can tell me in a few days' time if you were right."

"You worked in a bank, Sir?" Alex asks with surprise.

"Strange as it may seem, boy, I did. But not as a banker. I worked in IT security, trying to stop the bankers spending their time at work browsing porn once it became easily available on the web. I had to test their systems by trying different porn sites. And the porn I found was so terrible I decided to go into business making my own. Which is how my company started."

"Well I'm glad that porn was so bad, Sir, or else I wouldn't be here," Alex laughs. And with that he goes for a walk around the plane, leaving Damian to sleep.

A few hours later they land at Dulles airport and a hire car is waiting for them. Alex loads their bags in the back and starts to get in the car when he realises that he'd forgotten that cars drive on the right in the USA and his usual passenger seat has a steering wheel.

"I don't think you're ready to drive over here yet, boy," Damian laughs. And a red-faced Alex walks around to the other side of the car. Before Damian gets in to drive them to their apartment he retrieves Alex's chain collar and padlock from his suitcase and locks it on again.

"There, boy, feel better?"

"Absolutely, Sir."

As Damian drives them to their apartment, Alex feels like they're moving through a film set. He has never been to the USA but is surprised at how un-surprising it is. He has already seen so many of the iconic important places they pass on TV and in films that it makes the whole experience slightly unreal.

By the time they've settled into the apartment and feasted on oversized steaks at a neighbourhood diner they're both tired and Damian suggests they have an early night. Damian climbs into the apartment's king-sized bed and has to tell Alex that it's OK for him to get in as well.

At their home in London, Damian sleeps in his bedroom on one of the upper floors of the house while Alex always sleeps in his room off the secret corridor by the playroom.

"This is new to both of us, boy," Damian reassures him. "So just relax, take your clothes off, and get in with me."

Aside from the one time they snuggled together on his own bed for an afternoon nap, all Alex's close physical contact with Damian has been in the playroom where he's been restrained in bondage and tormented with impact and electro play. So he's not sure of the protocol when they get into bed together for the first time. Should he sleep well away from Damian or next to him?

His doubts are short-lived and soon Damian's body is wrapped around his in the bed and Alex feels Damian's hardening cock against his backside with Alex's chastity cage cupped in Damian's hand. Damian kisses him softly on his neck and Alex reaches back with his hand and holds onto Damian's cock, wondering if he should turn around and put it in his mouth.

"We could both do with getting lots of rest while we're here, boy," Damian tells his boy. "There will be plenty of time for play once we're at camp and neither of us might get much sleep once we're there."

CHAPTER 22

On their first day in DC, Alex and Damian visit some popular tourist attractions including the Lincoln Memorial, the White House and finally the US Holocaust Memorial Museum.

The high security at these places means that Alex has to spend some time without his collar and chastity cage so he doesn't set off the metal detectors, but they are soon replaced in the car in a quiet street.

Inside the Holocaust museum, they are both deeply moved by the tower of faces, a shaft with walls lined with photographs of those who died in the Holocaust, and the room of shoes. Damian spots that Alex is troubled by what he has seen so they go for a coffee afterwards.

"Sir, when you see reminders of all the brutality that has taken place in the world, and still does, doesn't it affect how you feel about your SM play?"

At points in his past Damian has needed to defend his SM porn in media interviews and is used to dealing with this issue.

"There is one word, boy, which separates what we do from what we have just seen in that museum, and that word is 'consent'.

"None of those people consented to being tortured or killed. And while there are some people who get off on dressing up as Nazis and wearing swastikas in their play, personally it's not something

I approve of. There are just some things I do not think should be sexualised."

Alex already knows that Damian thinks hard about what he does in his playroom. He remembers when Damian's anger about the vandal in his online porno films spilled over into Alex's punishment and how much he regretted it afterwards. So he isn't surprised that Damian has thought deeply about his sexuality.

"That helps a lot, Sir," Alex replies.

"Great. Now we're done with our coffee, boy, I'm going to buy you a present. I'm taking you to a leather bar here in the city tonight and you ought to have some leather to wear, so I'm going to buy you some. A boy's first leather should always be a gift from his Master."

Alex has never owned or worn any leather clothing. In fact he'd read somewhere that "boys" had to earn their leather so he feels really pleased. Not that he'd ever been to a leather bar either and wonders what it will be like.

At the leather store, Damian selects a black leather vest for Alex which looks good with his white t-shirt, jeans and black boots and he'll get him to wear it at dinner sometimes when they're at camp. After Damian has paid for it, Alex notices him writing something down on a piece of paper and giving it to the store manager.

"Right, boy, that's almost done. We need to come back in a couple of hours to collect it."

Alex is about to ask why they can't take it away immediately but decides not to spoil Damian's surprise.

They spend the next few hours doing more sightseeing and having dinner before returning to the store where Alex's vest is ready. On the right lapel is a gold-coloured metal badge with the words "Master Damian's boy" engraved on it. Alex smiles broadly "Guess they'll know where to return me If I get lost, Sir," Alex jokes.

"I don't plan to lose you, boy," Damian replies with a smile as they head back to the apartment to freshen up and change.

Damian dresses in his usual black t-shirt and combats and boots and over it he wears his own leather vest, with a matching, though somewhat less shiny, name tag on the left lapel reading "Master Damian".

Alex's heart swells at the idea of the two of them going out dressed similarly. "Sir, you should know that it makes me feel really proud to be out in public with you in our matching vests."

"Only the best for you, boy," Damian says equally proudly.

The leather bar Damian drives to is one he used to frequent on his previous visits to the city and he hopes to bump into some old friends, or at least some other early arrivals for the camp.

The bar is dark and there is loud music playing and Alex feels slightly scared. He doesn't know if 'boys' should behave in a special way there or even stand in a particular place. But Damian reassures him that he should relax and just follow his lead. But he also reminds him that, as his 'boy', he still needs to be respectful and remember his place and not be thrown off by the unfamiliar surroundings.

Damian pulls Alex's padlocked chain collar out from underneath his white t-shirt and lays it on top of the black bandana.

"That can stay out and visible now until we head back to the airport at the end of camp, boy."

Alex smiles and starts to relax and feel a little more at home.

Damian goes to the bar to buy them each a drink and Alex stands by the wall opposite, hands behind his back, feet apart, keeping his gaze firmly planted on Damian which proves difficult as the bar is filling up. If he lost sight of Damian he would have no idea where to find him or even how to get back to the hotel.

While Damian is getting the drinks and catching up on local gossip from the bartender a very tall bearded bear of a man walks by and stops in front of Alex, obscuring his view of Damian which makes Alex feel nervous.

He's dressed head to toe in leather, with a leather harness underneath his open jacket emphasising his hairy muscular chest and prominent ringed nipples. Alex feels intimidated.

The man looks at the gold-coloured badge on

Alex's leather vest and then speaks to him.

"Shame you're already owned, boy. You're pretty cute and if you didn't already have a Master, I'd snap you up myself. You here on your own?"

"No, Sir. I'm here with Master Damian," Alex replies hoping he has all the correct protocol words right.

"Jeez," the leather man exclaims smiling, "you're a bloody Brit. Is this Damian Hall?"

"Yes, Sir," Alex replies.

"Is he here? I haven't seen in him in years," the leather man asks.

"Right here, Bob," Damian replies from behind him before Alex can reply, his body totally obscured by the much larger man between them.

Alex breathes a sigh of relief, grateful that Damian is there to help him out.

The leather man swings around, spots Damian, grabs him in his arms and lifts him clean off the ground, planting a huge kiss on his shaved head before lowering him to the floor again, trying not to make Damian spill the drinks he's just bought.

"Well I never, where have you been all these years, you old scoundrel?"

Damian sees Alex standing there looking nervous and thinks he'd better explain.

"Boy, this is Bob Silverman, a very old friend of mine. He lives here in DC. He may look tough but he's a real pussycat underneath."

"Pleased to meet you, Sir," Alex says, still feeling a

little nervous as he shakes Bob's hand.

"Bob and I used to bunk up together at Hickoryswitch. I learned quite a few tricks from him. Are you heading to camp on Friday, Bob?" Damian asks.

"Sure am. I've been going every year and it gets better each time. I'm picking my boy up from the airport tomorrow and then on Friday we're driving down."

Alex decides that maybe Bob isn't so scary after all. And maybe he can make friends with Bob's boy as he feels it would be good to meet some other men in the same situation as himself.

But then Bob makes a suggestion to Damian, which scares him.

"Maybe you and I could do a two-hander on my boy and yours."

"Well, Bob, this is Alex's first time at camp and he's never played with anyone else but me. So let's see how he gets on. I don't want to overload him. How does that sound, boy?"

Alex looks at Bob and fears that this much bigger man will subject him to much more painful treatment than Damian. But he thinks carefully before speaking, realising that the camp weekend might give him some new experiences that would make him a better boy for Damian.

"I'm not sure, Sir. But as long as you're there, then I'll feel safer. I'm not sure I'm ready to go play with other tops on my own yet."

"That's a good answer, boy," Damian tells him, rubbing his head affectionately.

For the rest of their time at the bar Alex listens as Damian and Bob catch up on each other's lives. He still feels too nervous to leave them and explore the rest of the space, even though Damian had said he could if he wanted to. And when Damian tells Bob how he came across Alex and what a sad state he was in when they first met he tries not to feel too embarrassed.

Bob particularly likes the story of Damian's antics with the spilled coffee cup when they first met and this provides Alex with an opportunity to contribute a little to the conversation.

"I guess I learned my first lesson pretty quickly, Sir," he tells Damian.

"What a waste of good coffee," Damian says laughing. "But I did enjoy your muffin."

CHAPTER 23

The next morning Damian and Alex drive to Camp Hickoryswitch, stopping off on the way for some bottles of beer, water and some snacks at a convenience store. The road takes them through a few small towns and then open countryside until they reach the start of a more densely wooded area. To their right is a small track which they turn onto and about a mile along it they reach the campground's entrance. There's a high wooden arch with a barrier across it with a carved wooden sign in its middle.

"Here we are, boy," Damian says as an elderly man emerges from a guard hut and approaches the driver's window which Damian opens.

The man is wearing a slave collar and padlock like Alex's and Alex realises immediately that not all slaves are young.

"Good morning, Sir," the man says to Damian. "Are you here for setup?"

"Yes we are," Damian replies. "Damian Hall and Alex Jenkins"

The man checks his clipboard and opens the barrier to let them through before speaking into his walkie talkie. As he turns around Alex reads the word "SECURITY" on the back of his fluorescent orange vest. He wonders if security is to keep people in or out of the camp.

Damian drives into the camp along the perimeter

road and, as it circles around, Alex can see the camp's grounds gently falling away to the right through his window. After a while, they pass a long row of wooden cabins and through some of the wider gaps between them he can see an open green area sloping down, dotted with trees. There are some wooden structures amongst them and down at the bottom of the slope are three large barns and what looks like a single-storey administrative block next to one of them.

"Welcome to Camp Hickoryswitch, boy. We're going to drive around this perimeter road down to the bottom to sign in and find out which cabin we've been assigned to. Then we'll drive back up and take our bags into our cabin. There won't be many people here yet so we can have first pick of the beds."

Down at the bottom of the campsite Damian parks the car and he and Alex enter the open-fronted admin building. There are long tables and chairs scattered around what looks like a social area and piles of bedding in a storage area at the back. Damian instructs Alex to retrieve two bundles of bedding for them and bring them to the front desk.

"Holy, shit, Damian, where have you been." Alex hears someone saying behind him at the reception desk.

"Been busy, Graham, but I'm back here with my boy, Alex."

Alex joins them and is introduced. The stocky

older man has "Graham Tyler" on a name badge hanging around his neck and "Tape Master" written underneath it and Alex notes it says he's from Chicago.

"Graham here is in charge of all the admin and day to day running of the camp, boy. So if you need anything ask him and he'll sort it out for you," Damian tells Alex.

"Pleased to meet you, Sir," Alex says as shakes his hand.

"Welcome to Hickoryswitch, Alex," Graham replies shaking his hand firmly and looking at him with appreciative eyes.

Graham consults some lists on the desk in front of him. "You and your boy are in your old cabin 15 though it's been spruced up since you were last there. Do you remember where it is?"

"Sure do, it has that fine deck outside which I remember having you on your back, spread-eagled for a whole six hours one year," Damian laughs.

Graham gives them each a waiver form to sign and a large envelope. They take them over to one of the tables where pens are waiting. Inside the envelope is a run book with details of workshops, meal times and a map of the camp. There's also a name badge for each of them, Damian Hall/Master Damian/London UK and Alex Jenkins/Master Damian's boy/London UK.

Alex asks what the coloured stickers on their badges mean.

"The gold sticker on mine means I'm a member, boy. And the blue one on yours means this is your first time here. You're to wear it at all times, boy, unless it gets in the way of any play.

"You'll find that the badges will help you remember people's names. There's so many guys here it's easy to forget who you've already met and often I embarrass myself by introducing myself to someone I've spoken to already. And with your blue sticker, the more experienced camp members will know to look out for you and make sure you're OK.

"

Alex laughs, realising that he's going to be scrutinised and approached by many more people than he's used to.

He reads the waiver form, which seems to be some form of legal protection for the camp, signs it, and takes his own and Damian's back to Graham.

"Thank you, Alex," Graham says. "I hope we can get to know each other a bit better once camp starts. If you seem me around the play spaces be sure to come over."

"Yes, Sir. Thank you, Sir," Alex replies before quickly heading back to the car. He's still unused to people wanting to get to know him and shares this with Damian.

"You'll get used to it, boy. You'll find that the men here are very friendly and the fact that they want to talk to you doesn't automatically mean they want to play with you. But on the other hand they might."

"What does 'Tape Master' mean, Sir?"

"Graham's into mummification using plastic wrap and industrial tape. You'll not miss his work – a guy's whole body immobilised with layers of colourful tape and then left to stew or be edged or tormented. It's a sort of postal version of the sleepsack you've already been in."

"Well if I'm bad, Sir, you could always have him tape me up and post me back home," Alex laughs.

"Mummification is an activity I'm not very good at, boy, which is why I tend to use my sleepsack. But if you want to try it just go ask Graham. I'm sure you'll enjoy it."

Already Alex is already thinking this is something he'd like to try and he's sure that Damian would approve. "I'd like that, Sir."

"Well, boy, you have my permission to play with Graham any time he's free. You're probably best off going to watch him in action first, maybe even helping him out."

"How would I do that, Sir?"

"One of the things you'll find here at camp, boy, is that people are very keen to share their skills. So if they see you watching their play don't be surprised if they invite you over to take a closer look or help them. For example Graham might need a hand holding his subject up or turning him over or just applying more tape."

Cabin 15 is near one end of the upper side of the perimeter road close by the admin centre and in the front of it is a wide wooden deck with a wooden bench and some chairs under a porch supported by strong wooden posts and beams. Some of them seem to have eyebolts in them, from previous camps Alex assumes.

Damian parks the car off the road and Alex follows him into the empty cabin where wooden-framed single beds covered in plastic foam mattresses are lined up on either side. Alex can see a bathroom and toilets leading off at the far end through an open door. There's a shelving unit and power outlets next to each bed and more shelves and some clothes rails on the far wall.

Damian selects two beds in the middle of one wall and Alex places their luggage on them. "It's always a compromise where you select your bunks, boy," he tells Alex. "Near the door you are regularly disturbed by people arriving and leaving in the night. At the back, you hear everyone pass your bunk on their way to the bathroom. So in the middle always seems best."

Alex unpacks his suitcase, laying his white t-shirts and shorts and other clothes neatly on the shelves and hanging his spare jeans and combats and precious new leather waistcoat on the rail. He also helps Damian unpack, noticing that Damian has packed yet more black t-shirts and combats and a spare pair of high-sided boots.

Damian opens his second smaller bag and inside it Alex sees coils of rope, a bunch of bandanas, some wrist and ankle restraints, various hoods and gags and a selection of Damian's favourite whips and floggers and canes including the dreaded dragon which he hopes won't be used in anger. There's also some plastic tubs containing lube and some small toys including some of Damian's vicious nipple clamps.

Damian doesn't unpack this bag but slides it under his bed. "There, that's my toy box ready."

It's been quite a few days since they played and Damian thinks Alex needs a warm up.

"Take all your clothes off, boy, and lay face down on the mattress, feet towards the wall with your hands and feet at the corners."

When he's in position, Damian uses the wrist and ankle restraints and some rope to spreadeagle Alex tightly on the bed, his head hanging over the end of the mattress. He uses a large black bandana to blindfold Alex which he knows will help him settle into what is about to happen. There's no need for a gag, as Damian knows that the sounds of play are not only welcome at camp, but serve to add to the atmosphere.

Satisfied that Alex can't move, he takes one of his canes and starts warming up Alex's butt, starting with slow rhythmical strokes, then increasing the intensity as Alex's cheeks start to glow.

When they first started playing Alex hated the cane. He'd yet to allow himself to submit and enjoy the pain as pleasurable. Now he loves it and craves for the euphoric endorphin rush he gets as he slips into "sub space".

The strokes get harder and stingier and Alex feels his cock trying to grow in its cage as he experiences the waves of pain/pleasure spread through his body. He pumps up and down against the mattress to soothe himself but of course his cock can't get hard.

"OK, boy, now you're getting ten hard ones to finish you off," Damian tells him and then proceeds to cane him really hard, leaving ten neat bright red marks across his buttocks.

Alex clenches his teeth as the strokes bite in and a few tears emerge from his eyes, not from unhappiness but from the intensity and pleasure of what Damian is doing.

When he has finished Damian crouches down by Alex's head and uses the bandana blindfold to wipe his eyes before hanging it out of his own left back pocket.

"You have some fine red marks to show off there, boy. And now for something else you've been missing."

Damian removes his combats and stands at the foot of the bed, leaning over so he can tease Alex with his erect cock. Alex opens his mouth and starts moistening Damian's cock before taking it in so Damian can fuck his face. The sight of the red marks on his boy spurs Damian on and soon he cums down Alex's throat.

As Damian is giving his still restrained boy some

water to drink, the cabin door opens. Alex can't see who it is but he recognises Graham's voice.

"I think I'll leave you there for a while, boy," Damian tells Alex, and the two men go to sit outside on the deck to catch up.

Alex tries to look around the cabin as best as he can. He wonders who the other occupants will be and how he will feel playing with Damian in there with others watching or maybe even just sleeping or getting on with their own play or chores. And what if they snore? Spending the night in a room full of other men is something new for Alex and he hopes he will be able to sleep.

Damian returns and releases Alex. "Graham was just telling me about our work assignment, boy. We're to go help set up Dungeon Three first. It's the one mainly used for flogging and whipping as it has lots of St Andrews crosses in it. The guys who got here before us have already taken them out of the store but they need securing and the lighting set up."

Alex stands up and feels for the raised welts on his arse then stands to attention, hands behind his back, waiting his next instruction.

"Go wash your face and brush your teeth and then get dressed in your grey camo combats and boots, boy." Damian tells him.

Alex retrieves his toilet bag from the shelf by his bed and walks back to the bathroom. There's a full-length mirror on one wall and he takes the opportunity to admire his first trophy of the camp. "It's a shame I have to wear clothes," he thinks. "I'd sure like to show these off so people know I'm no novice at this sort of stuff, even with my blue sticker."

Damian and Alex walk down the perimeter road to Dungeon Three and Damian describes what the various buildings are, or at least those that were there on his last visit to the camp.

Some of the open wooden structures in the centre of the camp are quite large and Damian explains that these are probably where the demonstrations and workshops are usually held and where people play at other times. He shows him the large dining hall behind the admin building and Alex can hear the sound of dinner being prepared in the kitchen beyond it.

Inside Dungeon Three a stack of wooden crosses lays on the floor and Damian introduces himself and Alex to Larry, who is in charge of set up.

"If your boy can help me erect the crosses, Damian, perhaps you could unpack the medical and cleaning supplies and lay them out on the table by the door."

Soon Alex and Larry are done and Alex marvels at how well-equipped the dungeon is. Some of the crosses are secured to the walls. But a few are freestanding and joined together at the top, so the men tied to them face each other.

"No wonder Damian bought loads of stuff after he used to come here," Alex thinks. "These dungeons sure set a high standard."

Alex looks at the joined crosses and imagines himself on one side and Bob's boy tied to the other with Bob and Damian taking turns to work on their own and the other's boy while he and the other boy face each other. Far from fearing it as he did the previous night, he's now looking forward to it and resolves to tell Damian about this when the time is right. He ought to meet Bob's boy first before saying anything.

On the supplies table Damian has been stocking up there are boxes of latex and purple nitrile gloves, spray bottles of alcohol and other cleaning materials, paper towels and a first aid kit.

"Safety and hygiene are very important at the camp." Damian explains to Alex when he joins him at the table. "Everyone is expected to clean the equipment after use, for example."

"As for the first aid kit, sometimes accidents happen and guys end up with cuts that need cleaning and dressing. But no-one gets injured," he reassures Alex. "This is play, not fight club."

Larry comes up to them and asks them to help him with Dungeon Two, which is mainly set up for bondage. They erect the bondage tables and arrange the floor mats used for free-form bondage. Over in the corner Graham is talking to another man about the suspension equipment. There are chains hanging from electric winches attached to some horizontal steel girders and they are checking the controls are working.

Alex asks Damian about safety. "Do all the guys who use this stuff know what they're doing?"

"Good question, boy. Each dungeon is always monitored by a couple of experienced play monitors. It's their job to watch what's going on and to make sure guys know how to use the equipment and don't damage it or injure themselves or anyone else. In past years, my work assignment was often to do a shift as a play monitor.

"Before the camp decided to set up the dungeons for specific types of play, we had a problem with spectators walking around and crossing the path of guys doing flogging and single tail whipping. Now the spaces are arranged better and the play monitors don't spend so much time moving people out of the way for their own safety."

Alex notices that Damian has used the word "we" a lot and recognises that Damian probably considers the camp to be his spiritual home.

"How you feeling, boy?" Damian asks Alex, putting his arm around him.

"I'm getting into it, Sir, and that caning was a good start to the weekend. It sort of drove away a lot of my fears.

"I was looking at those crosses in Dungeon Three just now and thinking how much I'd like you and Bob to work on me and his boy," Alex continues, forgetting he'd decided he ought to meet Bob's boy before saying anything. The excitement of being at the camp has already started loosening Alex's inhibitions.

Damian smiles broadly. "I'll see what I can arrange, boy."

Finally, Damian, Alex, and Larry join some other men in Dungeon One where they are arranging more bondage tables, some interesting tubular steel frames and an area of floor covered in thick plastic sheeting with bondage tables on top of it.

"What's that for?" Alex asks.

"Larry told me that this is a new area reserved for wax play. The camp doesn't want us to get wax on the concrete floor, so this way at the end of camp, or when they get too covered in wax during camp, the sheets can be thrown away and replaced. But when they started this area there was still a problem with wax being walked off the area on guys' boots. So that's why we have now those rough mats at the edge to try to catch it all and a brush and dustpan handy. Hopefully the guys who use this area will clean up after themselves.

"The only thing not allowed in the dungeons is cigar play as they are no-smoking areas. But the guys into that use the open wooden structures in the middle of the camp or just out on the park benches. You should go watch that some time."

Alex has seen cigar play in porno films, with guys being put into a gas mask and a cigar plugged into it so they have no choice but to inhale the smoke. Alex wonders what that feels like. But as he's never even smoked cigarettes he isn't sure he'd like it.

In these films he also saw guys' bodies being heated up and even burned with lit cigars. And one time he saw a cigar used to singe off another guy's body hair, the top managing not to burn him at all, not even when it was his scrotum that was being done. But as Damian ensures Alex is always hairless from the neck down he realises this is something he won't get to try.

There's not many at dinner that night and Alex spends time talking to Graham and Larry while Damian catches up with the other men. He introduces Alex to the camp's chairman, Mark Dixon, and his partner Will, so now Alex knows a few more people. Mark and Will have never been to London and they discuss the best places for tourist to go. "We may have to come visit," Mark tells him and Alex is slowly appreciating the community spirit amongst the men. It's so different from the cold impersonal interactions he used to see in his favourite porno films.

CHAPTER 24

That night Alex and Damian sleep alone in their cabin, both tired from their travels and work assignments. The rest of the camp attendees aren't due to arrive until after lunch the next day and at breakfast Damian asks Larry if there's more they can do to help.

"We've still to get the ice bins and bottles of water and cans of soda and beer delivered around the site. Here are the keys to the pickup," Larry tells him, giving him directions to the catering-grade ice machine and the beverage store along with a list of places that the bins need to be placed and filled.

So Alex and Damian spend the morning driving around the camp distributing supplies, stopping occasionally so Damian can renew his friendship with guys he knows.

After lunch, Damian decides Alex should have his first experience of outdoor bondage and also provide a suitable welcome for the rest of the attendees, as most of them will need to drive past their cabin on their way to register.

Alex, dressed in just his boots, padlocked chain collar and black bandana and of course his chastity cage, waits on the deck outside their cabin while Damian goes inside to get what he needs.

Before long Alex is standing spread-eagled, wrists and ankles stretched out with ropes to the ringbolt fixing points on the porch supports. Damian puts a leather hood on him but leaves the blindfold off so Alex can watch people watching him. He also locks on the wide posture collar, which restricts Alex's movement even more. Alex remembers the first unhappy time it was locked on him, when Damian was punishing him. But now he welcomes its restrictive effect.

Finally, Damian puts a ball stretcher around Alex's balls and pulls them out in front of him with an elastic cord, attaching the other end to the deck. The tension on his balls makes his chastity cage stick out, glinting prominently in the sunshine for all to see.

Alex can't move at all. His field of vision is restricted and he can just about see into the side windows of the cars as other campers start arriving. Some of them slow down to get a better look and one or two of them call out words of approval to Damian who is sitting in one of the chairs drinking a beer.

Alex feels like a prized trophy and is enjoying being shown off. Occasionally Damian gets up and strokes Alex's balls or squeezes or sucks on his nipples, making his cock twitch in its cage.

"I hope we don't cause any of these guys driving by to veer off the road, boy. The ground's a bit soft once you leave it."

Alex laughs as best as he can in the hood and then sinks back into his idyllic immobilising bondage, eyes closed and enjoying every minute of it.

About an hour later, Alex hears a familiar voice

calling out from one of the cars, which slows down, and then stops and parks off the narrow road out of Alex's field of vision.

Two men walk up onto the deck. One of them is Bob, dressed casually and almost unrecognisable without his full leathers. Walking behind him, hands behind his back, is a short chubby bearded guy about his own age with short-cropped hair and a padlock and chain around his neck.

Damian and Bob embrace and Damian is introduced to Bob's boy, Mike, who seems equally friendly and quite cute.

"I'm afraid Alex is a bit tied up at the moment, Bob, but when you're settled in why don't you both come back here and we can have a beer and our boys can get to know each other."

Alex looks at the three of them, or as much as he can see through the small eye holes in the hood, and thinks again about the four of them playing together. His cock tries to grow in its cage, telling him that this is what he really wants.

After another half-hour, Damian decides Alex must be getting tired and releases him.

When Bob and Mike return they find Alex dressed in his boy's white t-shirt and shorts sitting at Damian's feet reading the run book, a bottle of water by his side.

Alex stands up and shakes Bob and Mike's hands. "Good to see you again, Sir. Pleased to meet you, Mike", he says with a confidence that surprises him.

He's not sure at what point handshakes stop and hugs start but discovers that this particular milestone has been passed when Bob and Mike both give him a big bear hug.

Bob sits down in a chair next to Damian and swigs on a beer while Mike sits on the ground between his legs drinking some water.

As Alex is about to sit down as well, Damian tells him to show Bob and Mike his marks from the previous day's play. "I thought Alex needed something to get him into the swing of things," Damian says proudly.

Though less prominent than before, the ten neat red stripes are still visible and Bob strokes them appreciatively while Mike looks a bit concerned.

"It's interesting, Damian, how different boys tolerate things differently. Alex seems to take the cane on his arse very well while my boy here can't but loves a good single tail whipping session on his back."

"Well, Bob, maybe Alex can help Mike with that. When I first took him on Alex found caning really difficult, not that he had any choice to start with as those first few canings were punishments. But after a while, he really got into the feel of my cane. Alex might have a few tips for your boy."

Damian sends Alex and Mike into the cabin so they can feel more relaxed talking out of earshot of their Masters.

"You're the first other 'boy' I've ever met," Alex

tells Mike as they sit on Alex's bed. "How did you and Bob get together?"

Mike explains how they met on a gay SM cruising web site. They only played online at first as they live at opposite sides of the country. After a while, Bob invited him to stay with him in DC for a week and they really hit it off.

"Sadly we're both stuck living where we are because of our jobs. But we go stay with each other a few times a year, and we have been meeting here at camp for the past few years as well."

Alex wonders how long-distance Master/slave stuff could work. But before he can ask more questions, Mike seems keen to asks his own. "How did you meet Damian, Alex? He's a real catch."

Alex is startled at his Master being described as "a real catch" and it makes him smile inwardly. He decides that the full grizzly truth about how he and Damian met is something he needs to put behind him and so gives Mike an abbreviated, sanitised version, saying that they met in one of Damian's interactive porn films and leaves it at that.

"Can I see your arse again, Alex?" Mike asks, and Alex drops his shorts so that Mike can take a closer look.

"Wow that must have hurt like fuck," Mike says, gently feeling the marks. "How do you cope?"

"At first the canings were punishments because I was having a hard time obeying Sir's orders as I used to be really disorganised. So I didn't see them as something pleasurable. But after a while, I got my life together and made fewer mistakes so Sir started using them as part of our play sessions as he really enjoys caning. He'd start slowly then build up the number and strength of his strokes. It always helped me sink into it if he tied me down really tight."

"I'm the same way with flogging and whipping," Mike tells him. "The less I can move, the more I can take on my back. But strangely, as soon as Sir starts caning or paddling my arse I sort of just snap out of things and get upset and start crying."

"Well," Alex says, feeling strangely wise for a change, "maybe it's not for you. Or maybe Bob isn't the right person for you for that particular activity. And there's no shame in crying. It happens to me a lot. Sir says it's good to release all that emotion."

"I agree, Alex. But I don't often play heavy stuff with anyone else so I don't know. Even here I usually only ever play with my Sir. We see each other so little that we spend all our time at camp playing with each other. There's great equipment here, much better than Sir has. Plus there's space. He lives in a small apartment in DC and I have a roommate in San Francisco so we can't play there when he visits, and we have to plan his visits to me around the local SM club play parties."

Alex thinks how lucky he is to be living with Damian and to have the luxury of playing in his well-equipped playroom as often as they want.

"That's a real shame," Alex tells him, deciding not

to boast about Damian's facilities back in London.

"Sir told me that I should play with others while I'm here which worried me at first," Mike continues." But this year I've decided it's about time I did and I'm looking forward to it."

"Same here," Alex replies. He wonders if Mike knows about the combined play Bob had suggested to Damian. "Our Sirs seem to be really good friends. In fact when Sir and I met Bob in a bar in DC, Bob suggested that the two of them work on the two of us together."

"Sir mentioned that when we drove by your cabin and saw you tied up on the deck," Mike tells Alex. "He said you seemed like a fun boy but that it was my decision."

As they're talking, Alex notices that Mike keeps looking at the cane which Damian had left hanging on the shelves.

"You seem fascinated by that cane, Mike?" Alex asks, finding himself strangely tuning in to what Mike is thinking. It's something Damian is very good at and Alex is surprised to discover that he is starting to have that ability as well.

"Oh, I don't know, Alex. It's just that maybe if you were to cane me a bit as a game it might be less frightening. But I wouldn't want to upset Sir by asking him."

Alex realises how much more comfortable and confident he is with Damian after only a couple of months than Mike seems with Bob after some years.

Maybe it's because he and Damian spend so much time together. Maybe it's because he himself was such a dumb ass that Damian had to spend so much time explaining things to him.

He's also surprised by his cock trying to grow in its cage as he thinks about caning Mike.

"Well, Mike, we'd certainly have to get permission from our Sirs before we did anything like that. Shall I ask my Sir first and see what he says?"

"That would be great, Alex, but don't let my Sir know what's going on. I don't want him to think I'm dissatisfied with him, because I'm not."

"Stay here," Alex tells Mike and he gets up to speak to his Master. He thinks he'd better speak to Damian on his own first, as he doesn't want to get Mike into trouble with Bob if he's stepped out of line.

Outside on the deck Damian and Bob are having a break in their conversation and Alex asks if he can have a private word with Damian.

"Sure, boy," he replies and leads Alex off across the road into the wooded area.

Alex describes his conversation with Mike and how he noticed Mike looking at the cane.

"It's a bit awkward, Sir, as I'm sure Mike doesn't want to appear disrespectful to Bob or to suggest he isn't a good Master. But maybe being caned by another boy might be a good intro for him – like trainer wheels on a bicycle."

"Well, boy, it's very observant of you to have guessed what he was thinking. You're definitely getting smarter. Maybe some of my intuition is rubbing off on you. More important, boy, do you want to do it?" Damian asks him.

"To my surprise, Sir, I found the idea quite exciting."

"OK, boy, I'll have a word with Bob. You go back into the cabin and reassure Mike that I'll handle this sensitively. I hope Bob agrees as I'd love to see you topping Mike."

As he goes back into the cabin Alex struggles to imagine himself as a top. But he can't deny the prospect is having an effect on his caged cock.

Inside Mike is pacing around nervously. "I'm worried I've done something which will upset Sir, and may be punished for it, maybe with a very painful caning."

"Don't worry, Mike, my Sir really liked the idea. And he is a very clever man and very careful not to hurt people's feelings. I'm sure he will devise something."

A few minutes later Damian and Bob enter the cabin, both of them smiling.

"Well, boy," Bob says to Mike. "I hear the two of you have devised a little entertainment for us which would be a nice way to start off the weekend."

Mike frowns a little and looks at Alex who gives him a look which indicates he should stay silent and see what happens.

"Damian here tells me you both thought it would be fun for us to watch our two boys playing. He suggested that Alex canes you, boy. What do you think?"

Mike smiles at Damian's ingenuity. "Yes, Sir, I'd like that a lot if it's OK with you."

"I'd love it, boy. And I'd rather you were topped by another slave than a Master who might want to steal you away."

Damian lifts the cane off the shelf and retrieves a second one and some rope and leather restraints and bandanas from his toy bag. "Let's go do this where others can see. Alex hasn't caned anyone before so I think they'll all enjoy the lesson. I hope his aim isn't too bad to start with or you'll have some marks in the wrong places."

They all laugh and Mike feels much better.

Over in Dungeon two, Mike undresses and Bob ties his boy tightly over a leather-padded wooden horse while Damian blindfolds him with one of his bandanas. He wants Mike to be able to give Alex some feedback so decides not to gag him. And he knows that a few shouts and screams will get Bob and himself excited and attract more attention.

He then hands a cane to Alex and gives him some instructions.

There are still not many men in the dungeon but a few of them gather around to watch, intrigued by the sight of one collared boy about to cane another.

"You want to stand here on the side, boy," Damian tells Alex. "Start with slow strokes so you can check your aim. And judge your distance. You don't want the end of the cane to hit him or you'll cut him, nor do you want it to wrap around and mark his thighs. When I hit a boy's thighs I do it deliberately."

Alex feels nervous holding the cane, but his cock is stirring and he knows he really wants to do this.

Slowly he starts tapping Mike's buttocks. Mike doesn't make a sound so Alex slowly increases the frequency and impact of the cane, following what he has learned from his own caning.

After a few more strokes, Damian walks quietly up behind Alex and whispers in his ear. "You need to check-in regularly with Mike to see how he's doing as he's being very quiet. See that he's OK and enjoying himself."

So every now and then Alex crouches down by Mike's head to ask him how he is.

"Doing good here, Sirs," Mike answers loudly.

Alex isn't sure if he is included in the "Sirs" but isn't bothered if he is. In fact, he feels quite good about it and stands a little taller than usual.

It doesn't take long for Alex to be hitting Mike quite hard and Mike's buttocks are glowing red with a few stripes showing. He does the strokes in sets of ten, with a break in between, each set being a little harder than the next. This is something he learned from Damian. For his part, Mike has started growling, showing that Alex's strokes are working well and he's not being too soft on him, nor too hard.

As Alex is about to start the next set, Bob moves

around behind him holding the other cane and moves him gently aside, holding a finger to his smiling lips to indicate to Alex that he shouldn't say anything.

Alex looks over at Damian questioningly and Damian nods his approval.

Bob gives Mike the next set of ten hard cane strokes and then an even harder set of ten after that. Mike doesn't notice the difference in the top's strength as Alex is not experienced enough to make all his strokes even, so they've been variable already. Damian just stands there trying not to laugh out loud.

By the end, Mike has received 100 strokes and his buttocks are bright red with quite a few visible red lines. He is released and when he gets up he gives Alex a big hug.

"I think your Sir deserves one as well, Mike," Alex tells him. "He gave you the last twenty strokes."

Mike's expression drops in astonishment and he looks at a beaming Bob. He's lost for words and Bob breaks the silence.

"Well, boy," he says. "I guess you're never too old to learn something, even from a slave. Maybe I've been breaking you in wrong when it comes to your arse."

Alex is on a high. Despite his cock stirring when Mike mentioned being caned by him, during the session it was quiet as he concentrated on holding the cane correctly, perfecting his aim and controlling the strength of his strokes. But emotionally he feels elated and very happy.

On his mental checklist for the camp, he ticks off two items – "Top someone" and "Play with someone other than Damian".

"Gosh," he thinks to himself. "Camp has barely started. I can't imagine what else is going to happen."

CHAPTER 25

As Mike and Bob had been to camp the previous few years and he hadn't, Damian suggests that Mike show Alex around before dinner while Bob does the same for him.

"It looks like there's lots of new play spaces and equipment here, Bob, and I have a few scenes in mind that I want to find the best space for. Let's meet up with our boys at dinner."

Damian is pleased at Alex finding a new friend and enjoys seeing the two boys bonding. He smiles proudly as Mike takes Alex into one of the other dungeons.

Inside two heavily tattooed guys are playing. The top is tall and skinny, bare-chested, and wearing just tight leather jeans and high-sided boots, his head sporting a bright red mohawk. His chest and back are tattooed with what looks like a barbed wire version of a string vest. Most striking are the large hoops in his ear lobes and rings hanging from his nipples and through the septum in his nose.

His hooded playmate is spread-eagled inside a metal frame, facing away from Alex. Alex can see coils of rough rope tattooed around his biceps and a matching length running around both his sides to the middle of his hairy back, but cut and frayed in the middle as if snapped by his muscular arms releasing themselves from bondage. All along his arms are dozens of brightly-coloured pegs and it looks very painful.

Alex keeps his distance as he walks around to look at the front of the suspended figure and stops suddenly. It's not the masses of pegs across the chest that startle him but the fact that the suspended person appears to be a woman. There are loads of pegs on what look like female genitalia.

Alex discreetly beckons Mike over to show him, trying not to make it too obvious which part of this person's anatomy he is pointing out, and then indicates for him to follow him outside.

"I thought this camp was for men only," a confused Alex asks in a whisper.

"It is, that's a trans man," Mike explains quietly, realising what Alex is referring to.

"I don't recognise either of them – I'd remember those amazing tattoos and piercings and that mohawk," Mike continues. "I think I saw a blue sticker on the top's name tag so it must be their first time."

Mike's explanation doesn't help Alex. "How can that be a man if he has women's bits between his legs?"

"Don't you know what a transgender person is?" Mike asks Alex, slightly reproachfully.

"I thought I did," Alex replies. "It's a person who was born with a woman's body but knows that they are really a man. But I thought they all had hormones and operations and things so they looked just like a man."

"Not always," Mike explains. "Or at least not all of them change everything about their bodies. If they have large breasts they may have surgery to reduce them. But many female to male transgender people don't bother with having their genitals remodelled."

"Go, on," Alex says.

"The operation isn't always that effective and many trans men prefer getting pleasure with the sexual organs they were born with rather than risk getting a poor fleshy imitation of the cock and balls a man would be born with and end up with reduced sexual sensitivity.

"The hormones help anyway and their clitoris can get much larger. A trans friend of mine back home refers to it as his 'cock' the same way you and I do and claims it can get bigger than many ordinary dicks he's seen."

Alex laughs. He didn't realise that the camp would provide him with an education in anatomy. And he's impressed that the camp's inclusive attitude meant that trans men were welcomed.

"I've made some great trans friends over the years and even played with one," Mike continues. "Not SM play, but going down on him and being fucked by him wearing a strap-on certainly broadened my outlook on what I thought of as gay men's sex."

"You're full of surprises, Mike," Alex laughs.

The two boys continue their discussion as they explore the outdoor areas of the campground. Alex tries hard to digest what he has just seen and learned. And he realises he admires Mike even more now. For all that he may have been a bit of a wimp when it comes to caning, Mike certainly seemed to have the courage to broaden his sexual repertoire way beyond anything Alex ever imagined.

Finally, it is time for dinner and as they stand in line, Alex and Mike spot Damian and Bob at the far end of the dining room. They choose their food and join them, sitting with their backs to the room in the free chairs opposite. Mike hasn't sat down since his caning earlier on and wriggles a bit on his hard chair, his buttocks still smarting from the caning Alex and Bob gave him.

"Still sore, boy?" Bob asks Mike.

"Yes, Sir, and thank you for allowing us to do that," Mike replies, being careful not to reveal how that play session came about.

Damian is very proud of his own boy's performance in the dungeon and marvels at how quickly he is maturing and gaining more confidence. Alex's puppy-dog eyes sparkle brighter than ever and his confidence that his boy would be a credit to him at camp has been borne out much faster than he expected.

"How was your tour, boys?" Damian asks them. Alex can't wait to talk about the two tattooed men he had seen.

"I think I know who the top is," Damian replies when Alex has finished. "He's called Paul and he and I have cam chatted on occasions. You're right that you don't see tattoos like that very often. Or ear lobe hoops that big or the red mohawk. I don't remember him mentioning a partner of any sort, let alone a trans one."

Damian scours the room behind Alex and Mike looking for Paul. As he does so, he spots someone familiar. He can't work out who he is or what looks familiar about the man until he looks back at Alex across the table and realises that the stranger and Alex look eerily similar, even down to the puppy-dog eyes.

And then Damian's friend Paul arrives with his food and sits down next to the strangely familiar man, greeting him warmly. Damian quickly rises from his seat and says a hurried "excuse me" to the others.

"Hey Paul, good to see you," Damian says shaking his hand.

"Hey Damian, good to see you in the flesh at last. This is my boy and partner, Rocky."

"Please to meet you Damian," the boy says as he stands up to shake Damian's hand. As he does so, a tattoo of coiled rope emerges from under his t-shirt sleeve.

"Is that a British accent I detect?" Damian asks Rocky. "Where are you from?"

"Well I grew up in a remote part of Norfolk which is a whole other world compared to Toronto."

Just as he's speaking, Rocky's nametag with its blue sticker swings into view.

Damian reads it. "Rocky Jenkins, Toronto ON, enigmaboy".

Damian's jaw drops and for once he is lost for words. Paul's boy looks uncannily like Alex. But Alex had a sister who moved to Toronto not a brother. Damian struggles to remember her name and then it comes back to him – Roxanne.

An extraordinary explanation forms in Damian's mind. Once in Toronto, Alex's sister must have transitioned to a man and by coincidence come to his first camp at the same time as his brother.

Damian regains his composure. "Welcome to your first camp, both of you. I'll let you get on with your dinner and catch up with you later."

Damian is glad that Alex hasn't seen this encounter as he thinks he needs to break the news to him gently.

Back at the table, Bob and Mike have left, leaving Alex there devouring his dessert. "Boy, when you've finished your food we should chat some more about what you did and saw this afternoon," Damian tells him, trying not to seem over excited or over anxious. He waits to make sure Paul and Rocky have left the dining hall before he and Alex do, padding out the time by treating himself to a second helping of cake.

Some minutes later Alex and Damian are sitting together on the sloping grassy area in the middle of the campground. Damian has chosen the spot carefully so they won't be disturbed as he expects this will be a very difficult and emotional conversation. He starts off slowly, discussing Alex's impressions of the camp and congratulating him on engineering the caning scene.

"From what I saw it looks like your initiative really helped Bob and Mike get closer to each other and you picked up the art of wielding a cane very well."

"Thank you, Sir. I'd almost forgotten it given how that encounter with the tattooed guys startled me. It's quite a coincidence that you knew one of them. Do you know who the other one is? The trans guy?"

"Well I've never met him before Paul introduced me to him at dinner. But…"

Damian stops, not knowing how to continue. If he himself was shocked at the discovery then the effect on Alex could be devastating.

Alex isn't used to seeing Damian flustered and senses something is up. "But what?" he asks, anxiously.

Damian take a deep breath. "But you do, Alex."

Damian never calls him "Alex" so he knows something important is about to be revealed, maybe something to do with his old life.

"Someone from London, Sir? Or a friend of Melissa's?"

Damian takes a deep breath. "Alex, that man is what your sister has transitioned into. It looks like moving to Canada wasn't just about Roxanne finding a new life but also about finding a new identity as a man called Rocky."

Damian starts to say more but realises that Alex has

already gone very pale and silent. He changes position and holds tightly Alex in his arms as Alex has started to cry.

"You remember, Sir, that when you suggested we come here via Toronto I said I wasn't interested in finding my family. Well deep down I realised I missed them, especially my sister. So when I went back to my room I searched for them online. I found my parents on Facebook but not Roxanne.

"Now you're telling me she is a he and is here. I don't know what to think or feel. It's all too much to take in at once."

Damian gives Alex the black bandana from his back pocket to dry his eyes. "I don't blame you for being confused and upset, boy. Nothing in your life has prepared you for this. Do you want me to go find Rocky and bring him over here? I assume you want to meet him. And I'll stick around if you like."

Damian referring to his sister as "Rocky" and "him" adds to Alex's distress. But he knows what he needs to do.

"Yes, Sir, I do. But can you find Mike first?" Alex asks. And he explains why, repeating what Mike had told him about his trans friends back home. "I think it would be a great help if I could talk to him first."

Damian totally understands what Alex is saying and doesn't feel at all upset at not being Alex's main support at this moment. He knows that being a Master of your own dungeon playroom doesn't mean that you will be able to cope with all the curve balls life throws at you, or your boy.

"Of course, boy. Let me go find him. You stay here and try not to worry too much."

Over at the social area Damian spots Bob and Mike. He isn't sure that Bob knows about what Mike gets up to on his own side of the country so finds an excuse to borrow Mike for a while and on their way over to the grassy slope Damian tells Mike what he has just told Alex.

"Holy shit, Alex. That's a bit of a stunner," Mike says excitedly when they arrive. "There we were in the dungeon watching these two sexy guys playing and it turns out one of them used to be your sister. That beats anything I've ever come across. Are you two going to meet up? Can I help?"

"Well, Mike, I'd like it if you were there when Roxanne, sorry, Rocky and I meet," Alex says quietly. "You'll be much better at knowing how to talk about these things than I am. But I'm not sure I'm ready to face my sister just yet, especially now she's a man."

Damian, wise as ever, cautions Alex. "Even though there are over 200 men at the camp it's inevitable that you and Rocky will spot each other at some point. It would be better if your first meeting was planned and took place somewhere quiet rather than a chance meeting at dinner."

"You're right, Sir," Alex replies softly.

"If you're willing, boy, I can go find Paul and explain things to him. It will give you two boys some more time together to chat," Damian says tentatively, knowing that Alex has to set the pace. He also realises that Paul may need to check that Rocky wants to meet Alex.

Alex sits there still crying while Damian and Mike sit either side of him with their arms around him, kissing him softly and allowing him to take his time to process what he's just learned.

After a few minutes, Alex is able to speak more clearly. "Let's do it now, Sir," he says, wiping his eyes and blowing his nose. "There's so much from my childhood I never understood and now I find out I knew even less about my sister than I thought. I don't want to walk around camp the rest of the weekend looking for her, sorry, him or worse, hoping I don't accidentally bump into him in the middle of a huge crowd."

Damian leaves the two boys to talk and deliberately walks slowly around the large campground so the boys have more time on their own. Eventually he finds Paul and Rocky in one of the dungeons watching a suspension demonstration and pulls Paul to one side, saying he needs to talk to him.

"Something strange and very serious has occurred which involves us both," Damian tells Paul. "Am I right in thinking that Rocky is transgender and used to be a woman called Roxanne?"

"Yes that's right, Damian. How did you know?"

"Well I was sitting there in the dining hall looking around and I spotted Rocky's puppy-dog eyes.

They're identical to my boy Alex's. And when I came over to say hello to you and you introduced me to Rocky I saw his name tag and that his surname is Jenkins, the same as Alex. What with that and that Rocky grew up in Norfolk, I put two and two together and came up with five."

"Well I never," Paul replies. "Rocky never talks much about his family other than to say he hated his parents. He mentioned he had a brother called Alex who was left behind in London who he often thought about and missed a lot. But I would never have guessed it was your Alex."

"This is going to be an important and difficult reunion for them," Damian warns Paul. "For Alex to meet his long lost sister is one thing. Coping with Rocky's transition is another. But he's with a friend at the moment who has some experience of these things and I'll be there to support him."

"And I'd better make sure Rocky is ready to meet Alex," Paul replies. "I'm sure he will be."

Damian tells Paul where he and the boys are sitting and leaves Paul to break the, hopefully good, news to Rocky. Back at the slope, he fills Alex and Mike in on his conversation with Paul and he and Mike holds Alex's hands while they wait.

Ten minutes later Alex looks up to see the unmistakeable Paul approaching them.

"No going back now," Alex thinks to himself, and shivers a little.

"Rocky collapsed in a flood of tears when he heard

you were here, Alex," Paul tells him. "He's desperate to see you again and will be here in a minute. I think he went to wash his face first."

In the distance Alex spots someone who, though more muscular and definitely a lot hairier than previously, is without doubt his sister.

Alex stands up and he and Rocky run towards each other and then stop and stare, unbelieving grins on their faces.

After a few minutes silence, Alex is the first one to speak. "Jeez, sis, what a handsome young man you've become, and how come you've got more hair and muscles on you than I can ever manage" he says and laughs.

"You're looking pretty good yourself, little brother. Even got a decent haircut for a change."

And then the disguising banter stops and they collapse, sobbing, into each other's arms. Damian, Paul and Mike stand back, giving the siblings space and time to adjust.

It is some five minutes before Alex and Rocky remember they are not alone.

"Alex, this is Paul, my partner and Master," Rocky starts. "He and I live in Toronto and run a tattoo and piercing store, as if that wasn't obvious."

"Sis, sorry, Rocky, this is my Master, Damian. We live together in London. Oh and this is Mike, he's from the west coast and he's a new friend I've made here."

Paul stands behind Rocky, massaging his shoulders

and asks him quietly if he's OK. "I'm better than OK, Paul," Rocky answers, touching his hand. And then, addressing Alex, he says to his brother, "It's OK if you call me 'sis' when it's just the two of us, but I confuse people enough as it is without having my little brother causing even more chaos." And he laughs.

Damian and Mike don't need to ask Alex if he's OK. They can tell he's also better than OK.

"Well," Damian tells them, "I think it's time for us to leave the Jenkins family and their strange sense of humour to themselves. We'll be down in the social area if you need us. And please don't have any family quarrels just yet. You haven't even started learning what a wonderful pair of men you've grown up to be."

Alex and Rocky talk late into the night, pausing once to grab some warmer clothes and a few times to get coffee from the social area where they move to sit by the open fire when it gets colder.

Alex learns about Rocky's transition from a woman to a man. How he stayed in Toronto so that their parents would be confronted with how much they had made him suffer as he grew up by their continual taunts about him being a tom boy and not wearing his hair long enough or using enough make up. And he describes how he met Paul at a tattoo convention in Toronto and how they set up their own very successful body art business with people coming from all around the world to be tattooed and pierced there.

For his part, Alex feels close enough to Rocky not to hide the details of how his life had declined since his family emigrated. And having seen Rocky play with Paul, he's relieved to be able to share with him the full details of his own transition from a sad solitary forever-wanking porno addict to a happy, proud, disciplined boy with a fine Master. And he shows Rocky his chastity cage and the tattoo above it.

"You know something, Alex," Rocky tells him. "If our parents weren't so hemmed in and blinkered by their own self-righteousness and prejudices they would be very proud of us now. I don't believe in rubbing people's faces in it unless sex is involved and it's my cock they're rubbing against. But maybe you and Damian should come visit Paul and myself in Toronto some time and the four of us could go visit them. Show them what they've been missing all these years."

"I'd like that very much, sis," Alex replies, laughing both at the prospect of taking revenge on their parents and the fact that Rocky now had a cock.

CHAPTER 26

The next morning Damian wakes up early as usual and looks over to Alex's bed expecting to see him fast asleep. But it's empty. Around him, the other men in the cabin are still sleeping.

Outside on the deck he discovers Alex sitting on the ground, naked apart from his collar and black bandana and chastity cage, polishing their boots.

"Good morning, boy. I didn't expect you to be awake so early. You came back to the cabin really late."

Alex stands to attention. "Good morning, Sir. I slept a bit but I had some strange dreams about my family and when I woke up I couldn't get back to sleep."

"Let's sit down, boy, I want to hear how it went with Rocky after we left."

Alex continues polishing the boots as he goes over the previous night's events.

"It went really well, Sir. Sis, sorry, Rocky and I always got on really well when we were growing up. It was as if we were protecting each other against the insults and lack of caring from our parents. I don't think either of us guessed that the other one also had a hidden secret. And now we have discovered those secrets in a really fortuitous way.

"I don't think we'd have been able to cope so well yesterday if we weren't surrounded by our partners and friends. So thank you, Sir, for your help."

Damian notices that Alex has referred to him as his "partner" and smiles.

"You're very welcome, boy. I'm really happy that it happened here. This camp is the safest place I know for guys to explore their inner desires and be open about who they truly are. I assume you and Rocky will be spending a lot more time together while you're here."

"Yes and no, Sir. We both want to make the most of our time here to play in this amazing place, so we agreed we'd maybe meet before breakfast over the next couple of days so we could talk more and leave the rest of the day for fun. He suggested we come to Toronto to see them some time and maybe even confront our parents."

"That sounds like a good plan, boy, though I'm not sure about confronting your parents. Paul also suggested a visit to Toronto after we left you and Rocky. What do you say to us making a detour on our way home? I checked with Jameson just before he went to bed back in London and things are fine back home and we can change our return flights."

Once again, Damian is one step ahead of Alex.

"I'd like that a lot, Sir, and that way Rocky and I won't have to worry about when we'll see each other again."

Damian agrees. "At breakfast we can run this past Rocky and Paul, and if it's still OK I can call Jameson when he's awake back home and ask him to change our flights and find us a hotel."

Alex smiles. "Thank you, Sir. You're very generous to me and I hope you know I'm really grateful."

"Well I'll get something out of it as well, boy. I'm thinking that maybe it's about time you got a septum ring in your nose and where better to do it than at their place?"

Alex's cock stirs in its cage at the thought of another piercing and wonders about asking for his tattoo to be permanently inked there as well, but decides it's best to let Damian make that decision.

"I'd like that very much, Sir."

"Oh, and I told Jameson about Rocky. It took him ten minutes to stop laughing. He's very pleased for you and I think a little bit jealous not to be here sharing in your discovery. You know he's very fond of you and very protective as well. Maybe you should start calling him 'Uncle Jameson'."

Alex laughs and feels even more secure and happy, knowing he has two emotionally strong men looking after him. "I love him a lot, too, Sir. I can see how the two of you get on so well. But I'm not sure about the 'uncle' bit. Adjusting to my new brother is enough for now."

Damian also laughs then continues his plans for Alex. "As for play, how about we put that foursome plan into action after breakfast? You and Mike seem to have got really close and you don't seem so scared of Bob."

"You were right, Sir, Bob really is a pussy cat under all that leather, though I expect when his claws are out he can be really mean, in the nicest possible way. Mike told me about some of the play they get into and it sounds like lots of fun."

"Oh, yes, boy."

Alex has finished polishing their boots and it is still some time until breakfast starts. Spotting that underneath all his excitement, Alex is really exhausted, Damian and suggests that he grabs some more sleep before breakfast.

"Actually I'm not that hungry, Sir, but I am tired. Is it OK if I skip breakfast and you wake me up when it's play time?"

"Of course, boy."

And with that, Alex goes back to bed and Damian gets dressed, admiring how well his boy had polished his boots. Fortunately, it's a dry day so they'll stay that way. He walks down to Bob and Mike's cabin and looks in. Bob and Mike are getting dressed but the other men in there are still fast asleep, a couple of them snoring loudly.

"I guess we lucked out," Damian thinks, realising that their cabin seems to be snorer free.

"How's Alex," Mike asks Damian as the three of them walk over to the social area for their first coffee of the day.

"He seems good, boy. I can't tell you how much I appreciate you helping him with all this."

"Yes, Mike told me about what happened last night" chips in Bob. "It sure beats any mind fuck I've ever come across. And Mike has a lot of experience of trans guys over on the west coast so it's fortunate he was around to explain things to Alex. Though from what he told me it seems like Alex and Rocky already had a good thing going between them so Mike didn't need to say much when they met."

Soon it is time for breakfast and Damian decides to look in on Alex beforehand. He's fast asleep so Damian leaves him.

After the previous night's play sessions, most of the men are still asleep in camp so the dining hall isn't very busy when Damian arrives. Paul and Rocky are already sitting with Bob and Mike at a table and Damian joins them.

"Good morning campers," he says as he sits down.

Rocky, barely awake, asks Damian how Alex is.

"He's getting some more sleep. He didn't sleep well when he finally got back to the cabin so I suggested he go back to bed after he and I had chatted this morning when I woke up. But he seemed really happy."

"I am too," Rocky replies. "But I'll feel a lot happier when I've had a nap after breakfast. I was hungry and needed some food first."

"Alex reminded me that you'd suggested we visit you both in Toronto some time," Damian tells Paul and Rocky. "Is that offer still on?"

"Sure is, Damian," Rocky replies immediately. "Whenever you can."

"I know it's short notice, but how about we make a pit stop on our way back to London? That way you and Alex will know you're going to see each other soon so you won't need to eat into your play time here. But do say if it's not convenient. You probably have a lot of catching up to do when you get back."

Rocky looks over at Paul. "What do you think?"

"That would be perfect," Paul replies. "Our business is pretty quiet at the moment what with it being just after the holidays and people not having much money. Plus they tend to get serious inking or piercings before the holidays so they can let them settle down before going back to work. So right after camp would be good."

"That's settled then," Damian replies. "When my assistant is awake back in London I'll get him to organise the flights. And if you let me have your address he can find us a hotel near where you live."

"Don't even think about that, Damian," Paul counters. "We live in big house on the edge of the city. And with our car and public transportation, there should be no problem getting around. How long can you stay for?"

"Maybe three days," Damian says. "I have some social and work meetings at the end of next week so we can't stay longer. But I'd really like to see Toronto and I'd also like to make use of your professional services. It's about time Alex got another piercing and I wonder if you'd do his septum."

"I'll be happy to do that, for free of course," says Paul.

"Yeah, you'd better do it," laughs Rocky. "Alex

never recovered from when we were kids and I used to torment him by trying to stick pins in him."

"Jeez," Paul says looking at Rocky. "I didn't know you started your piercing career so early."

Rocky laughs. "I guess I had hidden talents even then."

Damian turns to Bob. "How about we get our boys on the crosses this morning and do that double-hander you suggested?"

"Sounds good to me, Damian. Ok with you, boy?" Bob asks Mike.

"Absolutely, Sir. After the emotional roller coaster of last night I think I could do with something more physically stimulating."

When Damian gets back to his cabin Alex is showered and dressed in his whites, sitting on his bed talking to one of the other cabin occupants, who is dressed in a denim shirt and jeans and cowboy boots.

"Hey, Sir. I was just talking to Randy here. He's from Texas. Seems like your porno films are a great hit with him. In fact, he even mentioned seeing some guy in one of the interactive ones kicking the furniture. It's a small world."

Randy rises from Alex's bed and shakes Damian's hand. "Sorry we never got to chat yesterday. My flight got in late and you were all out playing or something when I went to bed. It's an honour to meet you."

"My pleasure, Randy," Damian says, noting Randy's name tag which says "Randy Hudson, Austin TX,

FlameTop".

Damian turns to Alex. "Are you awake enough to play, boy? "

"I could do with a coffee first, Sir, but after that I sure am."

"That works well, boy. We're meeting Bob and Mike down in Dungeon Three in an hour. But maybe you need to fill Mike in on how it went with Rocky first."

"That sounds like a good idea, Sir. I'll go find him now and meet you in an hour."

As Alex gets ready to leave, he spots some plain brown cartons on the shelf next to Randy's bed and a large box of cigars. "Interesting," he thinks to himself. "That's what I could smell on his clothes, cigar smoke. Quite nice, really."

Walking down the road from his cabin Alex bumps into Mike who had come to find him and they head back down together to get a coffee.

"How did it go?" he asks Alex.

"Pretty well," Alex tells him. "We talked for hours. Must have been 4am by the time I got to bed. It was really strange at first, talking to this person who both was and wasn't my sister. But once we started remembering things from our childhood and our old ribbing of each other surfaced it was like old times."

"Yes I noticed you two had a very strange sense of humour when you first met," Mike observes.

"And I hear you're going to stay with them in

Toronto on your way back home and Paul is going to pierce your nose."

Alex blushes slightly. He hadn't realised that Damian would share that last bit of information.

"It's good that we're going to see them again so soon. It means I can concentrate on enjoying what's here at camp. I feel like a kid in a candy store."

Alex senses that Mike has gone quiet.

"What's up?"

"Well, Alex, I guess I'm a bit jealous of you and Damian. Bob and I have a really great thing going but we're so far from each other. I wish he was closer so I could spend more time with him and serve him in everyday ways like you do with your Sir."

"Give it time, Mike," Alex says, sounding wiser than his age and experience would lead you to expect.

"Anyway, I hear the four of us are going to play this morning. I'm really looking forward to it."

"Me too," says Mike, rubbing Alex's thigh affectionately.

CHAPTER 27

Dungeon three is already filling up when Alex and Mike arrive. Bob and Damian are unpacking their toy bags around a pair of St Andrews crosses facing each other and joined at the top.

Alex and Mike look anxiously at what the other's Master had brought. Alex notices that Bob's floggers are longer and heavier than Damian's and they both spot some unusual impact toys poking out of the bag of the other's Master. But neither of them says anything, knowing that it's better not to spoil the surprise of what is in store for the other one.

The boys strip to their boots and are bound, outstretched to the crosses, facing each other. They look through the frames at each other and smile hesitantly but don't say much. They're each calming themselves for the intense experience they're about to have and wondering what it will be like to be topped by someone other than their own Master.

Bob and Damian stand behind their respective boys and start slowly, each teasing their own boy's back with a flogger. Bob's strokes increase in intensity faster than Damian's and Mike's eyes are screwed shut. Mike's grunts and groans give Alex an indication of what is in store for him when Bob is working on him. And as Damian changes to a heavier flogger, Alex too closes his eyes and sinks into his sub space to the soundtrack of the two floggers hitting their mark. He's unaware that Paul has walked by to watch for a while and decided to leave and see how Rocky is.

There is a pause in the flogging as Bob and Damian check in with their boys.

Standing close behind Alex, Damian asks Alex how he is doing.

"Just fine, Sir. It's good to have something physical to cope with after yesterday's emotional shock."

"You ready to be flogged by Bob?"

"Yes, Sir. I hope I can take it and don't embarrass you by wimping out."

"You'll be fine, boy. I'm sure."

Damian ruffles Alex's hair and the two men change sides.

Alex's body tenses. This is the first time he's been flogged by anyone apart from Damian and from what Mike has said, he fears there will be no warm up but intense impact from the start. So he's surprised when Bob starts slowly, even though he can tell that the flogger he's using is longer and heavier than the one Damian last used. He almost feels like Bob is kissing him.

Then Bob's strokes increase in their force, their solid impact resonating through his body, and he feels as he is being hammered into the frame.

Taking his lead from what Bob had told him about Mike and his capacity to take heavy stuff on his back, Damian picks up his rope flogger, which, despite its soft appearance, can be surprisingly painful. He starts by just dragging it across Mike's back, the rough fibres sensitising his skin even more. Then he starts hitting Mike with it, causing not a lot of sting but a great deal of thud.

Alex recognises the familiar sound of the rope flogger on Mike's back and starts to smile. But then his attention suddenly reverts to his own situation as Bob stops using the leather flogger and he feels something light but sharp and very stingy repeatedly hit his back. It feels like it's burning but in an unfamiliar pleasurable way. The frequency of the strokes increases until his back is on fire. Alex is in heaven, loving this new sensation.

When Bob and Damian decide to give the boys a break Alex opens his eyes to look at Mike. Mike has a huge grin on his face, even though there are tears streaming down it.

"How you doing, buddy?" Alex whispers to Mike.

"Brilliant, Alex. And you?"

"Amazing. I don't know what Bob just used on me but Sir should definitely get one."

Mike couldn't see what his Master had been using on Alex but can guess. "I think I know what it was. I'm sure he'll show you when we're done."

"OK boys, enough chat," Damian's orders them from behind Alex. And with that, he gags each of them with a knotted bandana. "I think the next bit might hurt a little."

Alex and Mike look into each other's eyes, their expressions a mixture of delight and anxiety.

Bob and Damian each have a cane in their hands

and they each give the boys ten strokes on their buttocks in turn, increasing the intensity with each round of the game as they move from one side of the joined crosses to the other. After maybe five rounds, both boys' arses are glowing and they are well off into their inner sub spaces, oblivious to anything but their own quivering bodies.

"You ready for more, boys?" Damian asks, laughing. As they can't make much noise, the boys just nod their heads in unison. "There will be ten more and then we'll be done," Damian tells them

Alex hears Damian whispering some advice to Bob and then feels the force of a dragon cane on his already sensitive cheeks. The dragon cane is denser and less flexible than a more common rattan cane so the energy penetrates deeper. Alex hasn't had the dragon used on him much since Damian used to use it for punishment, but this is different. It's not punishment. It's intense play and he's loving it more than he imagined he could.

He briefly wonders how Mike will cope with it, but this thought goes as the second stroke hits him.

Mike, who is surprised by how much he's enjoying the caning, is shocked by the first stroke of the dragon cane in Bob's hand. He's not sure he can take it. But he knows Alex can and he wants to learn and not embarrass Alex or his Master. So he calms his inner fears, stops fighting against what he is being subjected to, and sinks into the cross, preparing himself.

The dragon strokes still hurt like hell but Mike experiences a rush of endorphins taking him higher than he's ever been before. By the tenth stroke, his mind is still and he is all physical sensation and exhilaration.

Satisfied with their work, the two Masters lean close against their respective boys, stroking and kissing them and congratulating them on their performance. The gags are removed and the boys slowly open their eyes and look at each other. Their faces are drained but show how blissfully happy they are.

Alex closes his eyes again as Damian removes the restraints and turns his boy around to hold him.

"Thank you, Sir, that was beyond amazing," Alex whispers, finding it hard to speak. Behind him, he hears Mike trying to form words to show his appreciation to Bob but he seems even less able to say anything coherent.

When the boys have come down sufficiently they walk around a little and examine each other's backs and buttocks while Bob and Damian pack away their toys and admire their handiwork. Alex recognises the distinctive braided marks on Mike's back from the rope flogger and Mike spots the long scratches lined with bright red dots on Alex's back and knows exactly what caused them.

They go to hug each other and realise they need to be careful touching the other's now very sore body and they laugh a little.

"You OK, Mike?" Alex asks quietly.

"Sure am, Alex. Thank you for helping Sir and myself get to this."

Damian gives each of the boys a bottle of water and then returns to talking to Bob.

"Mike's a really good bottom to play with," Damian tells Bob. "And he took to the caning far better than I expected. Obviously his little chat with Alex helped."

"I think Mike probably saw it as a challenge," Bob says. "He didn't want to wimp out and that made him determined to ignore his fears and open himself up to it."

It is quite a few minutes before the boys start returning to the real world and, after thanking him for the play, Alex asks Bob what he was using on his back that stung so much.

Out of his toy bag Bob pulls a flogger made from strands of stiff plastic spaced along which are lots of small plastic spheres which caused the red dots on Alex's back.

"You like?" Bob asks him, beaming. "It's one of my favourite toys."

"Very much, Sir. It's very intense, like being burned, but in a pleasurable way."

"And it's good on other places as well, boy." And with that Bob grabs Alex's arm firmly and hits away at it with the plastic whip, leaving masses of bright red scratches and dots."

"Ouch," Alex laughs. "Ouch, ouch, ouch."

"I need to get one of those," Alex hears Damian say behind him.

"They have them in the store here in camp, Damian," Bob tells him.

Alex turns around to see Damian showing Mike his rope flogger.

"And I need to find out where to buy one of those," Bob says.

"Actually I made it," Damian tells him. "I just got a short length of thick hessian rope and some self-welding tape from a boating shop, folded the rope in half and used the tape to secure the two ends together to make a handle. You'd be surprised what a good source of great play toys boating shops are. And their rope is strong and much cheaper than what they sell in sex shops."

Bob isn't sure there is a boating shop in DC so Damian offers to make one for him and send it to him.

"Something for you to look forward to, boy," Bob tells Mike who barely hears, as he's still emerging from his inner reverie.

Some other men are waiting to use the crosses so they finish packing up and head out of the dungeon back to their cabins to drop off their toy bags.

Back in cabin 15 Alex is standing in front of the mirror in the bathroom admiring the marks on his back when he sees Damian come in behind him.

"How was that, boy?"

"That was amazing, Sir. And I didn't even freak out

when you started using the dragon on me. I've always feared that but somehow the setting was right and my mind was in the right place."

"I told you this place was special, boy. There are so many things that make it have that effect on people. It's the relaxed supportive atmosphere, the remote secure location and the fact that you meet such wonderful, genuinely friendly, supportive people.

"And you didn't seem to have any problem being flogged by Bob," Damian continues. "It's almost as if you forgot it was someone other than me."

"Well you were there, Sir, which helped a lot. And I'd met him and got to know him first. But I think I'm over that hurdle now."

"And what about seeing me play with someone else?"

"I felt really good about it and I've only just understood why, Sir. You are such a good Master and so skilled and caring that I realise it's selfish of me to prevent other boys experiencing that.

"I really feel close to Mike so I was truly happy for both of you and got a big thrill from being there when you played with him."

"Damn, boy. I've been training you to be a good slave and you're turning into a saint as well."

They both fall about laughing.

"So it's OK if I go play with someone else this afternoon, boy?"

"Yes, Sir, you should."

Damian slaps Alex playfully but hard on his bare

red buttocks. "Giving the orders now, boy?"

"Sorry, Sir," Alex says, though he doesn't really mean it.

Damian is happy because he really did want his boy to voice his permission for him to play with other men at the camp. "That's my afternoon sorted then, boy. What about yours?"

"Well I'll see if Mike's at lunch and maybe spend the afternoon wandering around the dungeons with him and see who's doing what, maybe check out the workshops. And if I see you playing with someone else and it upsets me at all then I can always talk to Mike about it.

"After this morning I can't see me wanting to play with anyone this afternoon anyway," Alex continues. "But if I see someone doing something I like, I'll try to remember who it is and check in with you about it for later on. I'll take my run book with me and make a note of their name in case I forget."

"You know, boy, if a few of months ago someone had told you that you'd be planning ahead, giving advice to other people and making new close friends in no time at all, you'd have thought they were crazier than you were. You've done so well to turn your life around."

"Sir, you led, and like a little puppy dog on a leash I just followed."

They both laugh and Damian gives Alex a deep kiss. "You know it was your puppy-dog eyes that first caught my attention when I saw you on cam that day we first chatted?"

"No I didn't, Sir."

"It's how I spotted Rocky in the dining room yesterday. They're the same."

"Well I never," says Alex.

CHAPTER 28

After lunch, Alex and Mike sit on the grassy slope in the centre of the campground discussing that morning's play.

"You know, Mike, for all that this morning was really intense fun, the bit I got the most pleasure from was doing it with you," Alex starts off. "When we were tied up there being flogged by our own and each other's Masters, I got the biggest thrill from looking at your face through the frame and seeing your expression as you were being hit."

Mike smiles. "I think I had my eyes closed much of the time, so I wasn't watching you that much, Alex. But I knew you were there with me and that made me feel really safe and relaxed, especially when the caning started. What sort of thrill?"

Alex blushes a little. "Maybe I'm becoming a bit of a top," he reveals with a laugh. "My cock got really excited in its cage seeing you all tied up tight and having to take what our Sirs were doing to you."

Mike laughs. "Not that trying to get hard seems to do you any good, Alex. What's it like being locked up in a chastity device? I've never tried one."

Alex explains a bit more about his previous addictive masturbation habit and how unsatisfying it was. "The main thing is that I can't cum whenever I want. Sir controls when that happens. So all the horniness just stores up. I suppose it means I get fewer, better orgasms."

Mike has more questions. "But what does it feel like wearing it? Doesn't it hurt when you try to get hard? What about pissing?"

"Well pissing is the easy bit. You just need to sit down or it goes everywhere. As for getting an erection, at first my cock did try to get properly hard, and this caused the cage to move forward and the cock ring pulled badly on my balls. So for the first week after I was locked in this cage I woke up often in the night with ball pain. Now it doesn't try to get that hard. I just get a delicious feeling of my cock being squeezed tight in its cage."

"Doesn't that mean you can't get hard easily when it's off?" puzzles Mike.

"Not at all," explains Alex. "Sir just takes his time coaxing it back to full size. He edges me for ages so by the end I'm really hard and desperate to cum. And when I do it's glorious. Mind you there's usually loads of electro stuff and nipple clamps and stuff going on at the same time so the actual orgasm is buried somewhere as my whole body sort of shudders."

"Wow," says Mike. "I wonder if my Sir would keep me locked up for a while. I expect it's not easy to do long-distance."

"Well maybe he could lock you up just when you're together, though lots of guys do have online keyholders. You two could start here at camp if he has a chastity device. Do either of you have one?"

"I don't, and I don't think Sir does either."

As they're talking, they see Bob approaching, holding a box in his hand. "Hey boys, how you getting on?"

The boys stand up at attention. "Good here, Sir," Mike tells his Master. "We were just discussing Alex's chastity cage."

"Well there's a coincidence, boy. I just bought one for you from the store here and came to find you. I really like the way that cage fits on Alex. In fact it's been getting me hard thinking about locking one on you. Let's go back to our cabin so I can lock you in it. Want to come help me Alex? You've probably got a few tips for me as I haven't done this before."

"I'd love to, Sir," Alex replies, feeling his dick twitch in its cage, and again priding himself at knowing something that Bob doesn't.

"Is that OK with you, Mike, that I come along?"

"Sure is Alex, I'd like that."

As they're moving off Alex notices a large bulge in Mike's tight black leather shorts. "I hope Bob bought a strong cage," he thinks, "because that is going to be a tough monster to tame."

Back at Bob and Mike's cabin Bob opens the box. Inside it is a chastity cage similar to Alex's but made of hard black resin rather than metal. There are a number of different sized cock rings, a cock tube and a padlock.

Mike gets undressed and stands with his hands behind his back while Bob works out how the device fits together. Mike's erection hasn't subsided.

"Sir," Alex says to Bob. "Mike's cock isn't going to fit in its present state and the more he thinks about being locked the longer it's going to stay hard."

"What do we do then, boy?" Bob asks Alex.

"I'll be right back, Sir," Alex tells him, and leaves the cabin, returning a few minutes later with a paper cup filled with ice.

He fetches Mike's damp face cloth from the cabin's bathroom. "See, Sir, all we need do is cool it down," he says as he puts the ice inside the face cloth and wraps it around Mike's cock and holds it there firmly with his hand causing Mike to squirm.

Some minutes later Mike's erection has subsided and Bob tries out the different-sized cock rings.

"You need the one that is just a snug fit, Sir," Alex tells Bob. "If it's too tight he'll end up with blue balls."

"What's that?" Bob asks.

"It's when there's too little blood getting in there, Sir. And if you make it too loose then the cage will slide down. You should just be able to slide a finger underneath the cock ring when it's on."

Bob fits the cock ring with the best fit, applies some lube to Mike's dick and slides the cage onto it. When he's happy it's all assembled correctly he snaps the padlock shut.

Mike looks down and realises that not only can he now not get hard or touch his cock, he can't even see it any more through the solid black cage. His cock tries to grow and he feels the hard resin tube constricting it which excites him even more.

Bob strokes Mike's balls with his hand, increasing Mike's excitement and frustration.

To take his mind off things Mike looks around and notices some numbered plastic locks laying on the bed with the rest of the packaging.

"What are those for?" he asks.

Alex explains. "They're so you can wear the cage if you need to go through metal detectors, for example when flying or going to government buildings. And they're numbered so a keyholder can check that the locked guy hasn't taken off the one that he put on."

"Well there's an idea, boy," Bob tells Mike. "I can send you home in this and you can show me on cam that it's still there."

Mike groans with pleasure. He's always regretted that Bob didn't control him more and now, inspired by Alex, that is going to happen.

"I'd like that very much, Sir," Mike says, beaming with delight.

Alex is standing back looking at the two smiling men. He's proud that what he learned from his own experiences has been useful and reckons that Damian will be proud of him. He can't wait to tell him.

"Do you know where my Sir is?" Alex asks Bob.

"Actually I do," he replies. "He was going to the chastity workshop which is about to start in ten minutes. Maybe we should all go over there and Damian and I can show off our locked boys."

"Sounds good to me," Alex replies.

"I'd like that too, Sir," Mike adds.

A few minutes later, they find the space where the chastity workshop is just starting. The bondage furniture has been pushed to one side and there is a circle of chairs. Damian is already there and Alex sits on the floor between his feet. Mike does the same when Bob sits down.

Alex is surprised at how many men are in the room, maybe 40, and some of them have already started undressing to show off their chastity devices. There are some full belts like the one he wore originally and a couple of guys are locked in what look like steel jock straps with solid metal covering both their cock and their balls.

The leader of the workshop, Thomas, welcomes everyone and asks for a show of hands for those who are currently locked and those who are keyholders. About 15 of the men are currently locked and slightly fewer are keyholders.

Damian raises his eyebrows when Mike puts his hand up as being locked and Bob as a keyholder.

"I didn't know that, boy," Damian whispers to Alex. "Mike wasn't locked when we played this morning."

"It's just happened, Sir," Alex replies with a smile. "I think we inspired them and I helped Bob lock Mike up."

Damian ruffles Alex's hair. "Well done, boy."

Thomas suggests a show and tell to start with. He asks everyone who is locked to walk around the room to show off their device, explain what it is and what they experience being locked.

Damian gives Alex a nudge and he stands up and does the first turn. The PA lock gets lots of appreciative looks and a couple of men play with it as Alex passes them, explaining as he walks around how he came to be locked and how comfortable the device is.

When Alex sits back down on the floor Damian says briefly to the meeting, "I just want to say that as a way of teaching a boy to be submissive and obedient you can't beat a good chastity device."

Eventually it comes to Mike's turn and he takes off his shorts to show off his new chastity device.

"I've only been in this a few minutes," he tells the others. "And from what you guys have been saying I think I'm in for an exciting and frustrating time."

The discussion continues for well over the allotted hour, with some of it devoted to keyholders sharing their experiences. There's lots of practical advice shared and even some warnings about devices to avoid. A few guys are not locked but interested in trying chastity and, from what Alex could tell, a couple of them manage to pair up with would-be keyholders.

After the workshop Damian and Bob and their boys chat outside.

"Well done," Damian tells Bob. "And you'll have a fun time ahead of you, boy, as I'm sure Alex has told you," he says to Mike.

Mike is already feeling the cage doing its job. "I already am, Sir," Mike replies grabbing the cage through his shorts.

Damian looks at his watch. "I have a play date shortly but what do you say we come back here after dinner. I have some ideas for how the four of us can have some more fun together. I'll tell you about them as we walk, Bob."

The other three agree and Bob and Damian walk off leaving their boys to enjoy the next few hours on their own.

CHAPTER 29

Alex and Mike walk down to the dungeons where Alex spots Graham the Tape Master starting a mummification scene. Stacked up on the floor are rolls of clear plastic film and silver tape. Alex doesn't recognise his subject but sees his nametag on the table and his name is Harry. He is naked and standing on the floor and Graham is wrapping him up in the clear plastic film like a sandwich. He sees the boys watching and invites them over.

Harry smiles at the extra attention he's going to get.

"Want to give me a hand, boys?" he asks. They agree and Graham asks them to hold Harry steady as he might find it difficult to stand once the film gets down to his legs and feet.

Soon Harry's body is totally enclosed in the clear film from head to toe with holes for him to breathe through and for his nipples, cock and balls.

As Alex and Mike hold Harry, Graham starts applying strips of the silver tape over the film until he is totally covered with only his nipples, cock, and balls visible, his cock quite erect.

"Are you guys strong?" Graham asks them.

"We're probably strong enough," Alex replies.

"OK, help me get him on the table."

The three men tilt Harry back and lift him onto the bondage table, sliding him around until he is in the centre. Graham produces some industrial ear defenders from his toy bag and puts them over Harry's ears to increase his isolation. He then adds some clamps to Harry's nipples and then moves the boys away from the table so the three of them can talk without disturbing him.

"What do you think, boys?"

"I'm not sure I'd like that," Mike answers first. "I'm a bit claustrophobic. Can't even cope with hoods."

"That's a shame, boy. But panic attacks aren't good. And what about you, Alex?"

"It looks really interesting. My Sir puts me in a sleepsack sometimes but it would be interesting to find out how different that feels. Can I try it some time?"

Alex realises he has just asked to play with someone other than Damian and mentally pats himself on the back for his courage.

"I'd like that very much, boy. How about late tomorrow morning?"

"That sounds good, Sir, but I need to check it's OK with my Master first."

"OK, let me know at dinner tonight."

Graham returns to Harry and pulls and twists the nipple clamps for a while, making Harry's erection grow even more. Then he gets some lube from his toy bag, which he rubs on Harry's cock, slowly stroking him but not letting him cum. Alex is familiar with this from his edge play with Damian but it is new to Mike.

"Gosh that must be so frustrating," Mike whispers

to Alex, his own cock straining in its cage.

Alex tells Mike that Damian can keep him on edge like that for hours and Mike goes light-headed at the thought. "There's some tricks I hope my Sir doesn't pick up here," he laughs quietly.

Alex and Mike decide to see what else is going on in the dungeon, making repeated returns to Graham's table to find that Harry is still being edged. Graham is now running a sharp spikey pinwheel up and down Harry's cock and Harry is moaning loudly and trying to wriggle but with little effect.

As they are about to move on Graham silently indicates for them to stay and watch. He pulls a tube of Icy Hot from his bag and spreads some over Harry's cock. Alex knows what this feels like and his own cock desperately tries to grow.

Harry's moans get louder as Graham massages the cream in further, stroking faster at times and then slower and then pausing for a while. Alex knows that Harry is desperate to cum and wonders if Graham will let him. His question is soon answered as Harry screams and his cock finally explodes, sending streams of cum all over the silver tape.

Graham removes the ear defenders and whispers into Harry's ear. "Well done."

Alex and Mike smile at each other and Graham comes over to talk to them, thinking Harry should be left to calm down a bit before being released.

"What do you think, boys?"

"Gosh, that looks so frustrating," says Mike. "It

certainly got me excited."

"Me too, Sir," adds Alex. "I hope I have permission to try it with you tomorrow, well at least the mummification part. I doubt my Sir would let me be unlocked and allowed to cum. I had an orgasm not so long ago and Sir likes to let things build up for a month or more before I have another one."

"A month?" Mike exclaims. "I don't think I've gone more than a few days without cumming. What have I got myself into?"

"Even more excitement, Mike," Alex tells him. "Being locked makes you less selfish and you focus more on pleasing others."

"But don't you feel horny all the time?"

"At first I did, but now it goes in cycles. Of course, being here with all these sexy men and exciting play totally disrupts things. But I know that when we're back home with our everyday routine things will settle down again."

Mike doesn't feel particularly reassured. "I find that hard to believe. But with my Sir holding the key, I guess I won't have any choice but to find out for myself. And if he changes the metal padlock for a plastic one before I fly home then it could be a while before I see my dick again."

"Don't worry, Mike. When we're both back home, we can chat online and share our frustrations and help each other out. And Sir introduced me to a great online chastity community you should join. It's full of locked guys sounding off about how frustrated they are. You'll enjoy it."

Over Mike's shoulder, Alex sees Rocky enter the dungeon followed by Damian and he wonders if this is the play date that Damian mentioned. He doesn't feel happy with Damian playing with Rocky. It feels a bit too close to home.

But then Damian and Rocky go their separate ways. Rocky spots Alex and starts walking towards him while Damian puts his toy bag down next to one of the paddling horses where another man is waiting.

"Phew" thinks Alex feeling very relieved but deciding nonetheless that he doesn't want to see Damian playing with the man.

As Rocky comes towards them, Alex turns to Mike and Graham.

"Sorry guys," he says, "I have some family stuff to do." And he walks away.

Mike and Graham look over and to where Rocky is approaching. "Is that Alex's brother?" Graham asks Mike, noticing the similarity between them.

"It is now," Mike says, watching Alex lead Rocky out of the dungeon.

Graham looks puzzled and Mike offers to help him unwrap Harry while he explains.

Outside the dungeon, Alex explains to Rocky why he left the dungeon.

"Sorry for hustling you out, sis, but my Sir is about to start playing with someone and I'm not sure I want to watch."

"That's OK, Alex, it's probably new to you. I sometimes like watching Paul play with others and seeing what he enjoys that maybe he hasn't tried with me. Are you having fun?"

"Oh, yes," Alex replies. "Far more than I imagined."

"And are you over the shock of meeting me again? We haven't spoken since last night. It must have been strange discovering I've now become the man I always knew I was inside when we were growing up together."

"It was at first," Alex replies. "But once we started talking I got over it and I'm really happy to have found you again. And you're obviously much happier now than you used to be. And Paul seems like fun."

"He is. We have a great relationship both living together and working together. Paul also came from a very controlling strait-laced family and for both of us our tattoos and piercings are a way of taking control of our bodies and shaping our lives as we want, not as our parents wanted."

Alex hadn't noticed before, but Rocky has some nipple rings clearly showing through his t-shirt. They were obviously hidden under the masses of pegs he had been sporting on his chest when Alex first saw him.

"What are you doing now?" Alex asks Rocky.

"I was just going to watch some play in the dungeon," he replies. "Paul and I played earlier and I'm still coming down."

"That's OK. We can chat more tomorrow before breakfast. Actually, maybe you can keep an eye on what my Sir is doing. I don't want to watch, but I'm sure interested at what he's going to do with that man."

Rocky laughs. "I'll be your spy, little brother. I'll tell you all tomorrow."

And Rocky gives Alex a big hug before returning to the dungeon while Alex wanders off to see what else is going on.

CHAPTER 30

At dinner later on, Alex remembers he needs to ask Damian if he can be mummified by Graham in the morning. But he decides to wait until they are alone. He's not sure how he would feel if Damian refused in front of Bob and Mike.

As he's thinking about this, he looks over towards the entrance to the dining hall and sees a man being manhandled into the room. He's in a strait jacket and leg irons, a leather muzzle locked onto his head and covering his mouth,

"What's going on there?" Alex asks Bob.

"Oh that's the hit squad. They get tipped off about guys who want to be kidnapped or put into restraints unexpectedly or humiliated in public. And one of their favourite activities is to bring their captives in here for everyone to see. The poor, or should that be lucky, victim has to go hungry and watch everyone else have their dinner."

"How long do they stay in bondage like that," asks Alex who hasn't seen anything like this before.

"Oh, some guys spend 24 hours like that. There's a prison cell inside one of the remote cabins and they're kept chained up there in isolation."

"Don't they get to eat or drink at all?" asks Alex who is now intrigued.

"They're given water, maybe in a dog bowl as they don't always have the muzzle on," Bob replies.

Alex asks what seems to him to be an obvious

question. "And what about going to the toilet?"

"They get put in a heavy-duty diaper so they don't need to, Alex."

Alex's cock stirs in its cage at the thought of long-term bondage and he wonders if Damian is taking mental notes.

"You know, boy," Damian tells Alex, "that there's facilities around the US where guys can pay to be held prisoner for days on end. Sometimes it's just cell holding. Other times it's an asylum scene and they're locked in padded cells in strait jackets. Some guys even go in for interrogation or chain gang scenes."

"I sure have a lot more to learn," Alex comments.

"And to experience, boy," Damian tells him, hatching another idea for Alex's entertainment at the camp.

As Damian and Alex walk back to their cabin after dinner to get ready for that evening's foursome, Alex asks Damian if he can play with Graham the next day and Damian readily agrees. He wants Alex out of the way so he can organise a more intense scene for him.

Not long afterwards Alex, Damian, Bob and Mike are back in the enclosure where the chastity workshop had been held earlier in the day but is now being used for play.

Bob and Damian move one of the available bondage tables so it is pointing out from a vacant St Andrews cross attached to some beams.

Alex and Mike smile at each other because they

know this means that they will both be tied up. Alex isn't sure what will happen when they are and tries to guess from the arrangement of the equipment. He's also eyeing up Damian slightly strangely, wondering what sort of play he got up to with the other man.

But his thoughts are interrupted when Damian addresses Mike and himself.

"OK, boys," Damian orders, "strip off to your boots and get on your knees, hands behind your backs."

The boys comply and Bob and Damian take their cocks out of their pants and stand in front of their respective boys so they can suck on them for a while.

Alex loves having Damian's cock in his mouth and the excitement makes his cock try to grow in its cage. He guesses the same thing is happening to Mike for whom servicing his Master while locked is a new experience.

When Bob and Damian are satisfied, Alex is told to stay where he is while Mike is attached to the cross, face out, and bandana-gagged. From here he will have a good view of what is happening on the table.

The bondage table top is made of wooden slats and Damian uses lengths of rope to lace Alex down to it, face up, with his head at the cross end. The rope is tight enough to make sure Alex can't escape but loose enough that he can wriggle a bit. Alex looks up and sees Mike above and just behind him looking down at him and trying to smile despite having a gag in his mouth, his chastity cage not far from Alex's face. Alex too is gagged with one of Damian's bandanas.

"OK, Bob," Damian says, "let's get started."

Alex realises that Damian and Bob have this scene carefully planned out and he is intrigued.

Bob puts some nipple clamps joined with a chain onto Mike, and Damian does the same with Alex. Damian is using the sharp ones and Alex winces as they bite in. From his toy bag Damian produces some elastic cord which he uses to attach the two chains together, maintaining some tension between them. If either boy moves at all they will both suffer.

Being a bit of a sadist Damian starts to tickle Alex which makes him squirm causing his own and Mike's nipple clamps to be pulled about.

"That's mean, Damian," Bob laughs. "But not mean enough." And with that he starts tickling Mike, so the two boys are both laughing and wriggling around, tormenting their own and each other's nipples.

Bob then produces a strange shaped vibrator from his bag which seems to be designed to sit around Mike's chastity cage. As he turns it on Mike groans as the sensations cause his cock to try to grow. It doesn't take long before Alex sees a few drops of pre-cum forming on the end of Mike's chastity tube and he recognises what Mike is experiencing as moans of frustrated pleasure emerge through his gag.

"Now for you, boy, we have something extra

special as you've been so good these past couple of days," Damian tells Alex.

Mike's eyes widen as he watches Damian unlock and remove Alex's chastity cage.

Alex's cock springs into life. For all that he hates the sharp nipple clamps, he can't stop himself being turned on by them.

Damian produces some lube and starts stroking Alex's cock. He does it slowly with not very much pressure so Alex doesn't get close to cumming too quickly.

Alex thinks back to the mummification scene he and Mike had helped with that day and wonders whether Damian will allow him to cum.

After a few minutes, Damian stops edging Alex and Bob takes over. He too can sense when Alex is getting close to cumming and abruptly takes his hand off Alex's cock, leaving it bobbing around in the air, desperate for more attention.

"You know, boy, it's another two hours until dinner, and with two of us doing this, and a few other men here who might like to help, we're not going to get tired.," Damian tells Alex, with an evil grin on his face.

Alex moans and looks up at Mike whose eyes are closed as he tries to cope with the frustration of his own cock being stimulated and denied pleasure at the same time by the vibrator on his cock cage.

Soon, some of the other men in the room have gathered around and are each taking their turn edging Alex.

Alex wonders whether these men might not be as skilled as Damian and might accidentally take him over the edge but Damian is wise to this.

"Of course, I don't want any of these helpers to go too far and make you cum, boy. So I've told them that they can join in on the understanding that if they allow you to cum they'll get five strokes of my dragon cane on their thighs. And I don't care if they think they're tops."

"Damn," thinks Alex. "Sir sure knows how to make things last."

The helpers are more cautious with their stroking of Alex's cock, which doesn't help matters as sometimes it goes soft, leaving him even further away from possibly cumming than before.

On the cross, Mike opens his eyes and watches Alex being edged. The vibrator is still causing him great frustration and as his body moves around trying to cope, he pulls on the connected nipple clamps which excites him further.

He looks down at Alex and thinks about how much he has to be grateful to his new friend for and how much Alex deserves to be allowed to cum. But he also knows that Damian is wonderfully evil and probably won't allow this to happen.

As for himself, Mike knows that he has only just started his chastity regime and so doesn't expect Bob to let him cum at all. But he sure is enjoying the constant arousal he's in.

Dinner time is approaching and Alex is almost out of his mind with the constant edging and torment of his nipples. And he still isn't sure whether Damian will let him cum. On the one hand, he hopes he will. But on the other hand, if Damian just locks him up again, Alex knows that he will enjoy the extreme horniness that is bound to follow.

Bob removes the vibrator from Mike's chastity cage and removes the elastic cord from Mike's nipple clamp chain, handing it to Damian who pulls it back and forth, exciting Alex's nipples even more.

Then Bob removes the clamps from Mike's nipples and Mike screams through his gag as the blood rushes back into them. And he screams further as Bob starts massaging them with his muscular fingers.

Alex watches, feeling both sorry for his friend and highly excited by seeing him being tormented. Maybe all that jacking off to porn he used to do turned him into a voyeur, he wonders.

But his attention sharply returns to Damian who has pulled the elastic cord tightly away from Alex's nipples and tied it tight around Alex's cock and balls. The constricting elastic cock ring makes Alex's cock even harder and as Damian methodically strokes Alex's cock, his nipples are pulled at the same time.

Alex closes his eyes sinking into the intensity of what he is experiencing. Damian strokes get firmer and longer until Alex's cock is almost ready to explode, and then Damian abruptly stops.

"That's it, boy. No cumming for you today," Damian tells Alex with an evil grin on his face. And he unties the elastic cord from around his boy's cock and balls but leaves it attached to the nipple clamps.

Alex sinks back onto the table, frustrated that he didn't get to cum but happy that Damian remained in control.

"Damn, boy, I think I'm the one who needs to cum," Damian laughs, rubbing his crotch where his erection is clearly visible. "And it's just tough if you thought that you would."

Alex lets out a contended sigh.

After a while, Alex's cock has finally gone soft and Damian locks him back in his chastity cage. He releases Alex from his bondage and orders him to turn around on the table so his head is hanging over the edge furthest from the cross. Bob has left Mike bound to the cross so he can watch.

Alex knows what is coming next and opens his mouth so Damian can fuck his throat. To encourage Alex and arouse himself more, Damian fastens the free end of the elastic cord around his waist so that the clamps are tugged as he thrusts in and out of Alex's mouth, Alex's groans spurring him on until he finally cums.

While this is going on Bob whispers to Mike. "I think you'd like a bit of that too, boy."

"Yes please, Sir," Mike mumbles through his gag.

When Damian has removed the clamps from Alex's nipples and massaged them back into shape, Bob releases Mike from the cross and has him lay on the table the same way that Alex had so Mike can suck him off, returning the chain-linked clamps to Mike's nipples so he has something to hold onto.

Finally, Bob and Damian are spent and their boys, horny as hell from their play, are getting dressed.

"Jeez, Alex, I don't know how you didn't explode down there when you were being edged," Mike tells him.

"I'm used to it. Sir is very skilled at edging. And it always leaves me extremely horny afterwards."

"Well I thought my cage was going to split open," replies Mike.

Alex laughs. "That cage you're wearing is a new design and I think it's much stronger than earlier plastic ones. So that's not gonna happen."

Across the room, Bob and Damian are talking quietly so as not to disturb the others playing nearby. "You know, I'm gonna miss playing with you and the boys when camp is over," Bob tells Damian.

"Not as much as I think the boys will miss each other," Damian replies, looking over at Alex and Mike.

Damian returns to Alex. "You glad you didn't get to cum, boy?" he asks.

"I'm not sure, Sir. I was desperate to cum after all that edging. And I got extra excitement from seeing Mike getting so turned on by it all. If I had cum I think I would have shot right over my head and onto him. But I wasn't surprised that you didn't let me."

"Well I certainly enjoyed it, boy. And sometimes you need a reminder that I'm still in control of you and your orgasms, even if you are starting to be a bit of a top as well."

"Yes, Sir, understood," Alex replies. "You'll always be in charge, Sir."

"And that's what keeps us both very happy, boy," Damian tells him as he ruffles his hair.

CHAPTER 31

As they had agreed, Rocky and Alex meet up before breakfast the next day in the social area. There are not many people around at 7am and they grab a coffee and sit by the open fire as it's still a bit chilly.

"So what did Sir and that guy get up to when you went back into the dungeon yesterday afternoon?" Alex eagerly asks Rocky.

"It was really heavy and I don't know how the bottom guy coped. I think his name is Ian. Damian strapped him down really tight over the horse and gagged him and then started hitting his arse. Damian used some really solid leather and wooden paddles and by the end Ian's buttocks were dark red, almost black. It drew quite a crowd. And Ian was in floods of tears. He had to be helped up off the horse and Damian spent a lot of time comforting him afterwards."

Alex is glad he didn't watch. Not because he felt jealous, but because he couldn't imagine himself taking that sort of a beating. And with Damian being the top in the scene, he felt he was bound to imagine Damian doing the same to him.

"Apart from here at camp where Sir and I have played with Bob and Mike I haven't seen him play with anyone else. I know I need to at some point, but maybe for now just hearing about it is a good first step."

"You should talk to Damian about it, Alex. You'll

find things easier if you don't bottle stuff up. Paul taught me that early on. He has a good line on this. If you see your partner doing something you want then you should ask for it. And if you don't want it then you shouldn't get in their way."

"That's very good advice, Rocky. In fact, Sir and I do talk a lot. He has this scary ability to guess what I'm thinking and feeling. So he usually raises things before I've had the courage to."

As they're talking, Ian walks into the social area, grabs a coffee and comes to sit by the fire as well.

Rocky decides to break the ice to help Alex out and introduces himself and Alex.

"I'm Rocky and this is my brother Alex. He's Damian's boy,"

As Ian starts to move away, thinking he's possibly intruding on a family discussion, Rocky keeps the conversation going.

"I saw what Damian was doing with you yesterday," Rocky tells Ian. "It looked pretty hard core."

"It was a real challenge. Want to see the results?"

Rocky glances over at Alex who is looking very nervous and he decides that his brother should face things rather than avoid them. "Yes please."

Ian lowers his shorts and turns around. His buttocks are just one big mass of black bruises.

"Wow, that's impressive," Rocky says noticing that Alex has gone a bit pale.

"Has Damian ever done this to you?" Ian asks Alex, which doesn't help.

"No he hasn't, and I think I'm glad he hasn't," Alex replies looking a bit scared at the extent of Ian's bruising. "It's taken me this long to cope with his serious canings."

"Yes I saw him in action with his cane when you and that other boy were tied up together. That's what prompted me to ask if I could play with him."

Alex remembers the good feelings he had about Damian caning Mike in that scene and tries to feel the same way about him playing with Ian but it's still proving difficult.

"Alex, I just want to thank you for sharing your Master with me. He's a very sexy man and you're very lucky to have each other," Ian tells him. "It's good that he feels able to explore play activities with men like me that perhaps he doesn't feel appropriate for you."

Alex manages half a smile. "I'm still learning to accept that I have to share him some times."

"I don't get to play very often so camp is the one time I get to try things out," Ian replies. "Whereas you have him whenever you want."

Alex relaxes a little and asks Ian how he managed to cope with the paddling.

"I set myself challenges. For example, last year at camp I wanted to be put in an isolation cell in a strait jacket for as long as possible. And the year before I was determined to try needle play."

Alex looks at Rocky when needle play is mentioned and wonders whether his piercing equipment gets used for more recreational purposes.

Ian continues. "This year I wanted to get the heaviest beating I could, just to prove to myself that I could take it. It wasn't easy, but I'm the sort of guy who always follows through with his promises, even to myself.

"It's devising and looking forward to those scenes and wanking over the memories of previous ones that keep me going through the year. I come from Hicksville Nowhereland so playing here is about the only heavy sex I get and I try to get the most out of it."

Alex feels proud to be so close and special to Damian and realises even more that he needs to feel good about sharing him with men less fortunate than himself.

The men around them are starting to move and the three of them realise breakfast is starting so they walk to the dining hall, grab their food and sit together. Ian wants to find out more about what it's like to be at the camp with your brother.

Just as Alex is starting, Damian joins them, kissing Alex on the head and giving Rocky and Ian an affectionate rub on theirs.

"How are you this morning?" Damian asks Ian.

"Very sore, Sir, as you'd expect. Thank you for helping me through it."

"You're very welcome, boy. I see you've met my boy Alex and his brother Rocky."

"Yes I was just asking them about that. Talking of

families, I really admire your relationship with Alex. It seems like you have a fine, open, trusting thing going between you. Most guys would get jealous if they saw their partner playing with someone else."

Damian realises that Ian hadn't spotted, as he had, that Alex left the dungeon when they started playing and decides that he should discuss how Alex felt about it when they are alone.

"Well it wasn't easy at first as Alex had a lot to learn. But he picked things up fast and has even started being a bit of a top. And he's generous enough to share me with other men at times."

"Before breakfast, Ian was showing Alex and myself his bruises," Rocky chimes in. "They're pretty serious. I'm very impressed."

"Oh, I had the easy bit," Damian laughs. "Ian was the one who set himself the challenge and stuck with it. My sore arm must be nothing like how sore Ian's arse is. Those bruises will take weeks to go away."

"Yeah," laughs Ian. "It's a good job I don't have a partner and live alone or they'd call the medics to have me locked away as insane."

After breakfast Damian tells Alex he wants to talk to Ian more to discuss their play and Rocky goes to find Paul. There's no sign of Bob or Mike, so Alex decides to check out what's happening in the dungeons.

In Dungeon One he sees some activity starting over in the wax area. A man is strapped face up to the table, naked apart from a blindfold, and he recognises the top as Randy from Texas who is in his own cabin.

"Hey, Alex, want to see what I'm doing?"

"Yes, please, Randy."

"Now this here is Simon and it's his birthday today so I'm making him a special cake with lots of candles. Except the cake is him so he's gonna have to take all the candles.

"Tell Alex how old are you today, Simon."

"43."

Randy points to a brown carton on the ground full of white paraffin wax night light candles.

"There's fifty in there," Randy tells Alex. "So I have a few spares in case some of them are faulty. Want to help?"

Alex has discovered that he likes being a helper so he readily agrees, the mystery of the carton by Randy's bed now solved.

"This is what you do," Randy tells him. "Get one of those night lights and take it out of the metal foil container. You'll see that the wick is stuck into a small metal disc underneath. Pull the disk off the wick and put the two metal parts in that rubbish bag. Then put the wick back through the hole in the candle and give it to me. Then do another one."

"Why do you take the metal off," Alex asks.

"Because if I didn't, the heat from the burning wick would transmit straight through the conductive metal into his skin and he'd get serious burns which might need a doctor. This way there's less direct heat from the burning wick."

As Alex disassembles and then reassembles each candle, Randy places it on Simon's body and then lights it. He waits until a bit of wax has melted, then moves the candle around until the molten wax drips down around the wick in the centre of the candle and solidifies, helping the candle stay in place.

Soon Simon is covered with 43 candles and his body is lighting up the dungeon.

"Now comes the fun part," Randy tells Alex mischievously. He pulls two pinwheels covered in sharp needle-like spikes out of his bag and runs them up and down Simon's body. As Simon wriggles and laughs, the molten wax spills out from the candles and heats up his skin causing him to wriggle even more.

Simon is laughing at the perpetual pain machine he's been turned into.

Randy starts tickling Simon around his middle and indicates to Alex that he should do the same with Simon's feet. Simon is alternately laughing hysterically and shouting "Ouch" as his movements cause fresh puddles of hot wax to spill out from the candles and land on his body.

Randy beckons to a couple of other men to come over and help them. "Make a wish, Simon, as we're going to blow out all the candles."

"I wish it wasn't going to hurt so much," Simon jokes.

At Randy's prompting they blow out the candles in

one go, their combined breath causing lots of hot wax to spill out of the candles making Simon's body tense up and try to free itself from the table.

"Almost done, birthday boy," Randy tells Simon as he removes the candles and throws them into bucket of water to make sure they're properly extinguished.

He reaches into his bag again and produces four stiff pet grooming brushes, one for each of his own hands and one for each of Alex's hands.

"We can't let you go back to your cabin all covered in wax, Simon. The camp management will complain."

"Oh, no," groans Simon with a smile on his face. "I think I know what's going to happen next."

Alex follows Randy's lead and uses the brushes to scrub all the wax off Simon's body, the bristles further punishing his already sensitive skin. As Simon is quite hairy, they both have fun teasing the wax out of it.

"You should be shaved like me," Alex tells Simon. "Then the wax would come off easily."

Soon nearly all the wax is brushed off but they have another go when Randy has untied Simon and he is standing up. Alex notices that some of the wax has run all the way underneath him and so he brushes away at Simon's buttocks, getting great satisfaction from leaving nice red marks.

"Alex, I think the wax around there went ages ago," Randy observes. "Seems to me you are just enjoying reddening up Simon's arse."

Alex blushes.

When they are done, Alex's now instinctive willingness to be useful kicks in and, without being asked, he grabs a broom and dustpan to collect the wax off the floor and put it in the rubbish bin.

"Thanks, Alex, you were a great help," Randy tells him.

"My pleasure, Randy. I'm sorry I got carried away."

"Don't worry. If you hadn't done that to Simon's arse, I would have."

Alex laughs, realising that his newly discovered sadistic streak is slowly growing and he worries a little about how Damian will manage this. Will he encourage it or slap it down?

Mike and Bob appear in the dungeon and come over to see what has been happening. Alex shows them the bucket of spent candles and the discarded metal components and explains what he and Randy have been doing.

"Now there's a fine way to celebrate a birthday," Bob says to Mike. And it's yours next month, boy."

"Damn," says Mike, "And I was hoping for a cake with icing on top and chocolate biscuits inside."

"Well you could have both, Mike," Alex tells him as he spots Graham preparing things for his own mummification scene.

"Be sure to send me some photos," Alex tells them as he walks over to Graham's bondage table.

CHAPTER 32

After lunch, Alex and Mike are in the social area, Alex telling Mike about the mummification scene he'd had with Graham before lunch.

"How was it," Mike asks.

"Actually it was just OK. I liked being immobilised, but it wasn't the same as when Sir puts me in a sleepsack. But I was glad I tried it. Maybe Graham is really into edging and making guys cum and the fact that I was locked sort of limited his options. Plus I told him that my tits were still really sore from our foursome after dinner yesterday."

"These things happen," Mike reassures Alex. "You can't always get it right. Was Graham unhappy?"

"Didn't seem to be. I think he gets plenty of satisfaction from getting the taping stuff done just right and he probably has a load of other less restricted men to play with still."

As they're sitting there, four heavy tall men in desert camouflage combats come over to where they are sitting at one of the tables. The boys look up and say "Hi" and are about to carry on their conversation when they are each grabbed by two of the men and lifted up in the air, knocking the chairs over. The men carry them out of the building head first.

"What the fuck is going on?" Mike shouts. "Put me down." He tries to free himself but the men are strong.

Though Mike had seen these kidnap scenes before

at camp, he'd never been part of one. And his resistance is a token protest to add some realism for the bystanders.

Alex smiles, realising that this must be a scene Damian had arranged after being inspired by the man in the strait jacket in the dining room the previous night.

"Relax, Mike, look over there."

Mike looks towards where Alex is indicating with his head and sees Bob and Damian watching and laughing.

"Bastards," mutters Mike. "And I was planning on going for a swim."

"Waterboarding can be arranged, boy, if you don't behave," one of the men carrying Mike tells him.

The boys are carried to an isolated cabin on the edge of the camp.

Inside, some more men are waiting and there appears to be lots of bondage equipment and a cage barely big enough to hold a person.

One of the men opens the cage and Alex is pushed into it and the cage door locked shut. Alex has to stand totally upright, his face pressed against the bars of the cage door and his arms pinned down by his side.

Mike is still struggling and shouting as the men holding him attach his wrists to chains hanging from the beams.

He isn't sure he likes what's going to happen. He's sure it will be safe and that Bob has agreed to it. But he's determined not to make it easy for the men. So he starts shouting at the men and trying to kick them with his boots.

Suddenly he feels a sharp pain in his buttocks which almost floors him.

The man behind him comes around to the front and shows him a stun gun.

"Now we can do this easy or we can do it hard, boy," he tells Mike.

"You're not my Master," Mike shouts at him, only to be rewarded with another zap on his thigh.

"Bastard!" Mike shouts at him.

The man grabs Mike's jaw firmly with his hand making it impossible for him to shout any more.

"We need to do something about your attitude, boy, starting with your mouth."

He holds Mike's head tightly while another man locks a leather muzzle on so he can't open his mouth properly. The muzzle has a narrow hollow gag built in to it.

While Mike is focussing on the muzzle, he feels metal cuffs linked by a short heavy chain being locked around his boots.

Alex is watching and getting turned on by what he's seeing and decides that when it's his turn he'll try to avoid being zapped, as it doesn't look pleasant.

The men cut off Mike's t-shirt and shorts and one of them cups Mike's chastity cage in his hand. "Poor boy, all locked up here as well. Wouldn't you like to be able to do this?"

Teasingly, he pulls out his dick and starts stroking it. Mike looks on jealously and his cock starts trying to grow in its cage, excited by the humiliation he's being subjected to.

Then he feels some lube being spread around and inside his arse hole and a long dildo being slid in. Mike hasn't had anything up there since he was locked and the pressure on his prostate surprises him and makes him even hornier.

Finally, a leather harness is fastened around his waist and between his legs, tightened up, and locked to make sure the dildo stays in place.

Satisfied that their first subject is ready, they open the cage door and manhandle Alex out of it, locking his wrists behind his back in heavy handcuffs.

The man jacking off orders him to his knees and tells him to make his cock happy.

Alex has never sucked anyone's dick apart from Damian's, and he hopes this was part of what Damian had arranged. He still feels a little scared but doesn't hesitate very long as he too feels a shock from the stun gun which causes his legs to tremble and weaken. So he drops to his knees carefully, not being able to steady himself with his hands, and takes the man's cock in his mouth.

It feels different from Damian's – not as fat or as long, which makes it easier for him to cope with as the man fucks his mouth for a while.

"That's enough for now, boy," the man says sternly.

And just as Alex pulls his head away, he too is locked in a muzzle with a hollow gag in it.

The men behind him pull him upright and, like Mike, his t-shirt and shorts are cut off and a harness is used to lock a dildo inside him. Finally, his ankles are chained together by heavy metal cuffs over his boots.

Mike is released from the chains and his wrists cuffed together behind his back.

The man who seems to be in charge speaks to them. "This is your sentence for the afternoon, boys. Your Masters thought you needed some exercise. So you are to spend the next three hours walking round and around the campground's perimeter road, past the dungeons and cabins and social area so all the camp can see what submissive, controlled boys you are."

Alex and Mike look at each other, anxiety showing in their eyes.

"Don't worry, boys, as long as you keep to the road there will be plenty of people around to make sure you're safe. In fact, they're doing more than that. They're checking that you are still walking and not sitting on the ground somewhere fucking yourselves on those dildoes. And they will make sure you don't get dehydrated by giving you water through those tubes in your gags from time to time.

"Understood, boys?"

Alex and Mike nod their agreement, both realising that if they don't go through with this they'll upset their Masters.

"Good, but we don't want to make it too easy for you. So we've decided to make it more challenging."

From a corner of the cabin one of the men produces two canvas strait jackets.

"Once again, boys, we can make this easy or difficult," the main man warns them, waving the stun gun in front of their faces.

The boys nod again and a few minutes later the handcuffs are removed and they are each strapped into a strait jacket.

They are each fed some water. In fact, with the tube going into their mouths through the gags they don't have much choice and have to take a lot more than they wanted.

Alex wonders what will happen when they need to piss and realises that they'll either have to hold onto it or just piss on the ground as they're walking. He hopes Mike is happy with this but can't ask him.

Outside the cabin, the two boys are led to the road where the final surprise awaits them. Rather than just walking alongside each other casually, they are fastened back to back, held together by leather belts attached to the sides of the strait jackets. And the cuffs around their ankles are rearranged so that Alex's left ankle is attached to Mike's right and Mike's left ankle to Alex's right.

Alex realises that they will have to walk in step and at any point one of them will need to walk backwards. He wonders how he and Mike will negotiate about when to change, as he doesn't think it fair that one of them should walk backwards the whole three hours.

"OK, boys, off you go," the main man orders, giving them each a short zap with his stun gun to get them started and setting the starting arrangement by facing Mike in the direction they are to go.

Mike starts walking slowly, trying not to make them fall over. He's glad the path is smooth and doesn't get very steep at all. For his part, Alex adjusts to walking backwards with his feet being led by the movement of Mike's. He realises that this could have been far worse. He could have been shackled to someone he didn't know, or worse, didn't like.

Soon they pass cabin 15 where they see Bob and Damian sitting, waiting for them to pass. "Well done, boys," Damian shouts before bounding off the deck carrying a bottle of water with a tube at the top.

Bob joins him and holds the boys steady while more water is poured into them. They each play with their own boy's chastity cage and see that the dildoes are having their effect as both boys' cocks are leaking.

Damian looks Alex in the eyes. "You enjoying this, boy?"

Alex tries to say "Yes, Sir," but it is all garbled because of the muzzle and gag.

"I'll take that as a 'yes', boy," Damian laughs.

By now, Alex and Mike have worked out how to communicate when the rear-facing one needs to change over – he grunts a couple of times. So they change directions a few times with each taking a turn at walking backwards.

Up near where the circular perimeter road joins the track out of the camp there is no-one around and they stop for a rest. They can't look at each other, and Mike's attempts to speak have them both laughing. After a few minutes Alex feels splashes on his bare legs and hears the sound of water and realises that Mike is having a piss and decides he should too.

They both giggle at what's happening to them. Far from being unpleasant, they're both enjoying it tremendously. The dildoes are keeping them horny and they're bonding in a way they couldn't have ever imagined.

By their second circuit, they've been force-fed lots more water by guys whose cabins they pass and their boots and socks are covered in piss. They haven't any idea what the time is and don't realise that their slow pace means they only have one more circuit to do.

As they approach the social area for the third time, they see Bob and Damian standing on either side of the road holding a finishing line tape across it. Behind them are a bunch of other men they recognise. And they all start applauding as Alex and Mike break through the tape, only just avoiding falling over in their haste to end their ordeal.

Alex feels like he's just finished a marathon race

and his legs are killing him. He imagines Mike feels the same way.

"Well done boys," Damian says, steadying them while Bob releases them from each other and removes the strait jackets and ankle chains.

"Jeez, boy, just look at your boots," Damian says to Alex. "And those socks were white when you put them on this morning. I hope there's a laundry here at camp."

Alex hopes that Damian is ribbing him.

Finally, the muzzles and gags are removed.

Both boys have sore jaws and find it difficult to speak at first. And Bob isn't surprised when neither of them accepts the offer of some more water.

"That was the hardest thing I've ever done, Sir," Alex is finally able to say. "Thank you."

"You're very welcome, boy. "

The men from the hit squad come over to congratulate the boys as well. One of them addresses Damian.

"I hope you don't mind, Damian, but I had your boy suck my cock for a while when we were prepping them."

"Well that wasn't part of my plan, Tom, but if it helped get them in the right frame of mind then I don't mind."

Alex looks over at Mike, who is buried in Bob's large muscular arms, and goes over to Bob to thank him too. Mike turns around and gives Alex a big hug.

"You know, Alex," Mike says, "finding you had a

brother was one surprise for you this weekend. But I don't expect you thought you'd end up with a conjoined twin as well."

They both laugh.

Alex feels closer to Mike and Bob than ever and once again marvels at Damian's evil ingenuity.

Damian suggests the boys go back to cabin 15 and have a rest, and as they walk, it feels strange to be facing forward for a change and be in control of their own steps. They also realise that the dildoes are still locked inside them.

"Do you think they forgot?" Mike asks Alex.

"No chance," Alex replies. "Sir is always in control and never forgets anything. Don't be surprised if we have to keep these in until morning."

Mike groans. Unlike Alex, he's not used to having his arse plugged for extended periods and doubts he will get any sleep.

A little later Damian and Bob call in at cabin 15 to check on their boys. They are both fast asleep on Alex's bed, curled around each other.

"Just like a couple of puppies," Damian tells Bob as they leave, quietly closing the cabin door after them.

CHAPTER 33

About an hour later Damian returns to his cabin to find Alex and Mike sitting naked cross-legged on the deck polishing boots, wriggling their bums occasionally.

"Hey, boys, what's up?"

The boys stand to attention, the dildo harnesses still locked on and drops of pre-cum leaking from the end of their chastity cages.

"I'm just cleaning our boots, Sir, and Mike's doing his and his Sir's. We thought they ought to be really well done for the drinks social before dinner tonight. I assumed you'd be wearing your high-sided boots. Hope that's OK."

Damian hadn't mentioned the social but Alex had clearly seen it in the run book. "That's good thinking, boy. You assumed that you'd be going as well?"

Alex's face drops. "Sorry, Sir, I did." Mike looks on warily having also assumed that he would be going.

Damian laughs. "Only teasing you, boy. Of course you're going, and you too Mike. After your performance this afternoon you're the talk of the camp and Bob and I wouldn't deny you all the attention you're gonna get."

Alex relaxes. "Thanks, Sir."

"Have you finished the boots, boys?"

"Yes, Sir," they both reply.

Damian examines the boots and sees that the boys

have done a fine job.

"I see you're having fun with those dildos," Damian continues, still laughing. "I watched you two wriggling around massaging your prostates with them with good effect."

"Sorry, Sir," Alex says.

"Not at all, boy, Bob and I always want you boys to enjoy yourselves."

He wipes the drops of precum off their cages with his fingers and rubs them onto the toecaps of his own and Bob's freshly-polished boots. "Mustn't waste those precious fluids, boys."

"Mike, you'd better go back to your cabin so Bob can get you ready for the social."

"Yes, Sir," Mike replies as he picks up his own and Bob's boots and heads back.

Inside the cabin, Damian thinks about what Alex should wear for the social. Definitely his leather vest and boots but what else? It's a warm night so he decides not to add anything. This will let everyone see Alex's chastity cage and the dildo harness and admire the still visible stripes on his buttocks. Of course the heavy padlocked chain collar and black bandana are, as always, around Alex's neck.

For himself he puts on his leather jeans, his freshly-polished boots and his leather vest.

Before leaving, he puts some handcuffs into his left back pocket along with a black bandana and Alex sees him put something else from his toy bag in his pocket.

There are plenty of men standing on the path outside the administration building drinking beers when they arrive and Damian orders Alex to get him one and a bottle of water for himself. As always, Alex isn't allowed any alcohol.

"Oh, before you go, boy, I have an addition to make."

Alex stands in front of Damian, hands behind his back, feet apart, and Damian retrieves some linked rubber-tipped nipple clamps from his pocket and puts them on Alex. "Just to add to your enjoyment of the event, boy."

"Thank you, Sir," Alex replies, wincing as he goes off for their drinks, his nipples still very sore and getting scabby from the rough treatment they've been having.

After Alex has returned, Paul and Rocky arrive. Paul is dressed in a very shiny black one-piece rubber suit with yellow stripes down the sides and hip-high waders. Following behind him on all fours is Rocky on a dog leash, his head is covered in a rubber puppy hood with ears and snout but an open mouth. He's instantly recognisable from the rope tattoo across his back and arms and his puppy-dog eyes which are clearly visible through the eye holes in the hood.

Rocky's legs are bent double and kept that way with red rope so he has no choice but to walk on his hands, locked in leather puppy mitts, and his knees covered in knee pads. Alex also notices a harness locked around Rocky's midriff securing a rubber pup tail inside his arse.

Paul is carrying a shiny metal dog bowl which he puts down on the grass before fastening Rocky's leash to a hook low down in the nearby wooden fence.

The excitement of the day means that Alex doesn't even consider how he feels seeing Rocky transformed like this. "I guess Rocky's puppy-dog eyes were the inspiration for this, Sir. It looks wonderful," Alex whispers to Damian, and Damian agrees.

Paul leaves Rocky chained to the fence and returns to congratulate Alex on his performance that afternoon. "You were amazing, Alex. You and Mike put on a really good show. And I loved it when you and Mike first stopped to have a piss up at the top."

Alex hadn't realised that anyone had seen them and blushes. "It took us a while to get the courage to do that but our bladders were bursting from all the water guys kept pouring into us. With those muzzles locked on and the hollow gags we didn't have any choice but to drink it."

Paul smiles. "That was my contribution to the scene. Rocky and I are really into piss play. In fact, I think Rocky must be getting thirsty. Wanna watch?"

Damian removes the tit clamps, which causes Alex to wince, and leads him by the hand as they follow Paul over to the fence where Rocky is sitting on his haunches, dog-style, on the grass by the fence.

Paul picks up the dog bowl, opens the zipper in the front of his rubber suit, and pisses into it making Alex feel a little uncomfortable.

He's slowly getting used to his sister now being a man. And he can just about cope with seeing Rocky as a puppy, but Rocky drinking Paul's piss is moving things a little faster than he's happy with.

"Are you uncomfortable watching this?" Damian asks, sensing Alex's unease as he squeezes his hand.

"It's a bit weird, Sir."

"Well you don't have to watch, but you see how happy Rocky is with Paul and if drinking his piss is what makes him happy then you should be happy too," Damian advises him.

Alex recognises the wisdom of Damian's advice and watches as Rocky eagerly laps up Paul's piss from the bog bowl.

"Good, pup," Paul tells Rocky, patting him on the head. "He'll be OK there for a while," he tells Damian and Alex as they walk back to the other men.

Soon Bob and Mike arrive. Bob is dressed in the same full leathers he wore when Alex first met him in the leather bar in DC. Mike is back in a canvas strait jacket and is muzzled again. Like Alex, he too is still locked in his dildo harness.

Bob gives Damian and Alex a hug. Alex looks over at Mike whose eyes are sparkling above the muzzle and decides not to approach him until he gets the lead from Damian or Bob and so just smiles at him.

More men come over to talk to them,

congratulating Alex and Mike on completing their challenge. Alex thanks them while Mike doesn't even attempt to say anything.

"That's the funniest thing I've seen in a long time," one of them says. Another asks whose idea it was and, as Alex expected, Damian owns up.

"These two boys were bonding so well, I thought I'd see how close they could really get," Damian tells him.

Bob asks the Alex how he's doing, pulling on Alex's cock cage which causes the locked-in dildo to move around inside him.

"Well this is sure keeping me on edge, Sir" Alex replies. "I've been leaking like anything."

"Well that's good, boy. Damian told me how he used this method to train you and I think maybe it's something I should use with Mike. He sure has a tight arse. And I really like the strait jackets the hit squad used. I'm going to save up for one."

Mike closes his eyes and groans.

"Just like old times, boy?" Damian asks Alex, referring to the dildo harness.

"Yes, it is. I'd forgotten what it was like."

"Then we'd better reinstate it when we get back home," Damian says with a laugh. "What do you think?"

"That would be good."

Once again, Alex doesn't include his respectful "Sir" in his reply and Damian decides that maybe he is getting a bit full of himself.

"Down on your knees, boy," he orders, after replacing the clamps on Alex's nipples. "With all this praise you're getting I'm worried you're forgetting your place and we'll need to widen the door frames when we get back home just so your head will fit through."

Alex laughs and then gets on his knees, hands behind his back.

"Yes, Sir. Sorry, Sir."

Damian handcuffs Alex's wrists behind his back.

"You did a fine job on my boots earlier, boy, and you remember I added a bit of you two boys' pre-cum just to improve the shine. Now get working on my boots with your tongue while I chat to these men. And do Bob's as well."

"Yes, Sir," Alex replies and remains bent over on the ground, licking Damian's and Bob's boots while they chat to the others, the clamps scraping on the ground as he does so. He feels a bit sad that he can't take any more praise but recognises that Damian is keeping him in check.

What he is glad of is that Damian hasn't ordered him to lick Paul's waders as well. Sharing a top with Rocky would be taking family closeness a bit far, he thinks. And he guesses Damian understood this.

Soon it is time for dinner and Alex is told to get up and the tit clamps and handcuffs are removed.

"That was an easy punishment for you forgetting your place, boy. Next time I won't be so lenient."

"Yes, Sir. Sorry Sir," Alex replies respectfully,

feeling good at being pushed back into his familiar slave role.

Paul retrieves Rocky from the fence and leads him on hands and knees to the dining hall. Mike follows Bob, having had no chance to join in the conversation.

Damian chooses a location at the back of the room where there is plenty of space around the tables and Paul parks Rocky on the floor in the corner, slipping the handle of the dog leash under his chair leg. He takes the dog bowl up to the serving area and fills it with some soup for Rocky, which he laps up as best he can.

Mike, on the other hand, isn't going to get any dinner and has to sit at the table, bound in his strait jacket and muzzle, watching the others eat. Occasionally, Bob feeds him some water through the gag from a bottle.

"Don't you go pissing on the floor, boy," he tells him, "or you'll have to lick it up."

Mike nods and mumbles a "Yes, Sir" as best as he can. He realises that his bladder is filling up and the dildo is putting some pressure on it so he tries to sit completely still.

Alex looks at the men around him and a shiver runs through his body. He feels like he's died and gone to heaven.

He turns to Damian. "You know, Sir, when you suggested that we come here I was full of apprehension. But it's been so wonderful I'm worried I'll wake up in a minute in my room back home and it will all have been a dream."

Damian laughs. "Maybe you don't have enough souvenirs yet, boy. I think tomorrow afternoon I'll put you back on one of those frames just to make sure you have something that will last well beyond our flight back to London."

Alex doesn't know what Damian is thinking of, but guesses it will be very painful and leave some lasting marks and bruises.

"Thank you, Sir," Alex replies immediately, having taken his warning from the boot licking duty earlier.

When they are back in their cabin, Damian asks Alex how he felt about him playing with Ian.

"I felt quite uneasy, Sir. So I left the dungeon."

"I noticed that, boy. But you seemed more relaxed about it when I was talking to Ian at breakfast this morning."

"Rocky is responsible for that, Sir. He made sure that I didn't run away from the situation but got to know Ian and saw the after-effects of what you had done to him. Those are some very impressive bruises."

"You see, boy, that's something I enjoy doing but which I don't think you're ready for. It might never be right for us. So here at camp I can do those things I can't enjoy at home."

"I understand that, Sir, and I'm much happier about it now. I'm so lucky to have you as my Master. And I shouldn't be selfish and want you all for myself."

Damian smiles. "I'm so glad you're feeling more confident about things. And while I enjoy playing with other men here, I'm still looking forward to having you all to myself when we get back home, boy."

"Thanks, Sir. But I do have another little worry. You probably noticed that I've started getting turned on seeing subs like Mike being played with. Do you think that I'll want that more and maybe start switching like you did?"

"I'm not worried at all, boy. I want you to enjoy yourself and fulfil your potential as a sexual human being. And if that means that I let you off the leash sometimes to go top someone, then I'm happy and I'll give you as much advice and support as you need."

"Thanks, Sir, that would be wonderful. Maybe at camp next year, if it's not too presumptuous to think that you'll bring me back here."

"You know, boy, I can't think of anything that would give me more pleasure than to see you here topping someone. As I've said many times, you're a smart boy and learn fast. But remember, you'll always be my boy and I'll stay in control."

"I wouldn't have it any other way, Sir," Alex replies, smiling.

CHAPTER 34

Before Alex goes to bed that night, Damian unlocks the dildo harness and lets him clean himself up properly. And Rocky's stint as a bound pup ends at bedtime too. So the two of them are able to chat without any encumbrances when they meet for coffee before breakfast the next morning.

"How you doing?" Alex asks Rocky.

"Really good," Rocky replies. "I felt a bit strange at first last night with you watching me all done up as a pup and drinking Paul's piss. But I thought, what the heck, my little brother has to see me like this some time."

Alex smiles. "You looked really great, sis. And you were right about the piss drinking. I did stop and think for a minute. But you obviously really enjoy it so why should I find it hard to see you happy? It was one of those 'growing up a bit more' moments."

Rocky laughs too. "I didn't have any problem watching you and Mike struggling around the campground bound together and one of you having to walk backwards," Rocky continues. "It was hilarious. In fact it quite turned me on."

Alex wonders if latent sadism runs in his family.

"Are you and Damian all set for coming to stay with us tomorrow?" Rocky asks.

"Tomorrow!" Alex exclaims. "Jeez this weekend has flown by."

"Sure has," Rocky agrees. "But there's all today and

this evening left to play."

"Sir says that Mr Jameson has managed to change our flights so we can fly back to London via Toronto. So when we've dropped the hire car back at the airport we'll be on our way up to you."

"That's great. I'll ask Damian what your flight times are and we can pick you up at the airport. By the way, what's this Jameson guy like?" Rocky asks.

"He's Sir's personal assistant, though it didn't start that way. When they first met Sir was Mr Jameson's slave and then as time went on they swapped roles."

"No way!" shrieks Rocky. "Damian a slave. This I would have loved to see."

"Shhh!" Alex says. "Keep it to yourself. I don't want to be punished for ruining his reputation here or elsewhere."

"Well he sure has one, Alex. Not just his skills as a top here at camp, but guys seem to really like his porno videos as well. You've certainly lucked out finding him."

"He found me, remember, wanking away over his web sites."

"Well your wanking days seem to be over," Rocky laughs, looking down at Alex's crotch. "In the past Paul suggested we investigate some sort of chastity device for me. But of course I don't have the balls for a device like that. And using piercings and padlocks on my genitals just isn't very effective and full-waisted metal belts are really expensive.

"So we gave up on that idea and I'm currently free

to play with myself whenever I want. But Paul may want to change that in the future if he can work out how. With his skill at creating innovative intimate metalwork I fear my wanking days may be numbered as well."

The memory of first seeing Rocky's genitals comes back to Alex and he feels like he's getting too much information. But he doesn't want to upset Rocky by saying anything so he just changes the subject.

"What have you planned for Sir and me when we're in Toronto?"

"Well, little brother, there's tourist stuff to do in town and we could go to Niagara Falls if you like."

"Oh yes, I'd love that. I found a pic of mum and dad visiting there on mum's Facebook page."

Alex realises that he's referred to his parents as "mum and dad" and is surprised. Rocky hasn't said anything to soften his feelings towards them. Just the opposite. But maybe talking to his brother took him back to when they were a family.

"Have you ever thought of getting in touch with them?" Rocky asks him. "Since leaving home and transitioning I thought about it but never have."

"Well Sir did ask me if I wanted to stop off in Toronto on the way here to maybe go see them and you. I said I didn't but I was still intrigued about what happened to you all. So I went searching online. I found mum's Facebook page and got really upset that there was no mention of you on it.

"Then I went searching for you and couldn't find

you anywhere. I assumed you'd got married and changed your name. Of course you did change your name but not for the reason I assumed."

Rocky laughs. "If you search for Rocky Jenkins you'll find loads of stuff about me and my work. But most of it is too racy for Facebook."

Alex continues to discuss what they will do in Toronto. "Of course I'm due to get my septum pierced by Paul. I'm sort of looking forward to it, as it's another sign of Sir's ownership. I originally worried about whether it would hurt and then realised how silly that was. The pain must be insignificant compared to what I receive from Sir when we play."

"You're right, Alex, and probably no worse than when you got your PA," Rocky says looking down at Alex's crotch.

"I forgot about that. My PA seems so much a part of me and my chastity that I barely think of it as a piercing. Anyway when it was done my head was somewhere above the clouds as I'd just had an amazing scene with Sir, so I barely noticed it. In fact it was the temporary tattoo that I remember hurting."

"You know, Alex, people freak out about piercings but are happy to have a tattoo. It makes no sense. A piercing is one needle going in once. After a few seconds it's over. A tattoo is dozens of needles going in thousands of times over a period of hours."

Alex remembers his idea of getting his pubic area

tattoo made permanent in Toronto. "Do you do the tattooing, or Paul," Alex asks, fearing that it would be Rocky which would be inappropriate he thinks.

"We both do, though I tend to do the more intricate stuff, and Paul does stuff like lettering, like yours. Do you think you or Damian will want to make that permanent some day?"

"I'm not sure," Alex replies. "I'm technically still in a trial period, so maybe it should wait. And I certainly shouldn't suggest it. Damian makes the decisions."

"OK then, little brother, I'll see what happens."

Soon it is time for breakfast and as they are walking towards the dining hall Alex spots Damian in the passenger seat of Graham's car heading out of the camp.

"I wonder where he's going," he says to Rocky. "I thought people couldn't leave the camp until it's over."

"Well Graham is in charge of day to day things so maybe he needs to get some supplies and Damian is probably just going along to keep him company or help carry things."

Were it anyone but Damian in the car then Alex would have accepted Rocky's explanation. But he knows Damian is planning something and he is sure that whatever it is, he will be involved.

CHAPTER 35

Bob and Mike are at breakfast when Alex arrives on his own. "Sleep well?" Alex asks Mike.

"Not at all," Mike replies laughing and looking at Bob.

"Sir kept me in the strait jacket and dildo harness all night strapped to the bed. And he put a heavy-duty diaper on me in case I needed to piss. It sure was horny, but I didn't get much sleep."

Alex is grateful he got off lightly but is turned on by the thought of sleeping in a strait jacket, dildo plugged and diapered and his cock grows a little in its cage as Mike is talking.

Damian doesn't show up at breakfast so Alex assumes he's still out with Graham or holed up somewhere planning something devilish. So he walks around the grounds to see what's happening.

Over on a park bench he spots Randy smoking a cigar and he goes over to chat to him and see if he's done any more candle scenes.

"Hey, Alex, come and join me."

Alex sits down, breathing in the smell of cigar smoke. It's not as bad as he thought.

"What you up to this morning?" Randy asks him.

"Not much. Sir has gone out into town for something, which I suspect is connected with a play session we're having this afternoon. So I decided to explore a bit."

Randy takes a drag on his cigar and deliberately

exhales it in Alex's direction, watching to see what Alex's reaction will be. Alex doesn't move away or cough and Randy is surprised when Alex says, "that smells nicer than I imagined."

"You ever smoked a cigar, Alex?"

"No I haven't and Sir doesn't smoke either. When I was a kid I tried some cigarettes but they never did anything for me apart from make me throw up."

"Want to try?" Randy says offering Alex the cigar.

Alex looks at it. It's fatter and longer than any cigar he's seen before and the outer leaves are far darker, almost black.

"I'm not sure Sir would approve," Alex says.

"Well you may not know it but Damian is partial to a cigar sometimes. Maybe not in London, but he and I smoked cigars together just last night. Maybe he doesn't want you to know in case you disapprove."

Alex laughs. "Sir is never concerned about whether I approve or not. He sets the rules and I obey. Maybe he just didn't think to mention it."

"So what do you think?"

Alex takes the cigar gingerly from Randy's hand and puts it in his mouth. The taste of the tobacco on his lips and tongue is unexpectedly bitter and the smoke curling up from the lit end starts to make his eyes water. And he hasn't even smoked it yet.

"Just take it slowly at first, Alex. Suck in a little smoke but don't inhale it. Leave the smoke in your mouth for a few seconds and then blow it out."

Alex follows Randy's instructions and after a few

attempts manages to get quite a lot of smoke into his mouth. The nicotine starts to have an effect and he feels slightly light-headed and nauseous.

Randy spots this, takes the cigar off Alex, and gives him some water.

After a few minutes, Alex has recovered and he asks Randy more about cigars.

"Do you just smoke them or do you use them for play as well? I've seen guys in porno films using them in the dungeon but never met anyone who did it for real."

Alex realises that he is varnishing the truth a lot as, before this trip with his Master, he'd never met anyone who did any sort of SM for real before besides Damian.

"Well I do lots of stuff. I use cigars to heat up parts of guys' bodies, and I sometimes tie them up and force the smoke into them."

Alex realises that his cock has started its regular futile attempt to grow in its cage. He'd really like to try some of the stuff Randy has described but isn't sure if Randy would be interested in doing it with him. Plus he'd need to get Damian's permission first.

"That sounds fun," Alex replies, hoping Randy will get the hint and invite him to play.

"Well how about we carry on?" Randy replies. "My toy bag is just over there and this is a perfect spot. It's quiet here so not too many people will see if you turn green and start throwing up."

"You sure have a fine way of making it sound

enticing," Alex laughs.

"I was joking about the turning green bit," Randy replies. "But if you're too eager and take in the smoke too quickly then you can start throwing up."

"There's one problem," Alex tells him. "I have to get Sir's permission before I can play with anyone but him. But he's still out of the camp."

"Can't you call him?"

"My phone is very basic and doesn't work in the US so I didn't bring it over here. Sir's does of course, because of work."

"Here, Alex, use mine. I can find his number in the run book."

Before Alex can stop him, Randy has dialled Damian's number and handed the phone to Alex.

Out at the hardware store Damian is surprised to see a call from an unfamiliar US number and wonders if maybe it's the camp calling and something has happened to Alex.

"Damian Hall," he answers.

"Sir, it's me," Alex replies.

"Are you OK boy? Has something happened to you?"

"I'm fine Sir. I'm sitting here with Randy from our cabin and I'd like to play with him. I told him I needed to ask you first, and before I could do anything, he called you. Sorry to disturb you, Sir."

"Yes that's fine, boy. You enjoy yourself with Randy. Can I speak to him first?"

Alex passes the phone to Randy who listens briefly

to what Damian is saying and then moves away out of Alex's earshot.

"Damn," thinks Alex. "Sir's plotting again. Or else he's giving Randy a warning about not injuring me."

Randy returns, having finished the call. "Damian was just checking on what I had planned and he approves. In fact he said that if you enjoyed it then maybe you could join the two of us tonight when we have our cigar together at the end of the evening."

Yet again Alex experiences Damian's caring for and controlling him in equal measure. He's reassured that Damian's checked things out for him. But he's also starting to be slightly irritated by Damian's total control. He feels himself growing up and wants to spread his wings and experience a bit more independence. He wonders if Damian recognises this.

"Right, boy," Randy tells him. "Take all your clothes off apart from your boots and put them on that bench over there. I don't want them to get damaged by any stray burning embers when we play."

Alex snaps out of his thoughts and does as Randy orders. "Yes, Sir," he says, realising that Damian has handed him over to another Master and he's not sure he's happy about it. So he is slow to get undressed.

"Don't worry, boy. Damian told me exactly how far I could go. He's looking out for you and might even call by to see how the two of us are getting on."

This doesn't help Alex who feels even more torn

between wanting to serve only Damian and the call of his swelling cock to explore play beyond that.

Randy notices Alex's unease.

"Listen up, boy. We don't have to do this. Damian told me that you have to want to do it and that at any time you can call timeout."

This option is something Damian has never offered him.

Damian had told Alex about stop words when they first started playing. But he'd also told him that he didn't believe they were always a good thing. His view was that a boy should trust his Master to take him on new adventures and only object if there was a real danger of injury or feeling ill.

Alex knows that, had Damian given him a stop word, he'd have wimped out many times and missed the wonderful, scary but ultimately exciting and satisfying play they'd had together. And he guessed that if that had happened too often he wouldn't have lasted long as Damian's boy and certainly wouldn't be where he is now.

Randy is patient and sits there smoking his cigar while Alex sits next to him, naked and silent. Alex thinks back to his less than successful mummification scene with George and wonders whether he's ready to play with other Masters.

"Tell you what, boy, let's do this slowly. I was going to tie you up but maybe you need to feel more in control to start with."

"For this first bit I want you to relax, boy, and let

me do all the work."

Alex isn't sure that he understands what he is to do or whether he will like it. But he can always say "Stop", so doesn't worry. And Randy's slow seduction is being very effective.

Randy places his cigar in his mouth and draws in some smoke before holding Alex's head with one hand and pinching his nose with the other. He places his mouth over Alex's and, with his own lung power, he forces some of the smoke into Alex's lungs then draws it out again, then in and out again so he's acting as a human rebreather bag.

When he's done, Alex is smiling. "That was cute, Sir" Alex tells him, feeling quite relaxed and a bit of a buzz.

Randy gets a gas mask from his toy bag and shows Alex how to put it on. The mask smells of rubber and cigar smoke and Alex finds he likes the enclosure and limited vision it gives him. But he is nervous and his cock has shrunk back.

"Now we sort of fit this tube in here," Randy says, screwing a corrugated tube into the mask.

For Alex, having his breathing being controlled through the mask is a new experience. But it feels OK, even a bit exciting, and his heart speeds up a bit.

Randy pulls on his cigar and then holds the open end of the tube in front of the mask's lenses and blows some smoke across the top of it.

Alex has his first experience of taking in smoke through a gas mask and it isn't as bad as he feared.

Randy repeats this a few times, letting Alex get used to the sensation.

Then, Randy tells him to hold the tube in one hand and Randy's cigar in the other.

"When you're ready, boy, hold the cigar against the end of the tube. Don't be too keen and push it in. Just let your incoming breath pass through the cigar a little."

Alex tries it and what he is breathing is part cigar smoke, part air. He coughs a bit and removes the cigar.

Randy waits, allowing Alex to set his own pace.

After a few minutes Alex tries it again, holding the cigar closer to the tube and takes a few breaths. He doesn't feel so nauseous this time and gains some confidence. He's enjoying the smoke entering his lungs and the buzz he's getting.

"Not bad, boy. When you're ready, put the cigar into the tube, breathe in and then out again and then take the cigar out."

Alex tries it and is surprised by the rush of smoke hitting his lungs. He takes the cigar out and welcomes the fresh air that replaces the smoke. The sensation of the smoke enveloping his face and being drawn down into his lungs excites him.

He tries it again, taking two breaths this time before removing the cigar and coughing a little.

Randy takes the cigar out of Alex's hand and puts it in his mouth before removing the mask. He asks Alex how he's doing.

"Well that was different," he tells Randy.

"Good different or bad different," Randy asks.

"I think good, Sir," Alex replies realising that Randy is sensitively teaching him and letting him maintain some control.

"Want to carry on, boy?"

"Yes, Sir, but I think I need to blow my nose first."

Randy hands Alex a large white paisley-patterned bandana and Alex blows his nose and hands it back to Randy who puts it on the bench next to Alex.

"OK, this time you still hold the tube but I'll hold the cigar. At any time you can pull the tube away."

The mask goes on again and Alex tries the game some more, taking more breaths of cigar smoke through the tube and mask and into his lungs.

Without Alex realising it, Randy is inching the cigar into the tube bit by bit so that Alex is getting less air and more smoke each time.

After a few breaths, Randy pulls the cigar away and takes the mask off so Alex can have some air.

"How was that?" asks Randy.

"Good, Sir, Alex replies, blowing his nose once again. Quite a buzz in fact." Alex notices some brown stains on the bandana from his smoky mucus.

"Want to ratchet it up a notch?"

"Yes please, Sir," answers Alex who is both challenging himself to face the unknown and feeling that, if Damian approves, then he probably knows his boy also wants it. Alex also can't ignore the fact that his cock has started swelling again, which means that, underneath his fears, something inside him is feeling aroused.

Randy goes over to his toy bag again and returns with some rope. He secures Alex's arms along the back of the bench and his feet together, attaching them to the underside of the bench so Alex is no longer touching the ground.

"OK, boy?"

"Yes, Sir," Alex replies looking nervously at the cigar in Randy's hand and the gas mask and tube laying alongside him on the bench.

Randy returns the mask to Alex's head and holds the gas mask tube in his hand.

"Here goes boy. If you feel like it's getting too much then just click your fingers. Show me you can do that."

Alex hadn't realised that some people couldn't, and demonstrates that he can.

Randy places the lit cigar in the tube and Alex takes in the cigar smoke. Except this time he has no control as he's bound to the bench. And he enjoys it. Randy lets Alex take just a couple of breaths before giving him some fresh air. Then starts again, lengthening the time between fresh air breaks until Alex starts to cough a little.

Randy removes the cigar and places it down on the bench before placing his mouth over the tube and forcing fresh air through the mask and into Alex's lungs.

"Wow, that was different," Alex tells Randy, his

voice resonating inside the mask.

"You're using that word again, boy. Good or bad different?"

"Good, Sir."

Randy notices Alex's cock straining at the end of his chastity cage and now knows for sure that Alex is OK, that he is enjoying the scene and that he probably wants more.

"This time it's five breaths, boy."

Alex nods his head and the tube moves up and down in time with it.

The cigar goes in and Alex paces himself, counting the breaths to himself. He wants to succeed. He doesn't want Damian to hear he's failed.

By the fifth breath of pure cigar smoke, he's almost out of his mind and his lungs are starting to protest. Randy removes the mask and lets Alex recover a little.

"Thank you, Sir. Can we do that again in a minute?"

"Sure, boy, as long as you want," Randy replies. He picks up the stained white bandana and helps the bound Alex blow his nose again before wiping away the few tears that have formed under his eyes. Alex notices how smoky the bandana is smelling and it excites him.

Their game continues a few more rounds, with Randy increasing the number of breaths each time. Alex's cock is straining harder than ever in its cage as the lack of oxygen heightens his arousal. And at one point he feels like he will spontaneously cum or pass out or both. But he doesn't do either.

Randy tells Alex that there will be a last round of ten breaths as he doesn't want to overdo it for his first time, and he fears that Alex might cum which would get them both into trouble.

Alex is feeling really buzzed by now and by the tenth breath he's struggling really hard as he counts. After the tenth breath Randy doesn't remove the cigar but forces Alex to take a few more and Alex starts screaming with excitement.

Randy removes the mask, worried about Alex. But underneath Alex is grinning, pleased with himself for facing the challenge. "Sorry, Sir, it was so intense I just had to let that out."

Randy falls about laughing, his concern now gone.

Alex greedily breathes in the fresh air and, as Randy moves away from in front of him, he spots a smiling Damian leaning against a tree opposite. As his Master walks over towards them, Randy releases Alex from the bench and walks over to greet Damian.

Alex remains seated, totally zonked.

"Thanks for letting me have this time with Alex," Randy tells Damian.

"My pleasure, Randy. I knew from our discussion on the phone that Alex would be in safe hands and have a good time with you. I only watched some of it as I've only just got back to camp. But it looked very hot."

Damian walks over to his boy and ruffles his hair before crouching down to ask him how he is doing.

But he doesn't expect an answer yet. Alex looks into Damian's eyes, smiling broadly, some smoke tears running down his face from the exertion of breathing pure cigar smoke.

Alex takes the white bandana which Damian has picked up from the bench and wipes his cheeks and then holds it to his face. It smells even more strongly of cigar smoke and he crumples it in his hand and holds it tight against his nose, greedily breathing in the lingering scent.

The two Masters sit down on the bench either side of Alex and hold him while he returns to the real world, offering him some water.

"That was amazing, Sirs," Alex eventually says in a quiet voice. "Thank you both very much."

"My pleasure, boy," Randy replies. "You might not want to repeat it. On the other hand, you might. I'm gonna give Damian some of my large maduro cigars to take back to London anyway so you might find yourself doing it again."

Alex looks at Damian.

"This isn't a scene I've much experience of, boy, Damian tells him. "But I learned a lot from watching and I can learn from you as well."

"That would be good, Sir," Alex whispers.

Somewhere inside him, Alex hopes he won't forget this moment when Damian told him that he could teach him something.

When he's recovered, the men prepare to leave and Alex gets dressed.

Looking around the bench to check he's got everything, Alex, spots the white bandana which he offers to Randy.

"Keep it, boy, as a souvenir," Randy tells him.

Alex holds it up to his face to breathe in the cigar smoke smell once again. This will be one of the treasured mementoes he takes back to London with him.

CHAPTER 36

After Alex has got dressed and thanked Randy again, Damian suggests he and Alex walk around the campgrounds a bit to clear Alex's lungs. Damian doesn't prompt any conversation, allowing Alex to process what he has just experienced. When they finally get to their cabin, Alex asks if it's OK if he has a nap before lunch.

"Of course, boy, and when you get up take a good long hot shower. You may like smelling like a refugee from a cigar den but I'm not sure the guys sitting next to you at lunch will."

Alex laughs and goes into the cabin and slumps on his bed and sleeps for over an hour.

His head still feels a bit strange when he wakes up but this soon goes after he's showered and brushed his teeth and put on a fresh set of his boy's white t-shirt and shorts uniform. He proudly hangs his trophy smoky white bandana over the end of his bed, knowing that Randy won't be able miss it as his bed is opposite.

As Alex is getting dressed he notices an orange plastic carrier bag poking out of Damian's half-closed toy bag. He can't quite read the white lettering on it, only seeing the letters "H" and "D". He's slightly tempted to take a closer look but then stops. He remembers how he knew it best not to spoil Mike's surprise when they did their four-hander. So he kicks the toy bag further under

Damian's bed and heads out for lunch.

The dining hall isn't very busy, as most men seem to have decided that, on this last day, play is more important than food. Damian and Randy are sitting together talking and Alex grabs his food and joins them.

"You OK, Alex?" Randy asks him.

"Just about, Randy," Alex replies sensing that the Sir/boy stuff was confined to their play session as Randy had addressed him by his real name and not as "boy".

"Your cotton wool head will go soon," Randy advises him. "Drink lots of water and get some more fresh air."

Alex isn't in much of a mood to chat as he's still recovering. He also knows that Damian has a special play session lined up for him later in the afternoon and he wants to be on top of things for that.

"Sir, what time are we playing later?" he asks Damian.

"About four should work. Meet me in Dungeon Two. If I'm not there just wait as I might be a few minutes late."

"Yes, Sir."

Alex picks at his food while Damian and Randy discuss the merits of various cigars and the properties of different candles. He's not hungry and grabs a bottle of water on his way to go sit in the sun.

Just before 4pm, he heads off for Dungeon Two and walks around the space, watching the various scenes going on. There's no sign of Damian but he doesn't worry as he had said he might be late.

A few minutes later Damian arrives, his toy bag in hand but completely zipped up.

"Give me a hand here, boy," Damian tells him and together they carry one of the wooden paddling horses out into the fresh air. As Damian decides exactly where to position it, Alex goes inside to retrieve Damian's toy bag. It doesn't feel very heavy which puzzles him. But it also reassures him, as it doesn't feel like it contains any heavy wooden or leather paddles like the ones Rocky said Damian used on Ian using the same paddling horse.

Outside Alex is told to strip to his boots and once he's positioned on top of the horse, Damian fastens him down with ropes around his waist and ankles and positions his wrists so his arms are tied parallel to his sides. He then blindfolds and gags Alex.

Alex listens intently as he hears Damian remove the plastic carrier bag from his toy bag and scatter its contents on the ground. It sounds like wooden sticks clattering together but he can't work out what they are. They don't sound like canes.

Damian moves around behind Alex and starts hitting his buttocks with the wooden sticks. He has one in each hand and is treating Alex like a drum kit. The strokes start slowly and soft, then increase in tempo and force, and then back down again. Damian is playing Alex like a musical instrument. As the strokes continue Alex's skin warms up and starts to redden, and then sting even more as Damian hits him faster and harder.

Alex growls into his gag.

Then the strokes soften again and, as he is concentrating on his rear, he feels strokes start on both his upper arms. Now he is being played by three people, each holding two of these sticks. Their paddling rises and falls in unison, sending waves of pain through his body.

And then he senses someone else standing by his head and they start using similar sticks on his back. So it's now four people working as a musical team, beating out a rhythm on his body. After a while, they stop and he hears them move around him, swapping places. The strokes get faster and heavier, then slow down and become soft before rising again. This routine is repeated many times, like a Caribbean steel band.

Alex is in ecstasy, his tense body shaking and glowing. They change positions again and the man now at his rear starts hitting the tender sides of his thighs. Alex opens his mouth and screams through the gag, venting his torment to help himself cope with the pain.

This carries on for what he guesses is about fifteen minutes, his skin bright red all over and tingling and burning like it is on fire.

One by one the men at his head and sides slow down and stop while the man beating his thighs speeds up, hitting him harder and harder until he thinks he can't take any more. There is one more really heavy stroke on each of his, now very sore, thighs, and then it stops.

Alex collapses onto the padded top of the horse, exhausted.

Someone bends down by his head and removes the blindfold and gag. It's Damian who uses one of the bandanas to wipe away his tears. "Well done boy. That was a present from all of us for being such a wonderful brave boy."

Damian releases Alex and allows him to take his time getting up and adjusting to the bright sunshine. He looks around and sees Bob, Mike and Paul standing there with large wooden paint stirrers in their hands, the words 'Home Depot' clearly visible on them. They are all grinning. Rocky is over by the wall and comes over to join them now the play has ended.

Alex looks at his upper arms, which are bright red, and then down at his thighs, which are an even darker red. Damian offers him some water and the five men surround him and give him a group hug.

"You're going to have some serious bruises down there, boy," Damian tells him, pointing at his thighs.

"Sorry about that, Alex," Mike admits. "I couldn't resist. I had to get my own back for you making me walk most of our round the camp hike backwards.

They all laugh and Alex gives Mike an extra big hug, his arms aching as he wraps them around his buddy.

"Thank you, everyone, for making my time here so

special."

"I think we'd all better have a quiet evening," Damian suggests. "I don't know about you but I'm all played out and we have to pack and be ready to leave in the morning."

Alex looks at Rocky. "Damian was right," he thinks. "Families are what you make for yourself, not necessarily what you're born with. And I'm incredibly lucky to have found both this weekend."

CHAPTER 37

Later that evening, after a nap and dinner, Alex and Damian are feeling refreshed. The excitement of the past days means they are both too energised to go to sleep yet so Damian suggests he and Alex have one last walk around the campgrounds.

In the grassy part of the slope near some large trees they come across Randy sitting on a bench, smoking a cigar and talking to Bob and Mike. Bob is smoking one too while Mike is sitting on the ground between his legs, coughing occasionally when the cigar smoke drifts his way. Randy calls them over and offers Damian a cigar which he accepts and he sits on the bench while Alex copies Mike and sits on the ground.

Alex enjoys the smell of the cigars as it reminds him of his play with Randy. And he inhales as much of the smoke passing by as he can. But he's aware Mike isn't that comfortable with it and is looking unhappy.

The three Masters are busy comparing notes on the play they've had at camp and Alex asks if it's OK if he and Mike sit somewhere else, so he can have one last chat with him before they leave in the morning. "I don't want to interrupt your discussions, Sir," Alex explains.

"Sure, boy," Damian agrees.

"Yeah, boy," Bob adds, laughing. "You and Alex go sit on the ground over there so we can keep an eye on you both. We don't want to miss anything if Alex starts hitting on you again."

The three men continue talking, Bob and Damian casting appreciating glances at their boys every now and then.

"I think Alex's body has probably taken enough for today," Damian comments.

"I don't think Mike has," Bob replies. "He's a real pain pig. But I'm too relaxed sitting here smoking one of Randy's fine cigars to want to do anything with him right now. What about you two?"

"Well Mike's really cute," Randy replies. "But from what you've told me, I don't think he'd last more than a few seconds in one of my gas masks before he panicked."

"I have an idea," Damian says. "I'll be right back."

Alex looks up from where he and Mike are sitting and sees Damian leaving.

"Be right back, boy, don't worry," Damian tells him as he passes them on his way down the path.

Alex recognises the mischievous tone in Damian's voice and wonders what he's up to. He hopes it won't be more hitting on his own body as he's extremely sore.

As the two boys look over at Bob and Randy, Alex tells him about his cigar scene.

"I could never cope with that, Alex. If I was put in a gas mask, well I'd just freak out. And as for what went into it, you saw how just a bit of smoke from Sir's cigar made me cough. I'm glad he doesn't smoke them when we're together."

Alex tells Mike that this was the real reason he suggested they move away.

"Thanks, Alex, you really know how to look after me."

Mike rubs Alex's thigh affectionately and apologises when Alex winces.

"Sorry, Alex, I forgot. Don't know why as I really enjoyed laying into you earlier."

Damian returns carrying his toy bag and talks quietly to Bob and Randy and then he and Bob walk over to the boys, leaving Randy to watch from the bench.

"How you doing, boy?" Bob asks Mike.

"Good here, Sir. Alex was just telling me about his scene with Randy. It sounds very exciting if you're into that sort of thing. But as you know, I wouldn't be able to cope with that."

"No worries, boy, there's lots you are into and I think you should get a little more from the trainee top sitting right next to you."

Alex looks around to see who Bob is referring to and then realises it's himself.

"What do you say, boy?" Damian asks Alex. "Want to have another lesson?"

"That depends on Mike, Sir. But I would really like that."

Mike looks down at Alex's heavily bruised thighs and fears that Damian is going to encourage Alex to get his revenge.

"Do I have a choice, Sir?" Mike asks his Master.

"Of course, boy. And this time I promise I won't take over from Alex part way through as I did when he was caning you. I'm just going to sit back there with Randy and finish my cigar while Damian takes care of things."

This doesn't help Mike who still fears Alex will get his own back. But he feels very close to Alex and if he can help Alex learn some things about being a top, why should he refuse.

"OK, Sir. I'm game."

Bob walks back to the bench and Damian tells Mike to stay sitting where he is while he talks to Alex.

Damian and Alex walk out of Mike's earshot.

"What do you think, boy, what do you fancy learning. What do you think Mike needs?"

"Well, Sir, there's a part of me that wants to whack his thighs really hard with those paint stirrers. But that would give me pleasure for the wrong reason. I don't think revenge should be the basis of a scene. Mike getting his own back on my thighs for me making him walk backwards so much was more playful and friendly than revenge."

"Good decision, boy. Now I remember you telling me a long time ago about your discussion with Lars where he suggested I teach you how to handle a flogger."

"I'd forgotten that, Sir, but maybe that would be good."

Damian opens his toy bag and Alex looks inside.

Amongst the floggers and rope he spots a brand new plastic flogger like the one Bob has.

"You bought one, Sir!" Alex says excitedly.

"Sure did, and it's probably easier for you to handle than a leather one with its heavier tails flying all over the place."

Damian and Alex plan the scene out some more, Damian telling Alex that he is now the "top" in the scene and to take charge of it. Damian watches as Alex goes over to Mike, carrying Damian's toy bag. Alex feels strange carrying it as a top and not as Damian's slave but it gives him confidence and helps him adjust to this change in role.

"You ready for this?" Alex asks Mike.

"Sure am, Alex."

"That's 'Sir' for the moment, boy."

Mike looks up at Alex and sees the serious expression in his face. It's one he's learned to instinctively respond to. He corrects himself. "Sorry, Sir, I am."

"Take your shirt and shorts off and follow me, boy," Alex orders Mike. He is amused at how quickly he is adjusting to taking a dominant role.

"Yes, Sir," Mike replies emphatically, responding to the firm tone in Alex's voice.

They walk to one of the stout trees nearby and Alex positions Mike with his arms encircling it. From the bag he pulls out some wrist restraints and rope and uses them to tie Mike tight against the tree. A bandana blindfold and gag follow and the tight bondage helps Mike sink into the tree and relax. He hears Alex and Damian talking quietly behind him and then Alex approaches him and whispers into his ear.

"This is going to be fun, boy. And you can be sure that my Sir will be advising me so I don't hurt you in the wrong places or the wrong way, only the right places and in the right way."

Mike nods his head and smiles. He's been turned on by Alex since they first met and the thought of Alex doing a solo top session with him excites him and his cock leaks a bit, leaving a damp patch on the tree trunk where his chastity cage is pressed against it.

Alex stands back, gauging his distance and starts slowly teasing Mike's back with the plastic flogger, more stroking than hitting.

Mike realises that Bob has never used this device in this way and he relaxes more, keen to experience Alex's own style of doing things once again. Being caned by Alex soon after they first met had been a hugely important experience for him.

Slowly Alex builds up the force and frequency of his strokes, taking breaks every now and then to get advice and feedback from Damian.

Back on the bench Randy and Bob are taking in Alex's gentler approach to things and admiring it.

"You know," Randy tells Bob, "we sure could learn a few things from these young-uns."

"Alex has already taught me a lot," Bob replies. "It's

not just about starting slow when caning or about being a chastity keyholder. It's also what he's shared with me about his relationship with Damian. I'd never realised how much Mike and I miss out on by not spending more time together."

Back at the tree, Alex is still being cautious. He measures his strokes carefully as he doesn't want to miss Mike's back and hit him on the sides or arms or for the plastic flogger to wrap over the top and hit his front. In fact, he discovers that by standing further back he can just graze Mike's back, the faster tips of the plastic flogger having a greater effect than when the force is spread across a larger area.

Damian stands well away, feeling very proud of his boy. He'd given Alex some basic practical advice, and then told him that the most important thing was to learn to read the bottom's body language, to spot what effect the strokes were having and when he was setting too fast a pace.

From where he is standing it looks like Alex has picked this up very quickly and Mike is obviously enjoying the scene. His body is moving around as much as it can against the tree. But this isn't the action of someone trying to avoid the strokes but someone luxuriating in them.

By now, Mike's back is covered in bright red scratches and a few drops of blood have appeared, so Alex stops. "Time for a break, boy," Alex says softly to Mike who just responds with moans of pleasure and gratitude.

Damian walks over and gives Alex some antiseptic wipes to clean up Mike's back. He whispers something in Alex's ear and hands him a cane before joining Bob and Randy on the bench.

Alex taps Mike lightly on the buttocks. "You know what's coming next, boy."

Mike nods eagerly, recognising the firmness of the dragon cane, and Alex feels ready to complete their play together the way it started what seems like weeks ago but was in fact just a few days.

As with the flogger, Alex starts slowly, making sure to stand in the correct position so the cane hits Mike squarely on his arse cheeks. As with his own experiences of the dragon, he knows he has a very powerful implement in his hand and needs to use it carefully.

He delivers the strokes in sets of ten, starting softly and then each subsequent set being slightly harder than the previous one. Mike's arse is reddening slightly, not reflecting the penetrating pain that the cane is causing.

Finally, Alex is ready to complete the scene and he stands behind Mike, pressing him against the tree, and kisses him on the back of neck, the way he loves Damian doing to himself.

Mike is almost purring with pleasure.

"You're doing very well, boy. Now I'm going to finish you off with something you won't forget for a while, or want to forget. These are going to be really hard ones."

Mike tenses himself against the tree, knowing what is coming.

Alex stands to one side of Mike and adjusts his position by just laying the cane across Mike's buttocks until he is confident he can hit his target accurately with the heavy strokes he intends to give.

"One," Alex shouts as he hits Mike's arse as hard as he can. Mike screams through his gag. "Two. Three. Four. Five," Alex continues. And then he stops, sensing from Mike sagging in his bonds that he has reached his limit.

"I think you're done, boy. Well done."

Alex hands the cane back to Damian and once again hugs Mike to the tree and kisses him and speaks softly in his ear.

"That was really hard, boy, and I'm very proud of you and honoured that you let me do that to you."

Alex removes the blindfold and gag and releases Mike from the tree. There are tears streaming down Mike's face and Alex uses one of the blue bandanas to wipe them away before handing it to Mike to finish the job.

Mike is finding it hard to speak, so shows his feelings by hugging Alex tight and kissing him on the shoulder and neck. In return, Alex kisses him on his head and face and strokes and soothes him. He finds himself experiencing something new – a caring protective feeling towards Mike, who he feels responsible for taking on a difficult journey.

Alex feels excited, but the arousal is emotional

rather than sexual and for the first time he understands the pleasure Damian gets from being a Master and having a boy.

Alex sits Mike down on the ground and fetches him a bottle of water from Damian's toy bag, which he has started to treat as his own.

Bob and Damian stay on the bench, fascinated by the way their boys are interacting. They know that this recovery and reconciliation period after a heavy play session is important for those involved and they let Alex and Mike cement their bond on their own.

The boys are quietly talking about what has happened, slowly transitioning from top and bottom to friends.

"Are you OK, Mike?" Alex asks, holding his hands.

"Sure am, Alex. That was wonderful and so unexpected. Thank you. At first, I was worried you would be too soft on me, or too heavy too quickly or your aim would be all over the place. But you were really good. You seem to have a natural gift for it. And you sensed when I was finding it hard to take any more."

"There's nothing natural about it, Mike. I've had a brilliant teacher."

Alex then realises he'd forgotten they were not alone and looks over at the bench where Damian and Bob are sitting, beaming smiles on their faces. Randy seems to have left.

The Masters get up and walk over to their boys, each sitting down on the ground behind their own boy with their arms around him.

"That was amazing, Sir," Mike says, tilting his head back as he speaks to Bob. "Thank you for allowing it to happen."

"And thank you, too, Sir, for arranging it," Mike adds, looking at Damian. "Alex sure picks things up well. You are a great teacher."

"You're very welcome, boy. I didn't do anything but awaken in Alex the ability to learn and be smart and apply himself."

Alex places his hands over Damian's, which are resting on his stomach. There's so much appreciation he wants to express but is stuck for where to start. So he decides to say very little rather than appear to be blubbing. "There's always two sides to any story and I couldn't have done it on my own."

It starts to get a bit cold and, after checking with Damian, Alex tells Mike he should put his clothes back on while he tidies up. Bob and Damian return to the bench to put the cigar butts in the nearby ash can, while Alex puts the flogger and ropes and bandanas in Damian's toy bag and takes it over to its rightful owner and gives it to him.

"Boy, I think you should give Mike something besides some fine red stripes on his arse to help him remember this evening," Damian tells Alex. And he opens the bag and hands Alex the now damp blue bandana he'd used as a blindfold. "It's a present from me to you to give to him."

Alex smiles, realising how significant his own black bandana around his neck is.

Mike and Bob return to the bench and Alex offers the bandana to Mike. "Mike, here's something to help you remember what a great time the four of us have had this weekend."

Mike takes the bandana and smiles broadly. "I know exactly what to do with this."

He hangs it around his neck, cowboy style, and knots it at the back before placing his padlocked chain collar on top of it, just as Alex does.

Next to them, Bob has his arm around Damian. "You know, Damian, in another reality we'd get married and adopt these boys. But for now we'll just have to be close relatives."

They all laugh and head off down the hill, walking in a line holding hands like a family at a theme park. For that is what this camp has been for them – an adult theme park full of exciting and scary rides which bring people closer together when they help each other face and conquer their fears and discover how to gain pure pleasure from their inner child.

EPILOGUE

Very early the next morning there are tearful, hug-filled farewells. Paul and Rocky are leaving early so they can get home to prepare before Damian and Alex arrive later on. And Bob and Mike depart soon afterwards.

The detour to London via Toronto goes very well and Alex gets his septum pierced by Paul.

Being older and a bit wiser, Paul and Damian advise Alex and Rocky against confronting their parents. Even so, Rocky posts a photo of the four of them together at the top of Toronto's CN Tower on his Facebook page hoping their mother will see it. And Alex shares this on his own Facebook page which he has resurrected. The caption underneath reads simply "Wish you were here." They both agree that it's best to let their parents make the first move at reconciliation when they're ready.

While in Toronto Alex gets to see Paul and Rocky's tattoo studio and this prompts a discussion about Alex's temporary tattoo on their flight home to London.

"I think, Sir, I would like it to be permanent," he tells Damian. "But that's your decision. After all I don't even know if I've passed my three-month trial."

"Boy, you've passed with flying colours. And when we're back home I think a special scene in the playroom is in order to mark the occasion.

Something tells me a spectacular orgasm might be involved. As for the tattoo, let's leave it a bit longer. I want the temporary one to have faded completely, and to find the right occasion and person to do it."

Alex is grinning from ear to ear. "I don't have the words to thank you enough for everything, including this," he says surveying the business-class cabin around them.

"Just seeing you grow into a fine, skilled boy is all the thanks I need boy," Damian replies, holding Alex's hand as the plane starts its descent into London.

Across their different continents, Alex and Mike video chat regularly, comparing the progress of their play and chastity. And they often laugh at their matching padlocked collars resting on their bandanas. They miss each other deeply but are certain that they will meet and play together again.

Damian and Bob keep in touch as well and plan further adventures for themselves and their boys at future camps.

Bob and Mike's relationship grows stronger and closer and Bob gets a transfer to a new job in San Francisco which enables the two of them to find a place to live together and eventually they get married.

Damian's business prospers and remains vandal-free and he never again asks for Alex's help with his business.

Jameson teaches Alex to drive and at times Alex

acts as Damian's chauffer, acquiring a smart black business suit for the job. He is allowed his freedom to explore the world, online and offline, without restriction and gets the fancy widescreen notebook computer he's always lusted after. He and Rocky talk on Skype regularly, keeping track of each other's adventures and progress with their Masters and Rocky's growing collection of tattoos and piercings.

The bedroom in the secret corridor by the playroom remains Alex's preferred space, though it becomes more comfortably furnished. Increasingly. he and Damian sleep together in Damian's bed at weekends.

Alex and Melissa meet often for a catch up at Café Noir though Alex doesn't reveal the full nature of his relationship with Damian or details of the interesting hardware and fading tattoo he has in his pants. And he replaces his septum ring with a keeper when they meet.

But he does tell her about meeting Rocky at a summer camp he and Damian went to, without telling her exactly what sort of camp it was.

He is still collared and Damian always keeps him locked in his chastity device. They play regularly and Damian has added new SM activities to their repertoire, including some cigar play. Alex gets edged by Damian often and he is rewarded with an orgasm whenever Damian sees fit. But in general, Alex enjoys his constant state of frustrated horniness as a reminder of the control Damian has over him and as a bond with Mike.

Alex's memories of topping Mike never leave him and on occasions he gets very excited at the thought of doing it again, both with Mike and possibly with other men.

The bond between Jameson and Alex grows stronger, sharing their love and service to Damian, and between them they maintain Damian's household.

Damian sometimes takes Jameson and Alex to SM social events and the three of them always attract a lot of attention.

Alex's wardrobe now includes more conventional clothes, albeit ones that still reflect that he is Damian's boy, and they are always chosen by Damian. On occasions Alex can still be seen around Damian's house wearing his white t-shirt and shorts, but the black and white camo outfit is never worn again as it has too many painful memories for both of them.

The gym workouts have given Alex's body more definition and he is now unrecognisable from the flabby self-centred porn addicted wanker he once was.

A tattoo convention in the UK provides the excuse for Paul and Rocky to visit London and they stay in Damian's house, their visit coinciding with the first anniversary of when Damian and Alex met. Paul gives Alex the permanent tattoo he'd asked for many months previously, with Alex holding Damian and

Rocky's hands while it happens.

"You know, boy," Damian reveals to Alex afterwards, "not long after we got back from Hickoryswitch I researched what might entice Paul and Rocky to come to London around our anniversary. And I couldn't believe there was a tattoo convention around the same time. I'm afraid this particular evil scheme has been in place for a very long time."

"I wouldn't have it any other way, Sir," Alex tells him. "Every day is full of your wonderful surprises."

Melissa fails to get a replacement for Alex from the pet rescue centre, so cleans up her flat and moves in one of her waiters who Alex meets over coffee one time. He looks very like he himself used to and Alex wonders if Melissa has a fetish for scruffy sad men.

Alex still watches online porn occasionally but it all seems like such a poor substitute for the exciting, and usually pleasurably painful, play he still has with Damian. Alex realises that what he was really looking for in porn, all those months ago, was the love of another man that he now enjoys, and he no longer needs to fill a void in his life with it.

On one of his rare visits to Damian's interactive porn films Alex comes across a cute-looking young submissive man who, he discovers as he still has his moderator access, is a regular visitor. His lurking desire to do some more topping rears its head as does his caged cock. Hoping Damian would approve, Alex takes a deep breath before sending the guy a cryptic private message.

"Hey boy, what are you looking for?"

www.ingramcontent.com/pod-product-compliance
Lightning Source LLC
Chambersburg PA
CBHW071207250626
47159CB00001B/232